PRAISE FOR THE NOVELS OF
TRACIE HOWARD AND DANITA CARTER

"Tracie Howard and Danita Carter have a ball chronicling the lives of several New York strivers from Wall Street to Park Avenue, in [this] glitzy romp." —*Essence*

"All the right energy. . . . It's a mix of money, sex, and power with a suspenseful story line that speaks to our aspirations." —Russell Simmons

"A sexy, stylish, and sophisticated glimpse into urban culture." —Antonio "L.A." Reid

"Consistently compelling." —*Booklist*

"A rich story that puts you in the heart of the city, with a sexy set of characters." —Keith Clinkscales, CEO and Chairman, Vanguarde Media

"A must read. Carter and Howard have written a witty novel with caché and heart. It is highbrow yet earthy, serious yet funny. A new dynamic duo is on the scene." —Yolanda Joe

"Gucci, glitz, and glamour . . . breaks exciting new ground in African-American fiction." —Kimberla Lawson Roby

Other Books by Tracie Howard and Danita Carter

Talk of the Town

Revenge Is Best Served Cold

Other Books by Tracie Howard

Why Sleeping Dogs Lie

Tracie Howard
and
Danita Carter

SUCCESS
IS THE
BEST
REVENGE

NEW AMERICAN LIBRARY

New American Library
Published by New American Library, a division of
Penguin Group (USA) Inc., 375 Hudson Street, New York, New York 10014, U.S.A.
Penguin Books Ltd, 80 Strand, London WC2R 0RL, England
Penguin Books Australia Ltd, 250 Camberwell Road,
Camberwell, Victoria 3124, Australia
Penguin Books Canada Ltd, 10 Alcorn Avenue, Toronto, Ontario, Canada M4V 3B2
Penguin Books (N.Z.) Ltd, Cnr Rosedale and Airborne Roads,
Albany, Auckland 1310, New Zealand

Penguin Books Ltd, Registered Offices:
80 Strand, London WC2R 0RL, England

First published by New American Library,
a division of Penguin Group (USA) Inc.

First Printing, April 2004
10   9   8   7   6   5   4   3   2   1

 REGISTERED TRADEMARK—MARCA REGISTRADA

LIBRARY OF CONGRESS CATALOGING-IN-PUBLICATION DATA

Howard, Tracie.
Success is the best revenge / Tracie Howard and Danita Carter.
p.   cm.
ISBN 0-451-21146-4
1. Manhattan (New York, N.Y.)—Fiction.   2. Bars (Drinking establishments)—Fiction.
3. Inheritance and succession—Fiction.   4. Investment bankers—Fiction.   5. Rich people—
Fiction.   I. Carter, Danita.   II. Title.
PS3608.094S83   2004
813'.6—dc22   2003024388

Set in Sabon

Printed in the United States of America

This book is dedicated to one of my two nieces, Korian Young, who has all of the essential ingredients for *Success*: intelligence, tenacity, sensitivity and talent! And of course, being cute as a button doesn't hurt either. . . .

Tracie

I dedicate this book to the "M" and the "E"—that's right, ME—for hanging in there when it would've been easier at times to let the grip slip. Thank you, God, for the strength to persevere!

Danita

ACKNOWLEDGMENTS

One of the main reasons I began my writing career was to offer readers a more diverse depiction of African-American culture and lifestyle. Most forms of media, including TV, film and publishing, depict a one-dimensional portrait of who we are, often ignoring the fact that—as with the mainstream population—we come in all shapes, sizes and levels. I'd like to acknowledge those people who have allowed me to have a forum to represent those African-Americans who are like my characters (Tyrone/Tess included!): fabulous, sexy, intelligent and sophisticated—in other words people just like you!

I'll begin by thanking my management company, *unzipped!*, for guiding my career into exciting, uncharted territory; my fabulous attorney, Denise Brown, for always getting the deal done; and Jacquie Lee with Moët & Chandon, for partnering with me on an awesome promotional campaign for *Why Sleeping Dogs Lie*. Imara Canady, Sheila Tenney, Dr. Walter Young, former mayor, congressman, and ambassador, Andrew Young, the Eclectic Café, and my wonderful sister Jennifer Freeman, and Lance Robinson for an incredible promotion in Atlanta, my hometown. Keith Clinkscales, your support is always priceless. I also thank my coauthor, Danita Carter, for always being on the same page (pun intended), which makes our joint projects so much fun for us both.

Of course, the staff at New American Library—I couldn't do it without you, literally and figuratively! I am appreciative of all efforts by Claire Zion, Marianne Patala and Craig Burke, and I am very excited to begin working with my new editor, Kara Cesare—I know that we'll create lots of happy endings together!

And my family—simply put, I wouldn't be here but for the love, support, encouragement and lessons that I've learned from: my amazing mom, Gloria Freeman; my sisters (whom I love dearly), Jennifer Freeman and Alison Howard-Smith; my favorite brother-in-law Donny Smith; my cousins April and Ted Phillips; my nieces, Chelsae Smith and Korian Young; and my mother-in-law-to-be, Margaret Mroz; and of course my incredible fiancé, Scott, who is the reason that my novels don't male bash—I definitely have one of the good guys!

And thanks to God for giving me breath each day, along with the courage, inspiration, health and strength to do what it is that I so enjoy . . . and I hope that you will too!

Much love,
Tracie Howard

The trilogy continues with *Success*, and I'd like to thank my friend and writing partner, Tracie Howard, for another awesome collaboration.

I've been blessed with some FANTABULOUS people in my life, so hold tight while I pay some much-needed homage. . . .

I'd like to thank my parents, Bill and Alline, for their support and unconditional love. Words cannot express what you two mean to me!

To my big brother, Ronald Carter, and his beautiful wife, Diana, though we live in different cities, your love transcends the miles. To my sister, Denise—Ms. Magic—the best makeup artist this side of the sun, thanks for making me look like a STAR, and to her tall handsome husband, Earl Milloy, thanks for sharing your Rolodex. My niece Danique Hughes, keep writing, girl—your stories are great! My nephew, and lifesaver, Ronald Carter II, the military man of the family, and his wife, Cathy, thanks for reading my books and giving me your honest comments. My niece Iman Carter, the Spelman grad who is now a bonafide businesswoman, go on, shawty. And to my younger niece and nephews who keep me on my toes: Daniel, Khary and Tamille, "I love you guys." To my Isom cousins, Joe, Ora, Ann, Charles, Jackie, Mitch, Monica, Tomika and the rest of the gang, thanks for your support. My cousins Henrietta Lamar; Nathan, Doris Hemingway and Ethel Hemingway; Alline, Jewel and the rest of my Memphis family, thanks for spreading the word in the South. To my cousin/brother Dane Woodard, his wife, Jill, and their boys, Quinton and Evan, thanks for supporting me at all the ATL signings. Aunt Elouise and Uncle Willie, thanks for your love. To Uncle Jerry, your sense of humor is priceless, and Aunt Marge, thanks for your support. Uncle Richard, thanks for letting me escape to Sag Harbor at a moment's notice. Alice and

Albert Allen, thanks for your support. To Vivian Bruce, thanks for your support (and the crab cakes). To my cousins Alton and Lil Gill, you guys are so special to me. To my cousin Oscar Gill, thanks for looking out for Dad. To Auntie Mill, my cousins Jackie, Victor, Charles, Priscilla, Milton and Collen, thanks for your support. To Aunt Louise and my Simms cousins, Iris, Adrienne, Chester, Joyce, Angela, Connie, Robert and the rest of the gang, I love you guys. To Auntie Nell, Warren, Cathy, Crystal and Allen, Love ya and thanks for your support.

To my friends, who understand when I'm in the cave creating and can't come out and play . . .

Kim, Carl and Britany Russell; Beverly and Eustace (Mr. Doctor) Lashley; Saunté Lowe; Tracey Rico; Norma Marshall; Charlene Oliver (write on); Kimberly Carmen; Terry Brantley; Katherine (Kitty) and Jerome Bell; Cathy, Dwight and baby Kristina Williams; Lou Melazzo (manager extraordinaire); DeLisa Peters; Bill Cooper (my dawg); Karen and Larry McDowell; Michael Newell; Mark Pickard; David Bolton; Melinda (Kelly Girl) and Richard; Charles Walton (meet me at the Den); Richard Walton; Steve and Dana Williams; Patricia Walton; Cheryl and James Cook; Martin Perry; Carmece and Charles McCullough; Debra and Dennis Turner; Thomas (Tommy Baby) Crown; Donna and Carl Mitchell; Linda Weaver; Lynn Mitchell (miss ya); Armand and Lana McCarroll; Craig Rex and Deanna Perry; John Early; and Ellen; Debra Simmons; Debbie Patrick; Robin Robinson; Edwina and Phillip Elliott; Daryl Myers; Ron Shipmon; Stephen Lazzaro; David Chase (u da man); Cheryl Patterson; Annette Dewberry; Regina Thompson; Jon (Exodus) Berry; Jennifer Moore (keep writing); Vincent Dimmock; The Grub Club—Val, Kaminsky, Al, Gail, Sharon and Ernest; Alan Specht; Darryl (Sconey) Jimerson; Mike Coburn, thanks for the hookup; Barbara Bates, thanks for your support, and Jerry Suqi at the Sugar Dessert Bar, your space is too "Sweet"—thanks for hosting our Chicago signing.

To my Novelnistas—Dywane Birch, I love our heartfelt e-mails; Eric Jerome Dickey, yo "e's" iz crazy funny; Yolanda Joe, thanks for your support; and Carl Webber, thanks for hawking our books.

And to YOU—yes, you, the reader—thanks for your support over the years!

Finally, to the awesome team of pros who keep me together . . .

Denise Brown, Esq., for no-holds-barred negotiating; Frank "Flash" Morris, my bombdiggity accountant; William Boyd Jr., the man behind the lenses, thanks once again for a sensational shoot; Saundra Warren for keeping my coif coiffed; Dr. Gregory Page, thanks for keeping my smile bright; Denise Milloy, for my flawless face; Scott Folks the marketing wizard; Imara Canady, for creating a tight P.R. schedule. To my former editor, Audrey LaFehr, I came a long way under your guidance, thank you! To my new editor, Kara Cesare, here's to a happy "marriage". To Rose Hilliard, thanks for fielding my endless questions, and the rest of the NAL team, thanks for the support.

Whew! That was a mouthful. Now get ready for a good read, 'cause Tyrone is awaiting!!

Love ya,
Danita

1

From nine to five, Tyrone's world consisted of an array of bright, explosive colors—not just your generic ruby reds or baby blues, but also more exotic hues, such as pomegranates, ceruleans and chartreuses. Each day he strolled the well-stocked aisles of Basicz, which was Canada's answer to Sephora. It was a cosmetics superstore, offering a staggering battery of makeup, skin-care potions, hair-care products, colognes and perfumes—everything but snake oil. The aisle for lip products alone boasted twenty feet of choices, from high glosses to tubed sticks and matte stains, from Succulent Sable to Fierce Fuchsia, and a vast cornucopia of brands, including Urban Decay, Vincent Longo, Stila and Philosophy.

Tyrone ran his long, limber fingers across a row of lipsticks, taking a visual inventory of the stock, checking to make sure that the reds were properly grouped, and that the browns were not jumbled in with the burgundies. As his hand glided over a tube of Juicy Fruit Mango, he discreetly slipped it into the pocket of his smock and continued perusing the aisle with no one the wiser.

Tyrone Nathaniel Thomas had been hiding out amongst the powder puffs and sable brushes since he skipped bail in New York City nearly two years ago. While his days were spent as a stock boy, his nights were dedicated to working his "womanly" wiles on unsuspecting men while dressed in full drag. He had been masquerading around town as the beautiful Contessa "Tess" Aventura. Exiled in the French Canadian environs of Montreal, he was inspired to create the persona of the biracial, illegitimate daughter of the Duke of Monaco after reading about Christopher Rocancourt, a brilliant thief whom he held in high regard. Mr. Rocancourt was a celebrity con artist who had swindled many victims out of millions, from Cannes to California, by taking on several personas, but most notably by posing as an heir to the Rockefeller fortune. His stock of personalities also included the son of Sophia Loren as well as the nephew of Dino De Laurentiis, the veteran Hollywood producer. All it took was a little creativity, Tyrone decided, and Tyrone was nothing if not creative.

Upon arrival, Tyrone had immediately secured bogus documents from Montreal's underground, using them to open several checking accounts at different banks. Playing three-card monte to make ends meet, he routinely floated one bad check to cover the other. But that game was short-lived when the various accounts were closed for insufficient funds. Now the banks were hunting him down like the Gestapo to press charges. His menial job at Basicz afforded him only the basic requirements. In fact, his monthly salary barely made a dent in the payment for the furnished deluxe flat he'd rented in the ritzier part of town. When the bogus checks were airborne, rent was a nonissue, but now he was three months in arrears and the landlord was threatening him with eviction. With all the demons looming over Tyrone's well-coiffed head, he had to come up with a solution, and soon.

He continued to spruce up the inventory with a feather duster. He mused to himself, *The last time I used one of these was on Tarzan.* He licked his lightly glossed lips at the memory of sexing up a no-name hunk costumed as the king of the jungle during a Halloween party in New York some time ago.

"Excuse me," he said absently to a customer who was loitering in his aisle and testing lipstick shades on the back of her hand.

"Do you have a tissue?" the woman asked.

Tyrone turned back around, thinking she was speaking to him, but the woman's friend approached, pulling a Kleenex out of her purse. The two women began chatting.

"Do you think this shade will match my gown?" asked the one with the lipstick-stained hand.

Her friend was dressed in a too-tight, unflattering teal suit with a skirt that hovered high above her knees. A tacky silver belt was buckled snugly round the waist of the seventies-era blazer. Her blond hair was pinned up in a messy imitation of a pompadour. Large silver-and-blue door-knocker earrings dusted the top of her padded shoulders. The pair brought to mind Eddy and Patsy, the best friends from the BBC sitcom *Absolutely Fabulous.*

"You need a bolder red," insisted the tacky one.

Lipstick Hand looked into the mirror. "You think?"

"If you want to stand out, most definitely."

Tired of this shabby display of nonchic, Tyrone was ready

to walk off, but stopped in his tracks when Tacky Momma said, "You know Montreal's who's who will be there."

His interest was piqued. He wanted the lowdown on when, where and exactly who was on that who's who list. The direct approach, coming straight out and asking, probably wouldn't work in this case, since they would no doubt view him as a mere underling toiling away in a discount cosmetics store. So instead, he wandered over to the next aisle, but he was careful to stay within earshot.

"You know the Black-and-White Ball is a rather conservative affair, so I think I'll tone it down a bit."

Aha! He smiled. *One question down, two more to go.*

"Suit yourself," said the tacky one. "I plan to add a bit of color to all that black and white."

Of course you *would*, Tyrone thought. Scheming, he ran through a mental inventory of the black and white evening gowns that hung in his closet. There was the black knit jersey Michael Kors, conservative but alluring at the same time. Then there was the slinky, silk, snow white Roberto Cavalli halter with thigh-high splits that oozed sex appeal. Since he didn't have the cash or credit to add to his options, one of them would have to do.

The store manager noticed Tyrone standing idly. He walked over and shot him the evil eye before asking in a condescending tone, "Don't you have something to do?"

Reflexively, Tyrone waved the duster in midair. "I was just cleaning off the lipstick display."

"Umm-hum," was the manager's response. "Once you finish tidying up here, I need you back in the stockroom. A shipment of pressed powder just arrived."

Tyrone wanted to say *Fuck the pressed powder*, but he desperately needed the paycheck, so with a phony smile he replied, "I'll be right there." He muttered underneath his breath, "As soon as I get the rest of the scoop on this big shindig."

The women were still gabbing it up. "Well, you know the CEOs of all the top companies are going to be there, and it's a prime opportunity for us to snag a husband," said the Eddy look-alike.

"I wonder if Edmund will be there. You know, he hasn't been on the social scene since his wife died a few months ago," offered the blonde.

"My friend Pearl works with him at Financier, and she told me that he's definitely coming—alone," she emphasized.

"Let's get out of here. I have to pick up my dress before the dry cleaners closes."

With that, the two women disappeared like the next tube of lipstick that Tyrone slipped in to accompany the one already in his pocket.

Well, I still didn't find out where the ball is, at least not yet, but I'll show up like Cinderella just the same. He chuckled to himself.

Tyrone saw his manager waving him back to the dreaded stockroom. The last thing he wanted to do was tag boxes full of pressed powder. Especially now that his mind was fixed on preparing for the big ball. So, as a bonus for the drudgery that lay ahead of him, Tyrone swiped yet another tube of lipstick, along with a matching lip pencil. He marched toward the stockroom like a prisoner headed to death row, counting the days until he could blow this joint.

* * *

Caché's offices were bursting the seams of the Harlem brownstone they had occupied for the last two years. Morgan Nelson had originally started the premier event-planning company out of her East Side condo, later moving it to a small garden apartment in the renovated three-family building that she and her husband had recently purchased. At that time she and her operations manager, Lisa Burrows, were the only two employees, unless you counted Morgan's best friend, Dakota Cantrell, who always pitched in to help.

Though it did have growing pains, the company was now on solid ground. It was on track to gross over two million dollars this year. To accommodate the growth, Caché had relocated to the three-bedroom apartment on the first floor of the brownstone, instead of the one-bedroom garden apartment below. It had six employees, all of whom reported to Lisa, who was now the general manager of Caché. Lisa and Morgan spoke daily, but Lisa was responsible for running the office, since Morgan was home on maternity leave with her baby girl, Zoë. The arrangement was perfect for both women.

Their business relationship hadn't started so smoothly. When Lisa initially began working for Morgan, she was unexplainably distracted and overly emotional at times. That caused Morgan great concern, given the shady dealings of her former partner, Tyrone Thomas, who'd proved to be a practiced con artist. She later learned, however, that Lisa was troubled by the health of her son, Justin, who had leukemia and was in urgent need of a bone-marrow transplant that his mother could barely afford. In the end, Morgan had put her company at risk by partially funding the operation out of her thin cash flow. Though it had almost cost her Caché, Morgan never once regretted the decision, particularly whenever she saw the blossoming, adorable little boy who was now like a big brother to Zoë.

"How's it going over there?" Morgan asked. Lisa could hear Zoë's jibber-jabber in the background.

"It's going." Lisa cradled the phone between her ear and shoulder while using both hands to flip through fabric choices for a party Caché was planning for the organizers of Fashion Week. "Oh, by the way, Dr. St. James called for you this morning."

"And how is the good doctor?" Morgan asked.

"You know him—he's all charm." Lisa chuckled. "But he did want to schedule a meeting with you to discuss the company's expansion plans, particularly into D.C."

"Cool. Go ahead and set up a meeting with him for anytime next week, except for Tuesday. Zoë has a doctor's appointment that day."

"Will do."

"How's Justin?"

"He's great! Now that David is back in his life, he's a different child. I never knew how much it meant for a child to have his father around."

Morgan paused for a significant beat. "But what about for you?" she asked. She was worried about the reemergence of Lisa's baby's no-good daddy. He had skipped out on her when she was six months pregnant without a job and had magically materialized now that Lisa finally had her life together. It didn't sound good to Morgan.

Lisa heard her friend's caution, but she couldn't help being enthusiastic. "It's cool. I've told him: It's about Justin, not about me. But of course, he's trying hard to change that."

Morgan said flatly, "If you ever get weak or confused, just remember the sacrifices that you had to make before the operation, and then ask yourself where he was then." Before Lisa confided in Morgan about Justin's medical situation, she had been working a second job as a stripper to make enough money for the operation.

Sobering, Lisa nodded her head. "You're right."

"And you know that a zebra never changes his stripes," Morgan warned. She turned sharply at the sound of Zoë happily tearing the pages out of magazines. "Hey, let me go," Morgan said. "Call me if you need me."

After Lisa hung up the phone, she stared out the window, trying to sort through her mixed feelings about David's reappearance in her life. On the one hand, it was great having him around, and not only for Justin. It made her feel good that he wanted to be a part of their small family. Though she had given up on fairy tales, what little girl didn't grow up harboring dreams of the perfect home, complete with the mommy, daddy and baby? Thanks to Caché, she had moved out of her grandmother's house, and she and Justin had their own apartment on a nice block in Harlem. The only thing that had been missing was the baby's daddy. That is, until two months ago when he showed up on her doorstep, along with a slew of apologies.

She could still see him standing in the doorway, holding a bouquet of wilting red roses, shuffling his feet while stammering through the awkward situation. Lisa had been so sur-

prised to see him that it took her several minutes even to respond. His reappearance felt like a bad dream. While he
poured out his litany of excuses, she remembered the last
time she'd seen him. Their positions had been starkly reversed; she was on his doorstep six months pregnant—or
more accurately, his mother's stoop—begging him to stay
with her and the unborn child. He had looked at her and
said, "That ain't my baby, so don't be tryin' to ruin my life
wit' it." Then he slammed the door in her face.

Standing on her own stoop years later, David shamelessly
went on and on about how he'd grown up since then, and
what a mistake he'd made, and how he had missed her and
his biggest regret in life was not seeing his son, yada, yada,
yada. . . . When she'd finally emerged from her daze, arms
sternly crossed, she could only stare at him in shocked disbelief. Until she felt a tug at her elbow.

"Mommy, who is that?" Justin stood at her side with a
puzzled expression on his cute brown face.

Before she could fashion a plausible explanation, David
had dropped to one knee and said, "I'm your dad."

Lisa stood up from her desk, cutting short her bumpy
trip down recent-memory lane. Justin's wide, glad smile had
told David all he needed to know. He could use the son to
get what he wanted out of the mother.

So why was she hanging on to this fantasy of a fairy-tale
ending?

2

"Mr. Johnson, a Monique is on line one for you." Lyle could tell by Hilda's icy tone that his longtime secretary didn't exactly approve of his female caller, who was one of the many bottle blondes that stalked the handsome, rich and charismatic Wall Street executive. If it were up to Hilda, he would already be married to a "suitable and respectable" mate and have a growing litter of offspring.

"Put her through," he said, ignoring Hilda's maternal disapproval. Though it had taken him a while, Lyle was finally coming around to his secretary's way of thinking. After years of enjoying the babes who flocked around the hotshot investment banker, Lyle was retiring his fully notched belt and hanging it next to the silk stockings belonging to Yvette Wesley, an accomplished New York socialite. They met at the Studio Museum's annual black-tie dinner and had been dating for ten months now. Recently the relationship had become exclusive. They were even talking about marriage. His boys would howl when they heard that piece of news.

"What's going on?" he asked. Putting the receiver to his

ear, he leaned way back in his desk chair, smoothing his Hermès tie over his crisp white dress shirt.

"Why don't we get together later tonight, and you can find out for yourself?" the caller cooed through the phone lines. He had met Monique last month at the trendy TriBeCa bar he owned, Street Signs. Since then, the bleached blond husband-stalker had been ringing his office phone an average of once a week, dialing for dollars. Usually, Lyle would feign a meeting, a long conference call or maybe even a trip out of the country, but he now decided to put an end to the chase. After all, Yvette Wesley had the ability to open all the doors he needed opened in order to make it to the top.

"I really can't," he said. "I'm kinda tied up."

She didn't catch the drift. "How about tomorrow night, then? Or the next one?" Though she had been trying for sexy and coy, a tinge of desperation crept into her voice.

"Look . . . um . . ." He'd forgotten her name.

"Monique." She sounded offended.

"Yeah, Monique, I really can't. I'm seeing someone." There. He'd said it, and it hadn't killed him. *So this is what monogamy is like*, he thought. Declining the generous favors of attractive women was new territory for him.

"Your loss," the woman snipped, before slamming the phone down.

Maybe so, Lyle thought, *but not likely*. Because Hilda was right: It was high time for him to settle down with one woman, someone who would be an asset to his career. Yvette was beautiful, smart, witty and, best of all, came from a good family that was well connected politically and socially. What more could a man ask for? Of course, Lyle was no slouch himself. He was highly regarded in his industry. Fate had chosen to bless him with movie-star good looks—his complexion was a deep mocha with rich red undertones—and he was wealthy beyond the imagination of the young boy who grew up in Newark, New Jersey. Lyle had the Midas touch. Everything he laid a hand on turned to gold.

Lyle's remarkable ability to navigate the highest and tightest ropes made him the lone star of the three-ring circus called Wall Street. Since graduating from Columbia with his prized MBA, he had demonstrated an uncanny ability to anticipate the often-unpredictable whims of the market and then make moves that made vast fortunes for his clients.

A rap at his door pulled him away from his thoughts. "Come in," he said.

Hilda stuck her head in. "Just wanted to remind you of the cocktail party for the Democratic Election Fund at Lincoln Center tonight. It starts at six thirty, and Yvette called—she's having her driver pick you up here at six. Since it's five now, you need to start returning these calls so that you won't be late," she said, handing him a call sheet. Though Hilda looked down on the likes of Monique, she did approve of Yvette.

Hilda was like a mother hen, always careful to nudge her brilliant offspring in the right direction. Though she was a mother of three—all boys—and the grandmother of seven, she was still a very elegant woman. Her shiny gray hair was always gathered in a neat French chignon, without one strand daring to be out of place. Her wardrobe consisted of vintage Chanel suits that were much better made and designed than today's flimsy ready-to-wear, which she referred to as garbage. Hilda was from the era of cashmere twin sets and single-strand pearls.

"Thanks, Hilda. Anything else, or do you think I can handle it?" he teased.

"That's all for now, but I'm sure I'll think of something else. And when I do," she assured him as she turned to leave, "you'll be the first to know."

"I'm sure I will," he said. Sometimes he wondered who was the boss in their relationship—him or her.

An hour later, right on schedule, Yvette's black Town Car rolled to a stop in front of Lyle's office building. When he eased into the backseat to join her, she favored him with an openmouthed kiss, which he returned with equal vigor. Another thing that he loved about her was her passion. She actually kept up with his vigorous sexual appetite.

"How was your day, baby?" she asked, snuggling close to him.

"Hectic," he answered. "You know how crazy the market gets whenever Greenspan opens his mouth."

"My poor baby," she cooed as she began gently massaging his neck.

"I can't complain—I could be flipping burgers," he joked. Given his poor upbringing in Newark, he was right. Raised in a single-parent home in the middle of the ghetto, he'd made it out. He couldn't say the same for his brother, who'd never made it further than from one jail cell to the next.

Yvette couldn't fathom a world other than the one they now shared. "*That* would never happen," she insisted, dismissing the notion as preposterous. Yvette owned a PR firm whose client list included a who's who of politics, film and TV. Her father, a five-term congressman, and her mother, a white socialite from old New York money, had raised her on Fifth Avenue.

Lyle reached into his breast pocket and pulled out his cell phone. While the call rang through, he covered the receiver and said, "Gotta check in with the bar. I'll just be a minute."

Yvette settled into the leather seat and crossed her arms.

"Hi, Jeanine? Just checking in," Lyle said into the receiver.

"Hey, boss. You coming in tonight or are you off to another fancy-shmancy party?" Jeanine, the head bartender, also doubled as the assistant manager. She shot straight from the hip, which was the reason Lyle had hired her.

He ignored her directness. "You joke while I'm out here bustin' my buns so you guys can drink and party every night."

"If drinking and partying are involved, I must have gotten the wrong job."

He chuckled. "How's it going tonight?"

"The crowd is small, but they are buying premium, so all in all it's a good night so far."

"Cool. Call me if you need me."

"Will do."

As soon as he hung up, Yvette slid closer. "So where were we?" she asked as she turned his head toward hers for a long, steamy kiss.

When they arrived at the party, Congressman Wesley greeted them near the door. "How's my girl?" he asked, reaching out to Yvette for a hug.

She kissed him on both cheeks. "Daddy, you remember Lyle," she said, gesturing his way.

"Of course I do," the congressman answered, flashing a broad politician's smile as he reached out for the younger man's hand.

"Congressman Wesley, it's good to see you again."

"Likewise. How are things on Wall Street these days?" He wrapped his arm around Lyle's shoulder.

"Like riding a bull without a whip."

"Spoken like a true ringmaster," the congressman chuckled, patting Lyle on the back. "Hey, there's someone I'd like you to meet."

"Oh, Daddy, don't keep him all to yourself," Yvette said.

"Don't worry—I'll bring him back unharmed," her father teased. "I just want him to meet Senator Neuman," he said, leading Lyle off into the crowd.

"Hey, beautiful!"

Yvette turned to see Spence Ellis standing next to her, wearing his trademark Colgate smile. They shared an air kiss. "How are you?"

"I can't complain."

"I guess that means that the real-estate business is still treating you well."

As usual, Spence was dressed to kill in a blue seersucker suit, white shirt and blue tie with yellow stripes, a combination that would have been atrocious on most men—but on Spence it was impeccable.

"Speaking of real estate, how is Lyle enjoying his new apartment?"

"He loves it." Six months earlier, Yvette had introduced the two, which resulted in the purchase of Lyle's three-million-dollar penthouse apartment on the Upper West Side.

He winked. "Thanks again for the referral."

"You're welcome. I'm glad it worked out for you."

"It seems to me that things are working out pretty well for you too," Spence said, glancing in Lyle's direction.

Yvette blushed. "He's a great guy."

"If your dad likes him, he must be." Spence and Yvette pretty much grew up together; they'd attended the same private middle school in Manhattan.

"What's not to like? He's handsome, rich and educated."

"Well, here comes Mr. Handsome, Rich And Educated now."

"Oh, I forgot one other attribute," she said, smiling slyly.

"What might that be?"

"Sexy," she said, winking at Spence.

When Lyle came within range, she swept him into a torrid embrace. Feeling the eyes of everyone on them, he tried to pull away, but she wouldn't let go. "You're mine now, sexy," she purred into his ear.

3

The annual Black-and-White Ball, Montreal's grand social event of the year since 1903, had a guest list that rivaled that of the exclusive Inaugural Ball. The city's crème de la crème—bankers, politicians, business professionals, along with their status-seeking spouses, were the headliners. The ball was originally conceived by a group of bored housewives wanting to subsidize the budgets of the city's museums. Over time, the event grew in scale, as did the donations and the evening's social prestige. The men, competitive by nature, all tried to outdo each other by upping the financial ante each year. So now the coffers tipped the scales at a half billion Canadian dollars.

This year's gala was being held at Musée des Beaux-Arts de Montréal. The crown jewel of Montreal's art community, the museum boasted two expansive pavilions. The original structure, dating back to the early 1900s, had a Greco-Roman design with Corinthian columns that flanked the impressive entrance. Directly across the street was the modern pavilion with its partially slanted facade. The juxtaposition between the new and the old was deliberately reminiscent of the Louvre in Paris, with the I. M. Pei–designed glass pyramid in the center of the palace courtyard.

For tonight's event, a custom-designed platinum runner in honor of the ball's centennial celebration replaced the usual crimson carpeting. It began at the entrance of the museum, flowed down the steps, and stopped curbside. A matching runner also ran the length of the underground passage that joined the two pavilions.

The driver held Tess' hand as she stepped out of the black stretch limousine. A coy smile spread across her lacquered lips the moment her Ann Demeulemeester–clad feet sank into the plush silvery carpet. After logging several hours on the phone dialing a small network of friends, Tyrone had not only found the location of the ball, but also scored a highly coveted ticket. His networking also produced a car and driver from a friend who owned a limousine service. After much consideration, he decided to wear the black Michael Kors gown and a single strand of pearls rather than the overtly sexy Roberto Cavalli number. To complete his transformation into Tess, he donned a shoulder-length auburn wig styled in a loose flip. His makeup was not over-the-top drag queenish, but had an understated professional quality that hinted at a "natural beauty."

Tess arched her back, held her head high and sauntered up the welcome runner as though she owned the place. At the entrance were two attendants dressed in Louis XIV–style wigs and white tights with platinum-and-ruby embroidered capes.

"Welcome, mademoiselle." The attendant extended his gloved hand. "May I have your invitation, please?"

"Gladly," Tess said, smoothly sliding the invitation from her evening bag.

Once inside, she marveled at the tiny pin lights that twinkled overhead, accentuating the splendid works of the Renaissance masters—Michelangelo, da Vinci and Botticelli—that hung on the palatial walls of the museum. The overall effect was a surreal romantic vision.

She mingled amongst Montreal's elite, keeping a keen eye out for a suitable target. One of the servers—all of them were dressed in the same Louis XIV costumes—presented her with a crystal flute of champagne. As she sipped the bubbly elixir, she caught sight of the tacky Eddy and Patsy clones from the store. Tess had to stifle a laugh at their outlandish getups. One had on a black gown with huge white ruffles surrounding the neck and hemline, while the other woman wore a hideous beaded black-and-white gown with a bloodred shawl draped around her shoulders. That mess would never have passed inspection by the fashion police—if they could have gotten past the trail of bugle beads that she left abandoned in her wake.

Shaking her head, Tess surveyed the crowd. Aside from herself and the two hideous misfits, almost everyone was coupled off. She thought back to the conversation at the store and remembered that the two had spoken of a newly widowed gentleman thought to be coming alone. Tess was certain that the pair had their crosshairs set on him, but not if she sighted the man first. She moved among the flock, trying to spot the pigeon, but all she encountered were married stiffs.

Maybe he's in the new pavilion, she thought.

Tess joined a throng of people who were headed in the direction of the underground corridor that led into the modern wing of the museum. When she ascended the stairs on the far end, the masterpieces of Monet, Renior, Cezanne, Degas and Sisley greeted her. She strolled the gallery, leaving the impressionists behind, and walked into the modern era. Feigning interest in Picasso and Calder, she stopped every few feet as if passionately admiring their works. She stopped in front of a painting by Dalí, cocked her head slightly to the side, trying to decide what exactly it was.

"Don't you just love the surrealism of his work?" asked a male voice from behind her.

Tess' heart began to race. This was the moment she had been waiting for. *This must be Mr. Available,* she thought. Before turning around, she patted her lips together, making sure that her lipstick was evenly distributed. She readied a smile, then executed a slight pivot, turning around to face her destiny.

"He's one of my—" Her words caught in her throat at the sight before her. Standing nearly eye level with her fake breasts was a stout man in an ill-fitted tuxedo. The shoulders of the jacket were too tight, and the sleeves were too long. His bald head glistened like a smoothly greased cue ball. She looked down and could nearly see her reflection in its top.

"He's one of my favorites," he said, completing her sentence and gazing up into her eyes.

Tess assessed the vapid, unattractive little man and wondered how many zeros were in his bank account. He wasn't her type physically, but her motto was that money could make anyone look good. She decided to turn on the charm, just in case the man before her was Prince Charming disguised as a frog. "Mine too," she replied enthusiastically as she batted her false eyelashes and extended her manicured hand. "I'm Tess Aventura. And you are?"

"Ed—"

Before he could get his name out, a stout woman waddled up behind him. "Edward, there you are." She glanced up at Tess, then said to the fat little man, "I've been looking all over for you."

"Well, here I am," he said, sounding disappointed that he had been found. He then attempted to make introductions. "This is Tess Aven . . . Aven . . ."

"Aventura," Tess said.

His face flushed a bright red as if embarrassed. "Of course. Ms. Aventura, may I introduce my wife, Imalene?"

"Nice to meet you," Tess said, shaking the woman's chubby hand. *So he's not the eligible one,* she thought, relieved. Before turning to leave, she plastered a fake smile across her face. "Nice meeting you both."

As the night wore on, her patience wore thin. She made the rounds through both pavilions twice. Thinking that the third time would be the charm, she took in a deep breath and retraced her steps, but again, all she encountered were couples. *Maybe Mr. Available decided to stay home tonight,* she said to herself. *And that's exactly where I'm headed.* Tess walked the length of the underground passage feeling deflated.

A light mist had begun to fall over the city when Tess reached the doorway of the entrance. She peeked down the street, looking for her car and driver. "Great," she mumbled under her breath as the mist turned into a steady downpour. The forecast hadn't mentioned rain. Irked, she raised the hem of her gown and slowly began her descent down the hill of stairs.

"May I offer you my umbrella?"

Tess turned around. Standing before her was a tall sixty-something specimen with Paul Newman blue eyes and Richard Gere gray hair, dressed in a custom-tailored tuxedo. He opened his plaid Burberry umbrella, sheltering her against the pelting rain. As they walked down the steps in silence, her heart was thumping against her chest so loudly, she was sure he would hear each rapid beat. He waited with her as her car inched closer. "I'm Edmund Dubois," he finally said, breaking the silence.

Her mind flashed back to the conversation at the store. *Didn't they say his name was Edmund?*

She smiled. "Contessa Aventura."

Before she could refluff her feathers and puff her chest, the car pulled up to the curb. The handsome stranger walked over and opened the passenger door. "Nice to meet you, Ms. Aventura," he said, helping her into the limousine and shutting the door for her. As mysteriously as he'd appeared, Edmund disappeared again into the night.

Settling into the plush leather seat of the car, Tess felt like Cinderella back in her pumpkin after the ball. Except this scenario was strangely reversed, for she would be the one scouring the city in search of her Prince Charming. Only, he didn't have to fit into a magical glass slipper. All he had to do was be fabulously rich.

4

Lisa was very proud of the small two-bedroom apartment in Harlem that she and Justin called home. It was on the bottom floor of a six-family walk-up on 135th Street, only minutes from the office. More important for Lisa, it was tangible proof of her hard-won independence.

Like a lot of naive young girls, when she first learned of her pregnancy, she was sure that a baby would keep David in her life forever. Even after he slammed the door in her face, she stubbornly held on to a shred of hope that he would come around in time, especially once the baby was born. After Justin was delivered, she sent pictures of him to David weekly and called almost daily, until three months crept by, leading to the painful realization that there would be no happily ever after in this storybook. The other shoe dropped one Sunday morning as she sat alone in Harlem's Abyssinian Baptist Church, cradling her beautiful four-month-old son. To her left was a young black woman about her age, who sat contently nestled between her toddler daughter and her handsome husband while she lovingly cradled a newborn swaddled in a soft, light blue blanket. The woman appeared to glow from an inner peace that Lisa did not remember ever having had. The epiphany was as clear to her as if Moses had hand-delivered it from up on the mountaintop. She would forever be solely responsible for the care of her child. It was up to her, and her alone, to make sure that Justin could succeed in life. With or without a father.

When she returned to her grandmother's house later that afternoon, she locked herself in the white-tiled bathroom that they shared, turned on the shower to buffer all sounds, and let a stream of hot tears and choking sobs cleanse her soul. After drying her eyes, she vowed that those would be the last tears she'd ever shed for David. She had to move on with her life and, by doing so, create a better one for her son. Throughout his later illness and surgery, it was a hard time, but she realized that she would not trade a moment of her struggles for the pure joy that her son brought to her. Whenever she looked into his innocent brown eyes, she knew she would suffer all over again just to see his bright smile as it lit up her heart.

That was why David's sudden reappearance in their life bothered Lisa as much as it made her hopeful. Since Justin had been old enough to have playdates with other kids, he'd been deeply troubled by the fact that God hadn't given him a father. It was no comfort to him that some of his friends were also from single-parent homes. His longing remained constant, as did his questions. Where is my daddy? Why did he leave? Is God going to send him back for my birthday? Lisa did the best she could to answer his questions, but her elusive replies were never quite enough to quench his desire to know his father. So when David suddenly appeared that day, Justin was certain that God had answered his prayers. He had never been happier—he talked incessantly about his daddy. It was her deepest fear that David would do something to wipe away that smile.

"Mommy, what time is it now?" Justin asked, jumping up and down while craning his neck up to the wall clock that hung over their kitchen table. He was so excited that he could barely stand still. He shifted his weight from one foot to the other, trying to make time go by faster than sixty seconds per minute. David was coming over this afternoon, and the three of them were going to Central Park.

"It's ten minutes after two o'clock, baby." She smiled down at his worried face and pinched his little cheek lightly. "Don't worry—he'll be here any minute now." Justin had his backpack already stuffed with his drawings from school, plus some of his favorite toys to share with his dad. It had been packed since Thursday when Lisa okayed the excursion. David had initially asked to take the boy out alone, but Lisa would have no part of that plan. As a compromise, she agreed to tag along with them.

"Do you think Dad'll wanna play baseball?" Justin asked with a look of wide-eyed anticipation usually saved for the night before Christmas.

She put the last dish into the dishwasher and turned to face him. "I don't know, but you can ask him," she answered, rubbing his head.

That answer was enough to send him scampering back to his room, in search of the baseball glove that David had brought with him on his last visit.

After she closed the dishwasher to start its wash cycle, the doorbell rang. She took off the apron that covered her Baby Phat sweatsuit and headed for the door.

"Hey, baby," David said as he thrust a large bouquet of flowers into her arms. "Where's my boy?" he asked, smiling, knowing that Justin was probably within earshot.

Lisa stood back to let him in, not quite sure what to do with the flowers. It was easy for him to charm an innocent six-year-old, but after all she'd been through, charming her would not be nearly so easy. "Justin?" she called out over her shoulder.

Before she finished the second syllable, a blur headed in the direction of David, who squatted on the balls of his feet with outstretched arms to greet his son, like a catcher waiting on a fastball. "Daddy! Daddy!"

While the two carried on in the small living room, Lisa headed to the kitchen to get the bag that she'd packed for the park. She also had to find a vase for the flowers. Despite her trepidation, she couldn't help but be happy for Justin.

After bear-hugging the little boy, David stood up and asked, "So, how is my little man?"

"Ready to go to the park. Do you wanna play catch?" The smile on Justin's face was radiant, and his eyes twinkled with happiness.

"I think that I can arrange that." Smiling, David turned toward Lisa as she returned to the room. "Can Mommy play too?"

A puzzled look came over the boy's face. "Mommy can't play baseball," he announced. "She's a girl." He shrugged his little shoulders and spread his arms, as though that explained everything.

"What do you mean, I can't play baseball?" Lisa challenged. "I'll have you know that I was the best shortstop on my block."

David picked up the backpack and put it on Justin's shoulder. "We'll see about that," he snorted.

Since when did he become Mr. Athletic? The only exercise she'd ever seen him do was running to escape responsibility. "Let's go," Lisa said, sourly grabbing her bag and ushering the two of them out of the door.

Street Signs was located on SoHo's Broome Street, a half block from West Broadway. The dark, cozy enclave was mannish enough—with rich, dark woods and brick-faced walls—to make the testosterone-drenched alpha males feel welcome, but was chic enough, with flickering candlelight and plush velvet lounges, that the femmes fatales felt sexy while on the prowl. Like a high-maintenance aquarium for breeding an exotic species of fish in, Street Signs was a delicately balanced ecosystem whose structure was necessary to produce a truly hot bar.

Like his customers, on many nights Lyle floated through the bar on his way home to his elegantly appointed Columbus Avenue penthouse. Sometimes he was in and out of the bar in fifteen minutes, but other times he was there until the wee hours of the morning, depending entirely upon his mood, the scene—more specifically the eye candy available— or whether there was pressing business that Marc, the manager, needed his assistance with. Since Lyle was so hands-off with the bar's management, the latter was hardly ever the case.

Lyle walked in and waved to Jeanine. He smiled as a red-headed fox gave him a slow once-over. Since buying the hot bar last year, he'd had all sorts of fun. Leggy young women flocked to Street Signs by the dozens looking for a rich Wall Streeter to help finance their blond-streaked highlights and frequent trips to Prada. Lately the problem was stocking the bar with enough alpha males to lure the females, since the stock market had become about as bullish as a small yapping dog. The big spenders were staying at home these days, licking their bleeding wounds. All except for those who, like Lyle, were at the very top of the Wall Street food chain, and therefore had excess cash to cushion the market's blow. He hadn't bought the bar to make a mint; he'd already had that. His reasons were to add a little texture to his otherwise smooth, structured banker's life; still, there was a difference between not making money and losing it, and lately Street Signs was crossing the centerline.

He headed to one of the cozy booths that surrounded the space. They were recessed nooks with thick burgundy velvet drapes drawn back seductively to frame the semiprivate lairs. They were also the perfect little hideaways from which to lie back in the cut and survey the room. Lyle was chilling in his reserved booth when one of his colleagues, Renwick, lumbered over to join his table. He was a sales trader at Merrill Lynch.

"How's the market treating you these days?" he asked, sliding into the seat opposite Lyle.

"Hey, man, you know the score," Lyle said, leaning far back into the cushions. "It's a bloodbath." He then shrugged his shoulders nonchalantly.

Renwick shook his head. "Tell me about it. Just when I didn't think the blue chips couldn't possibly go lower, they nosedive again."

"The market definitely isn't for the faint of heart."

"I've been following your picks—you're not doing so bad. You obviously have a pretty strong pulse." Renwick squinted at him. "Why don't you share some of your secrets with an old friend, or at least lend me your crystal ball?"

Lyle was one of the few African-American men on Wall Street who ran the investment banking divisions of major brokerage houses, and his track record was impeccable. He laughed, his head resting on the back cushion of the booth. "I wish it were that simple."

"You certainly make it look that way."

Lyle motioned for one of the cocktail waitresses. "Would you get my friend here a drink, and I'll have another gimlet martini." He turned to Renwick. "What are you drinking?"

"I'll have a gin and tonic."

After dutifully writing down the order, the waitress turned to Lyle. "Can I get anything else for you?" she asked, her eyelashes batting suggestively.

"I think that'll be all for now."

When the willowy brunette was out of earshot, Renwick leaned over and lightly punched Lyle's forearm. "You are the man!"

"What are you talking about?" Lyle asked, though he knew perfectly well where Renwick was going with that one. He did have a well-earned reputation of being a ladies' man.

"Not only do you have access to all the hot babes that slither in and out of here every night, but I'd forgotten about the help. Man, it's like picking a winner in a one-horse race. You can't lose," he chortled, looking around the room. "No wonder you bought this place."

The waitress reappeared with their drinks in tow. After

bending coyly at the waist to set the glasses on the table, she smiled brightly. The performance continued even after she left, giving them a show of her retreating, undulating backside.

Renwick whistled lightly. "Man, oh man. She's hot. You should introduce me."

Lyle shook his head. "Don't waste your time," he said dismissively.

"Easy for you to say."

"Trust me, the hardware really looks good, but I don't think the software has been installed yet."

"Hey, beggars can't be choosers. We can't all be Lyle Johnson."

Renwick was the kind of guy who found it hard to score chicks, money or no. He was short and round and had fat, stubby little fingers. His mousy brown hair was thinning rapidly, and he'd started swooping the longer side strands across the top in an attempt to cover up the obvious, while only drawing more attention to it. Lyle had often wondered what form of dementia made white guys do that.

They settled into a comfortable silence as they sipped their drinks and watched the procession of women who sauntered in wearing the latest, most skin-baring designer wear. The women came solo, in pairs, in entire man-hunting packs. Usually more white girls than black. Very soon their table was swarming with women, all trying to outmaneuver one another for Lyle's attention—until suddenly Yvette arrived with a friend. She made a beeline for Lyle, confidently brushing past the other "ladies in waiting."

"Hey, honey!" she chirped, leaning over to plant a lip-locking kiss.

"Hi, babe. Didn't know you were stopping by."

"Samantha and I were out to dinner, and I thought we'd stop in for a nightcap." Yvette turned toward her friend. "I'm sorry—I don't think you two have met. Lyle, this is Samantha. Samantha, this hunk here is my honey, Lyle."

Samantha and Lyle exchanged greetings before Lyle introduced a beaming Renwick, who couldn't seem to take his eyes off either girl. He was watching the action like a front-row spectator at Wimbledon.

Yvette slid into the booth next to Lyle and wrapped her arms around him possessively. Then she leaned in to coo into his ear, "I can't wait to get you home."

Lyle slid his hand up her thigh. "You know, we can leave now."

She ran her hand up his chest and covered his mouth with hers, causing the other women to scatter to the winds. "Maybe I should pass on the nightcap. I think I'd rather have a bedtime story instead."

She stood to leave, extending her hand to him. Lyle followed with a smile. Renwick sat with his mouth agape.

5

Like Cinderella after the ball, slaving around the house in her shabby clothes, Tyrone was back at Basicz sans his beautiful evening gown, makeup and wig, pushing brooms, unpacking boxes and doing any other menial job the wicked store manager could conjure up. He couldn't keep his mind off that magical night. Finally, after roaming the museum for hours, he'd met Edmund Dubois, his Prince Charming. Edmund was polished, sophisticated and appeared to be the epitome of the corporate-executive-making-seven-figures-a-year-plus-bonus—and he was a gentleman. Tyrone had felt like Audrey Hepburn in *Roman Holiday* when Edmund appeared and offered his umbrella. It was all so romantic. The only downer was that it had now been several days since the ball, and he still had not been able to find his leading man.

Because he was daydreaming, he didn't see the manager trying to get his attention, until the man walked over and stood directly in front of him.

"I'm not paying you to stand around idle."

Tyrone snapped out of his trance. "Uh? What did you say?"

"I said, you're skating on thin ice around here, mister."

"What do you mean?" Tyrone asked, playing dumb.

The manager raised his eyebrows. "I mean, either you do the work you're paid to do," he snapped, "or else!"

Tyrone wanted to snatch off the stupid smock and storm out the door, never to return, but he had to bide his time. Instead he asked, "Did you need me in the stockroom?"

The manager exhaled loudly, blowing his hot breath directly into Tyrone's face. "The price stickers you put on the pressed powder the other day are wrong. Those stickers were for the loose powder, not the pressed powder. Now I need for you to scrape those stickers off and replace them with the correct stickers. You think you can handle that?" he asked in a condescending tone. He was talking to Tyrone like he was the world's biggest imbecile with the smallest brain.

I think I can kick your Barney Fife–looking ass up one aisle and down the other, Tyrone wanted to say, but once again he bit his tongue. "Sorry for the mix-up. I'll be right there."

As soon as the manager turned to walk away, Tyrone pocketed a pack of false eyelashes. Made from genuine sable fur, they were the rage among jet-setters. Tyrone could barely afford the regular synthetic ones, let alone the fur lashes, which retailed at more than fifty dollars a pair. *Since they ain't paying me nothing, I might as well subsidize my income*, he thought, and swiped another pack for good measure.

With his goodies in pocket, Tyrone went back into the stockroom and began the tedious task of removing the stickers. When he was halfway through the first box, his mind began to drift back to the night of the ball. *If only I had the money to hire a private investigator to find Mr. Right, my troubles would be over*, he thought. And then as if from nowhere, he remembered that the tacky women had mentioned where Edmund worked.

Did they say First Federal? he pondered. *No, that's not it.* He continued to rack his brain, running a list of names through his mind. *Federal Lending, Federation, Financier.* Tyrone popped up like a piece of toast. "That's it!" he said in a hushed cry. "That's it, Financier." He hurried over to the phone on the wall of the stockroom and quickly dialed 411.

"At the tone, please speak slowly," said the automated voice. *Beep*.

"I need the telephone number to Financier," Tyrone said nervously.

After what seemed like forever, the automated voice returned with the phone number. Tyrone cleared the line and then quickly dialed the number.

"Good afternoon, Financier LLC. How may I help you?" asked a pleasant voice.

Tyrone went into Tess mode and said in an octave higher than his natural voice, "I'm trying to reach Mr. Edmund Dubois." He held his breath, hoping he had the right company.

"Hold on, please. I'll connect you to his office," said the receptionist.

A few seconds later, he was speaking to Edmund's assistant. "Good afternoon, Mr. Dubois' office."

"Is he available?"

"I'm sorry, he's at lunch, miss. Would you care to leave a message?" asked the efficient secretary.

Tyrone really didn't want to speak with Edmund, at least not yet. Since they hadn't exchanged information the night of the ball, Edmund would become suspicious if he were cold-called out of the blue. "I just wanted to double-check your address. I have a delivery for Mr. Dubois."

The assistant spouted off the address, then asked, "Is there anything else I can help you with?"

"No, thank you. You've been quite helpful."

Tyrone hung up and danced around the small room, raising his long arms in the air. He now had a new sense of purpose.

There was a popular restaurant near Edmund's office where most of the local businessmen lunched. *I bet he's at Elsa's,* Tyrone thought, referring to the restaurant. He wanted to bolt out the door and run straight over there. *Well, tomorrow I'll be there and* accidentally *run into my prince.*

As Tyrone continued his victory dance, the manager came into the room. "And what do you think you're doing?" he asked, looking at Tyrone strangely.

"Oh, just a little exercise to loosen up the old muscles." Tyrone grinned.

The manager gave him a look that read, *You're pushing it.* He then said, "Well, get back to work."

The manager walked out, and Tyrone went back to scraping stickers. But he knew it was just a matter of time until his days of scraping by were over.

Tyrone called in sick the next morning, to the dismay of the manager, who ranted about the store being understaffed.

Tyrone didn't care. He had lunch plans. Tyrone settled in at the ornate vanity table in the dressing room of his posh subletted apartment. He started by slathering on makeup, the first phase of his "Tess" transformation. He expertly applied foundation, pressed powder, eye shadow and lipstick to his creamy caramel complexion. Tyrone had clipped enough of the store's inventory to open his own cosmetics boutique. He also possessed an array of wigs in black, auburn and platinum and of varying lengths, which were set atop Styrofoam heads on their own vanity table. He chose the same auburn wig he wore the night of the party. *I want to make sure he remembers me,* he thought as he secured the wig to his head with extra-large hairpins.

With face and hair intact, he walked over to the vault-size closet and opened a dresser drawer filled with an arsenal of padded bras and panties to enhance his slim figure. After padding his assets, he selected a conservative but seductive black formfitting wrap dress. He wrapped the ties around his slender waist, then slipped on a pair of black Ralph Lauren pumps to complete the look. Standing in front of the full-length mirror, he admired the transformation. It was perfect. Tyrone grabbed a black leather purse from the vanity, swung it over his shoulder, and headed out the door.

Elsa's was an upscale restaurant with outdoor seating. The tables were situated closely together, reminiscent of the cafés in Paris along the Champs-Élysées. The neighborhood comprised a scattering of office buildings, restaurants and boutiques. Tess strolled past people having leisurely lunches underneath the huge mustard awning. Beneath her dark shades, she cut her eyes to the right, trying to sneak a glimpse at the outdoor patrons. She didn't spot Edmund, so she proceeded inside.

"*Bonjour, mademoiselle,* welcome to Elsa's," said the maître d'.

"*Bonjour,*" Tess responded, checking out the handsome Canadian.

"A table for one?"

"Yes, *s'il vous plaît.*"

Taking in the bustling dining room, she followed the maître d' with movie-star sex appeal through the crowded restaurant to a table near the back. Once seated, Tess scanned the room: no Edmund. When the waiter appeared at her table, she ordered a Belvedere and tonic to soothe her nerves and watched the door, anxiously hoping that Edmund had decided to dine out this afternoon. The first drink went down effortlessly, so she ordered a second. After twenty minutes and no sight of Edmund, an empty glass and a full bladder, Tess decided to go to the ladies' room.

As she was exiting the rest room, a man brushed against her slightly on his way out of the men's room.

"Excuse me," said the debonair-looking gentleman.

Tess looked into his ice blue eyes and nearly fainted. She couldn't believe her lucky stars. It was Edmund. "You're excused," she replied, playing it cool.

He regarded her a second time and hesitated a moment. "You look familiar," he said, puzzled. "I know that sounds like a line, but have we met before?"

Tess played right along with a puzzled expression of her own. "I can't say that we have." She extended her hand. "I'm Contessa Aventura."

"Pleased to meet you," he said, taking her hand in his, and giving her a quick once-over. "I'm Edmund Dubois."

Tess flushed as Edmund released her hand. Men were so easy to figure out, and if there was one thing Tess knew about, that was the male species.

"Nice to meet you, Mr. Dubois," she said as she turned to walk away.

"Edmund. Please call me Edmund," he said, trying to prolong the conversation. Then as if a bolt of lightning had struck him, he blurted out, "The ball!"

"Excuse me?" Tess asked as if she was completely clueless.

"We met at the Black-and-White Ball. I walked you to your car in the rain."

"Oh, that was you?" Tess feigned surprise.

"Are you here alone?" Edmund asked.

"Yes, just having a quick lunch before my next appointment," she answered, glancing at her watch.

"Do you mind if I join you?"

This is going to be too easy, Tess thought, then said, "Of course not—my table is this way."

"Are you new to town?" Edmund asked once they were settled at the table.

"Relatively," Tess simply said, playing coy.

Edmund stared into her eyes. "Where are you from originally?"

"New York," Tess said. She didn't want to give away too much information on the first meeting. She knew men loved the thrill of the chase. Letting him fish for information would keep him baited until she was ready to reel him in.

"I don't mean to stare, but you're simply gorgeous."

"No need to apologize for that." She blushed coquet-tishly.

The waiter came and took their orders. Over lunch she learned that he was the president of Financier LLC, Mon-treal's premier brokerage house. Tess hardly heard the rest of his conversation for the loud *ka-ching*s that rang in her head as she tallied up his money.

Once lunch was over and he had paid the bill, he asked, "How can I get in touch with you?"

Tess hesitated. "Not to be rude, but I don't give out my number." She knew a man of his stature was accustomed to getting what he asked for. Besides, she was not about to wait around, hoping that he called.

He looked taken aback but quickly recovered. "I under-stand. Here's my information," he said, handing over one of his business cards. "Please give me a call. I would love to take you to dinner."

"Thanks for lunch, Edmund. I'll speak to you soon." Tess tucked his card in her purse and sauntered out of the restaurant.

Mission accomplished, she said to herself as she walked home.

6

"Yes, sure, Mom." Lyle nodded obediently into the phone, which was wedged between his right ear and his shoulder. "I'll be there on time, I promise." Assured of that point, she switched gears, downshifting into a new line of chatter about how Pathmark had raised the price of chicken breasts. Lyle clutched his chest, shocked as he watched his computer monitors in real time while the Dow suddenly took a nasty dive. Investors from Wall Street barons to Ma and Pa Kettle in Paducah, Kentucky, were fleeing the market in droves, taking their hard-earned money with them. It was not a pretty picture.

The only thing his mom cared about was that both her boys would be present at her dinner table come Sunday for the first time in years. Ernie, Lyle's older brother and the black sheep of the family, had just been released from jail last week, and Mrs. Johnson was eager to welcome him back into the warm bosom of her family. She was sure that her love—and a good home-cooked meal—would miracu-

lously do what the justice system so far could not, and that
was to straighten out his crooked ways.

Lyle scowled at the thought. He had not spoken to Ernie
in over eight years, not since the time his brother had stolen
checks and forged their mother's name in order to finance a
drug deal. She had immediately forgiven him, after he'd shed
a couple of crocodile tears and spouted forth a rote apology,
but to Lyle, stealing from their mother was the last straw. He
hadn't seen his brother since, and he had refused to provide
bail money during his subsequent journeys through Newark's penal system. Not one to be deterred, Mrs. Johnson
was determined to bring her two boys back together.

As much as Lyle disliked the idea of seeing his brother
again, there was something else that he dreaded even more.
"Mom, don't forget that Yvette will be coming to dinner
with me."

For the last month, Yvette had been quizzing Lyle about
his family, and when she learned that he would be visiting his
mother this weekend, she insisted that he include her. After
all, he had met her family, and besides, their conversations
were turning more and more to the subject of marriage. Lyle
tapped his pencil impatiently. As much as he wanted to put
off the inevitable, she had to meet his family sooner or later,
so Sunday was as good a time as any. That way they'd get
past the ex-con issue early.

"Oh, yes, the young lady you've been seeing. I can't wait
to meet her."

Lyle only wished that he were as thrilled with the
prospect.

"Okay, listen, Mom, I gotta run," he said, anxious to get

off the phone. He had to stem the hemorrhaging that his firm's clients were suffering.

He also had to turn off the image looming in his mind: that of Yvette's mouth open wide at the sight of where he'd grown up.

Whenever Lyle entered his mother's aging two-family walk-up in Newark, the age-old sounds, baked-in smells, and conflicting emotions of his childhood swallowed him like a ripple sucked into a fast-moving tide. It led back to a place worlds away from his everyday existence. Twenty years ago, he'd left for college with one barely full suitcase, yet sadly and miraculously, almost nothing had changed at 5762 Liberty Street. The house's worn siding was still puke green. The tin mailbox that hung to the left of the front door was still crooked. Like post-riot Newark, his family home was frozen in a decrepit time warp.

Emma Johnson didn't care to be any other place on earth, which was a sore topic between them. Since Lyle landed his first six-figure job on Wall Street, he had repeatedly offered to move his mother out of the old neighborhood, but she would have no part of his grand schemes. "The only way I'm leaving here is in a pine box," she would say. So finally, Lyle gave up. Every so often he'd have to take his trip across the river, and down the streets he'd worked so hard to escape.

Lyle glanced at Yvette, who seemed reluctant to step across the threshold. Her dress screamed New York chic in the shabby surroundings. Lyle gave her a slight tug, and she flinched, startled.

"Hey, baby," Emma said when Lyle walked in, reaching up to grab his face between both hands to plant a generous kiss on his smooth cheek. She was a short, wiry woman that seventy years of living had failed to slow down.

Lyle leaned his tall frame over to wrap her up in his arms. "Mom, I want you to meet Yvette Wesley. Yvette, this is my mom."

Yvette stood in the doorway, clutching her Louis Vuitton purse for dear life. She tried in vain to remove the distasteful look from her face. It was clear that her Gucci mules had wandered to the wrong side of the tracks. "How do you do?" she said too formally as she stuck out her hand for a quick shake. She was hyper today even by her own standards, and Lyle groaned inside.

"Come on in, you two, and have a seat," his mother said too brightly. "Dinner's about ready. I fixed greens, some fried chicken, potato salad and lemon pies." As she spoke, she went about removing Lyle's jacket and hanging it up in the tiny coat closet just inside the front door, then ushered him a few feet into the living room. She offered to take Yvette's pashmina wrap, but the younger woman declined, holding it tightly around her shoulders.

Lyle entered the living room; he saw Ernie already slouched down into the plastic-covered chair in the corner of the room, looking like a street thug forced to sit through Sunday school.

"Yo, man, wassup?" Ernie asked, not bothering to stand up. He wore a sweatshirt that was about four sizes too large over a pair of large jeans and Timberlands. A Newark Bears cap was still on his head, turned to the back.

Lyle turned to see Yvette cringe at the sight of his brother. "Nothin' much," Lyle managed to get out as his mother watched on hopefully. Why had he ever thought it was a good idea for Yvette to meet his brother? "Ernie, this is Yvette. Yvette, Ernie."

She was at a loss for words. Was this person before her really related to her Lyle? She'd realized that Lyle was from a modest upbringing—nowhere near the height of her crust, but then, who was? But never would she have imagined this. "How do you do?" she managed weakly.

"I do just fine," Ernie answered, pleased with the tight grimace that Lyle wore.

When no other words came forth to fill the spreading void in the room, Emma jump-started the chatter she had begun at the door. "I remember when you boys couldn't wait to get to the table on Sundays after church. Remember those days?" she asked, looking between the two men on the opposite sides of her life.

"Sure I do, Mom," Lyle answered.

What he remembered most about growing up was a string of disappointments. The first one was the day that his father failed to return home from a day out looking for a job. Though Lyle was only nine years old at the time, he knew right away that his dad would never be back, though his mother was convinced that he was laid up in a hospital somewhere unconscious. Even after a week, when he hadn't shown up in area hospitals or jails, she clung tight to the belief that he must be wandering around somewhere with amnesia. To this day Lyle wasn't sure exactly when she finally realized that he was never coming home.

"Yvette, can I get you something to drink? Some iced tea?" Emma offered.

"No, thank you." Yvette was unsure what to do with herself. Lyle seemed to be frozen in place. Ernie was leering at her as though she were the punch line to a bad joke, while Mrs. Johnson stood by, wringing her hands.

Lyle finally came to her rescue. "Have a seat," he said, guiding her to a chair opposite the sofa.

His mother hastily disappeared into the kitchen. The two brothers sat glaring at each other while Yvette studied the polish on her nails. Finally, Ernie cocked his head and spoke from one side of his mouth. "Long time, no see."

"Yeah, it has been a long time. What was it, six to ten?" Lyle said disdainfully. He regretted the statement as soon as he said it, if for no other reason than Yvette hadn't yet been told that his brother was an ex-convict.

The sharp barb hit home. "Why you gotta go there?" Ernie shifted his weight on the sofa to reach into his back pocket, fishing out a half-empty pack of Camels. "You know, I don't need this shit."

"Watch your language," Lyle threatened.

"Oh, excuse me," Ernie snarled, "Mr. Holier Than Thou." He fished a pack of matches from his other pocket and struck one, holding the flame to the cigarette's tip.

Yvette looked on in shock and horror. All the while, she had thought Lyle was as sophisticated as she was, but how could he be if these were his roots?

Seeing her dismay, Lyle leaned forward. "What's your problem, man? You come in here, fresh outta jail, complete with an attitude. You know how important this dinner is to

Mom. So why don't you try to just chill out and at least get through the damn dinner?"

Ernie laughed unpleasantly, leaning back in his chair. "You know, that shit's easy for you to say as you bark down orders from on top of your throne. Not all of us can chill out in a penthouse on the Upper West Side, or cruise over to Jersey in our Jaguar, paying a quick visit to the common folk."

Eight years of anger boiled to the surface. "Don't give me that shit, man. You had the same chances I did—you just decided to make some fucked-up choices. That's the only difference."

Ernie paused with the cigarette inches from his lips, the smoke curling toward the chipped ceiling, and pinned Lyle with a challenging look. "You really think so? I guess it's easier for you that way."

Lyle had not seen this intensity in his brother for a long time. What was he getting at? "No, I don't think so. I know so."

"Oh, that's right. I forgot," Ernie said, thumping his forehead with the heel of his hand. "You know everything. You've got all the answers."

Before Lyle could respond, Emma reappeared in the room. "Dinner's ready," she said in her most chipper voice, though Lyle was certain that she had heard their argument.

Lyle rose to his feet. He extended his hand down to Yvette, who was staring at Ernie like he was a one-man freak show headlining in the circus. At last she shook free of her spell. Smiling awkwardly, she took Lyle's hand and stiffly rose to her feet.

Ernie scratched his head, puzzled. "Lyle, who do you think you are, with a woman like that?" He stood up with the lithe grace of a panther. "You really don't know as much as you think you do. What, do you think about your past at all? Or are you too wrapped up in your future?" With that, he stared pointedly at Yvette.

Though confused, Lyle wasn't backing down. "I think about my past. I just choose not to think about everyone in it."

Ernie snorted. "Go on, keep foolin' yourself, baby bro. Let's go have a nice family dinner," he said sarcastically.

7

Tyrone drifted into work fifteen minutes late, still floating on a cloud from his dinner with Edmund the night before. He didn't care if he had to scrape the price stickers off every single item in the store, because he knew it was now just a matter of time until he was rescued from the working-class poor. Soon he would join the ranks of the privileged few.

He had purposely waited a few days after their "chance" encounter before calling Edmund at work.

"Mr. Dubois' office," said the secretary.

"Contessa Aventura for Mr. Dubois," Tess announced in a professional voice.

"May I ask the nature of your call?" inquired the efficient assistant.

"It's personal business," was all Tess said.

The assistant hesitated a moment, at a loss for words. "Oh. Hold on, I'll see if he's available."

"Trust me, honey, he'll take the call," Tess mumbled after hearing the click of the hold button. And sure enough, after a brief pause Edmund came on the line.

"Ms. Aventura, how kind of you to call," he said with a hint of excitement.

"Tess. Please call me Tess."

"Tess, I thoroughly enjoyed our conversation the other day." Tess could tell by his tone that he was smiling. "I would love to take you to dinner tonight, if you're available," he said, getting right to the point.

"Hold on a second, let me check my calendar." She paused, perusing an imaginary appointment book. "Actually, I do have a cancellation this evening."

"Well, it must be my lucky day. How does seven thirty sound?"

Normally, Tess would have put off the first date for at least a week, but with the bills mounting, she had little time to snare him. "Seven thirty sounds fine."

"I'll pick you up, then," he said eagerly. "What's your address?"

She gave it to him and said, "See you tonight."

"What to wear? What to wear?" Tess sang as she danced around her dressing room later. The key tonight was to make sure her outfit was provocative yet elegant. She didn't want to wear another wrap dress like the one she wore to lunch, so she surveyed the other dresses that hung waiting in her closet. She eyed a magenta minidress with thin spaghetti straps—too clubby. Then there was the emerald green dress with the empire waist—too matronly. Finally, after trying on every single dress in her closet, Tess chose a sapphire silk organza blouse and a matching skirt with sexy side slits.

After a leisurely bubble bath, she went through her makeup ritual. It took a while to get just the right feminine look. She had to make sure her face was flawless. Her future depended on this high-stakes game of deception she was playing. She had to lure him with her good looks, enchant him with her charm, and then hold him at bay physically until snagging enough of his money.

She unbuttoned the first four buttons on the slightly see-through blouse to allow a teasing glimpse of her chest. The sheer fabric enhanced the imprint of the fake nipples that she wore. Walking back to the vanity table, she picked up the crystal atomizer and spritzed Chanel No. 5 on her wrists and neck. She knew the scent was dated, but figured an older gentleman like Edmund would appreciate its sophisticated fragrance. The doorbell rang at precisely seven thirty. Tess smirked to herself and whispered, "It's show time."

Edmund was dressed in a midnight blue pin-striped four-button suit with tone on tone ice blue shirt and tie, which matched the color of his eyes. He gave Tess an appraising look, with his gaze landing on the erect nipples. "You look delectable," he said, his eyes darting from her face to her beckoning breasts.

She nearly laughed out loud. Men were so predictable. She knew he would be drawn to the rubber nipples like a newborn to a wet nurse. "Thank you," she said, picking up her evening bag from the Parsons table near the door. "Let's go."

Edmund had made reservations at City Lights, a romantic restaurant high atop a hill. The hostess settled them into a choice table near the huge picture window, with a clear view of the twinkling city lights below. Throughout a dinner of chateaubriand, haricots verts, potatoes au gratin and several bottles of vino, they exchanged life stories.

Tess lied effortlessly about being raised on the shores of Monaco as well as on the Upper East Side of Manhattan. With a straight face, she told him that she was the love child of the Duke of Monaco. He seemed to swallow that lie as easily as he did the wine. After remembering the comment that the tacky women had made about him being a widow, for good measure she even spun a tale about a husband dying of a rare brain disease.

This forged an immediate bond between the two. Edmond empathized with her loss and went on to tell her that he too was a widower. His wife of twenty-five years had died just eight months ago after a seven-year battle with Alzheimer's.

"The ravishing effects of that dreadful disease robbed Ella of her vibrant spirit, leaving her bedridden for the last two years." Tears welled up in his eyes. He dropped his head, then in a faraway voice said, "In the end, she didn't even recognize me."

Tess reached across the table and gently touched his hand. "I'm so sorry. That must have been awful for you," she said softly. From the sadness in his eyes, she could tell that the poor man was starving for affection.

He nodded. "What I missed most throughout the illness was the companionship we shared. Ella and I did everything together."

"Well, you don't have to worry about that now. I'm here," Tess said, getting in her bid. She waited a moment to see his reaction. When he didn't say anything, she began to

worry, thinking that maybe she had overstepped her bound-
aries.

Then he squeezed her hand and said, "And I'm glad."

It can't be this easy, Tess thought. She knew that for
someone who'd been married for as many years as Edmund
had, his natural instinct would be to drift back into the comfort zone of a committed relationship. But still, catching
him, so far, was like shooting crabs in a barrel.

After dinner, they strolled hand in hand to his car. Once
they arrived at her apartment, she pondered the notion of
inviting Edmund up for a nightcap. But thought it better to
end the evening with a mildly passionate kiss in the car.

"There you are," ranted the manager, dragging Tyrone back
to the present. "I need to see you in my office. Now!"

Once inside the cramped, dingy office, the manager said
without preamble, "You're fired!"

Tyrone froze like a deer caught in the glare of high
beams. "Fired?" He didn't want this job, but he wasn't
ready to give it up, at least not yet. "You can't fire me. You
said just the other day that the store is understaffed," he
pleaded.

"Don't tell me what I can't do! You waltz in here late,
take off whenever you want and, when you are here, you
barely do any work." He handed Tyrone a sealed envelope.
"Here's your check. Good-bye," he said, ending the conversation.

Tyrone opened the envelope and looked at the amount.
"This isn't my full check."

"You didn't work a full week. Like I said before, good-bye," the manager reiterated. Then he stood and opened the door for Tyrone to exit.

The cloud that Tyrone had floated into work on had now turned dark. As much as he hated to admit it, he needed this penny-ante job, since it was his only source of income. All his bills were past due, and he had promised the landlord that he would pay his back rent on Friday. He couldn't ask Edmund for money. It was too soon and would definitely turn him off.

Tyrone moped home with his head hanging low. "What the hell am I going to do now?" he wondered.

He unlocked the door to his sublet. Once inside, he noticed a message on his answering machine. "It's probably the landlord." He wasn't going to play the message, then thought that it might be Edmund calling. Tyrone pressed the PLAY button.

Hey, T, it's me. Call me when you get in, I got some news, Jimmy said.

Jimmy Brown and Tyrone were friends and former lovers who once upon a time shared a seedy walk-up in Harlem. Jimmy had supplied Tyrone with his first dose of estrogen a few years ago, compliments of the OB-GYN office where Jimmy worked as a file clerk.

When Tyrone called back, he listened as Jimmy told him all about his impending promotion to clerk supervisor. "Man, if I get this position, I'll also get a hefty raise," Jimmy said optimistically. "With the extra loot, I can finally quit selling them fake bags 'cause you know I ain't trying to get busted out there peddling on the street."

"I know that's right," Tyrone said dryly. He was happy

to hear the news about Jimmy's looming promotion, but couldn't help feeling gloomy about his own dire situation.

"What's wrong with you?" Jimmy asked, picking up on Tyrone's dark mood. "Did Mr. Moneybags find out about that private package between yo' legs?"

"Naw, man, and he ain't gonna find out until I got him locked down."

"What's yo' problem, then?"

"I got fired today." Tyrone told Jimmy the sordid details of his finances. "My plan was to stay there until I got my hands on Edmund's money."

"How soon you think that's gone be?"

Tyrone relayed the sad tale about Edmund's dead wife, and how desperate he seemed for affection. "Chile, he ain't had none since it had him. He's so hungry for some ass, all I gotta do is lick him up a few times and, trust me, boyfriend'll be opening up real soon. All I need to do is buy some time." Tyrone paused. "Hey, you got any extra money? I'll pay you back as soon as I start milking my cash cow."

"I got a little somethin' stashed away. How much you talkin'?"

"Two Gs? Yeah, two grand will keep the bill collectors away for a few weeks."

"I—I—I don't know," Jimmy stammered. It was a lot of money.

"Aw, come on. I'll have it back to you with interest before you know it's gone. I promise."

"Interest? How much we talkin'?"

"I'll do better than interest—I'll pay you back an extra two grand. Edmund's so loaded that, once I tap in, money won't be an object." He was desperate to get his hands on

Jimmy's cash, and frankly, would have promised him the deed to Graceland, if he thought that would seal the deal.

"Four Gs! Now we talkin'." Jimmy had always liked Tyrone's penchant for the lavish gesture. "I'll overnight a check to you."

"Make it cash, 'cause you know I can't show my face in the bank until I pay 'em back their money," Tyrone reminded Jimmy.

"Okay. I'll send you twenty crisp hundred-dollar bills tomorrow." Jimmy was now a bona fide businessman, from fake purse distributor to loan shark. He had turned two thousand dollars into four in a day. Not even the stock market yielded returns like that.

"I owe you big-time, Jimmy."

"True dat, true dat. Just remember when you start milking Mr. Moneybags, get an extra pint or two for me," Jimmy said.

8

Lisa gazed fondly at the framed photo of Justin, David and herself that she set among the stacks of plans, reports and notes on her desk. The picture was taken in Central Park on the Sunday the three had all gone out together. The following week, David surprised her by dropping the framed photograph by the office. The camera lens captured a grinning Justin with his Yankees baseball cap turned backwards, while he held a fielder's glove that was almost as big as he was. David kneeled, smiling, on one side of the little boy, and Lisa was on the other. Though her smile wasn't as broad as either of theirs, the photo still showed rays of happiness that lit up her eyes.

Her desk phone rang, interrupting her thoughts. "Good morning. Caché."

"Good morning!" There was a song in Morgan's voice.

"Hey, what's going on?"

"Let's see. Where shall I start? With a new high-profile client or with the green light for our expansion plans?" Morgan's excitement resonated through the phone line.

Lisa sat up in her chair, smiling. "Something tells me that your meeting with Dr. St. James went well."

"That's an understatement. In fact, he's setting up meetings for me with some of the key members of the Democratic National Committee. He thinks we have a really good chance of landing the convention next year, which I'm sure I don't have to tell you would be a major coup. In fact, it would be the perfect entrée into Washington, D.C., where he thinks we should plan to expand next year."

Lisa was thrilled. This was just the break that Caché needed to establish credibility for their expansion plans. It was one thing to be a rousing success in New York, where Morgan and Miles both had such great contacts, but breaking into D.C. would be another matter altogether. "Wow! I'm speechless. How are we going to handle all of that?"

Morgan laughed at Lisa's response. "Don't worry—by then I'll be back in the office full-time, and of course we'll hire a lot more staff."

"That's good to know," Lisa said, exhaling audibly. "With the company, employees, Justin and now David, my plate is pretty full."

There was a pronounced silence on the phone line before Morgan finally said, "David?"

"You know, Justin's father," Lisa answered defensively.

"Hey, I'm just asking." Morgan backed off, at least for the moment. It bothered her, though, that this scoundrel could suddenly pop back into Lisa's life as though nothing had ever happened.

"It's nothing to worry about. It's all good. In fact, he's been spending a lot of time with Justin lately, and I've never seen my baby happier."

Morgan couldn't help herself. "What about his mother?"

Lisa sighed. "Honestly, I don't know how I feel. But I do know that having a positive male role model has been good for Justin, and what's good for him is good for me. Plus, I can't fault any black man who's trying to do the right thing by his child."

Morgan could tell that this spiel had been rehearsed, probably while Lisa was in the process of trying to convince herself. "In this case," she said pointedly, "it's the child's mother that I'm concerned about. I just don't want to see you get hurt by him again, that's all."

"Why are you coming down so hard on David?" Lisa responded, though she knew full well why. "He's learned his lesson. Everybody's entitled to a second chance."

"It's just that I happen to be a believer in the zebra-stripe theory."

Lisa sighed impatiently. "Morgan, not everybody is perfect like Miles."

This comment hit home, especially after last year. As good as Miles was, he had been caught in an unseemly situation with a female coworker. Morgan took the hint. "We both know that Miles isn't perfect. No one is."

"Then at least give David a chance," Lisa begged. "You've never even met him, and he already has three strikes in your playbook." When Morgan didn't answer, Lisa continued. "Why don't you make a point to get to know him at the Ecstasy party? You guys are coming, aren't you?"

"You know Miles will be there. For him it'll be work. Dakota and I'll stop by to see if we can help out."

"Great. Just give him a chance. Okay?"

"Sure," Morgan said. "Gotta go. The princess summons. Call me if you need me?"

Lisa could hear Zoë fussing in the background. "Will do."

"And by the way—not that you need it—but good luck with the Studio Museum party tonight."

"Thanks. I'll let you know how it goes."

Lisa hung up the phone feeling better about her budding relationship with David. It was disconcerting that Morgan thought so badly of him. Not that she could blame her boss, given David's shady past, but he had changed. That she was sure of.

The Studio Museum was in Harlem on 125th Street, between Lenox Avenue and Adam Clayton Powell Jr. Boulevard. In recent years, thanks to generous benefactors and the hiring of Lowery Stokes Sims and Thelma Golden, it had garnered prominence in the highbrow, hoity-toity art world of New York City. Its permanent collection contained more than 1,600 impressive works by African-American artists such as Romare Bearden, Jacob Lawrence, Betye Saar, Norman Lewis and James VanDerZee. Tonight's party was to celebrate the opening of a new exhibit called Harlem World: Metropolis as Metaphor, and it was just the kind of bourgeois affair that attracted elite African-Americans throughout Manhattan, from investment bankers and corporate tycoons to entertainment executives and rappers. And of course, it was planned by Caché, which was now a status symbol in and of itself.

Lisa shook her head at the rampant pretentiousness that prevailed in these social circles. The women seemed to spend more time matching nail polish to lipsticks than they did anything else, besides coordinating dates at the spa, highlights at Josephs Salon, and shopping forays through Bergdorf and Barneys. All to catch the men, who wore their success like feathers on a peacock. She looked around the room, taking in the scene. Waiters doled out glasses of chardonnay, sparkling water and an array of gourmet appetizers, while patrons stood around either engrossed in animated conversation with each other or the more serious art enthusiasts stood back, admiring the exhibits. This was where she found the dapper Blake St. James.

She walked up behind him and leaned in close. "Well, hello, Mr. St. James."

Blake turned around, then reached out to her for a hug. "Lisa! It's good to see you. How are things going?"

"I can't complain," she said, smiling. Blake always brought a smile to her face. He was one of the nicest guys she knew. *Why couldn't he be straight?* she thought. "How are things at the gallery?"

"Couldn't be better. After a year of struggling to attract the best artists and clients, I'm finally being taken seriously."

"So I hear." Blake had recently been featured in a *Vanity Fair* article about fresh new talent on the art scene. "Congratulations on the article—I am so happy for you."

"I hear that things are going well for Caché." Blake's father, the prominent United Nations executive Dr. St. James, was Morgan's silent partner.

Lisa nodded. "Thanks in large part to your dad."

"He might be pulling a few strings, but it's Morgan's vision and your hard work that really make it possible."

"I just know I don't hear this man talking about hard work."

Blake and Lisa turned to see Spence Ellis, Blake's long-time best friend, standing off to the side with a disbelieving look on his face. The two had known each other since attending a private high school together on Manhattan's Upper East Side. After college, both traveled the world before landing back in the Big Apple.

"Look who's talking," Blake said as he embraced Spence. "At least I have a few calluses to show for hauling and hanging pictures. I don't think you can claim any for escorting the rich and famous around looking at multimillion-dollar properties." Spence was one of the most successful real estate agents in Manhattan. He handled only high-end properties and clients.

"It's dirty work, but somebody's gotta do it." He buffed his perfectly manicured nails brusquely across the lapel of his Ferre suit jacket. "How are you, sweetie?" he said, turning to air-kiss Lisa's cheeks.

"I'm well, and by the looks of you, I'd say that you were too."

"I can't complain."

"And if you did, I'm sure no one would bother listening," Blake teased.

"Fancy meeting you here," a female voice whispered in Spence's ear.

It was Yvette, who was dressed to kill in a Valentino suit, matching spectators and diamond stud earrings the size of walnuts. "I should have known I'd see you." He hugged her before kissing both cheeks.

"You know I am on the board for the museum, so missing this wasn't an option."

"Where is that handsome boyfriend of yours? Or should

I say, fiancé?" Spence lifted her left hand for inspection. The last time they'd talked, she confided in him that they'd been discussing marriage, but that was before her trip to Newark.

"He's here somewhere," she answered with a dismissive frown that set Spence to wondering. Had the bubble of amour somehow popped?

"Well, as fine as he is, I'd suggest you put a leash on that man. A *really* short one." When Yvette didn't respond, Spence asked, "Trouble in paradise?"

She took a deep breath. "Let's just say, I didn't know that paradise included a detour through Newark. That's where Lyle's from, you know?"

Though Lisa and Blake were having a casual discussion nearby, she overheard the remark and rolled her eyes. Whoever this chick was, she should be a poster child for the snotty black woman.

"I know this may come as a surprise to you, but not everybody was fed by a silver spoon," Spence said.

"I know. It's just—well, his mother lives in the ghetto, and his brother is fresh out of prison."

"And?" When she didn't answer, Spence asked, "What's all that got to do with Lyle?"

Before she could answer, Lyle himself walked up. "Hi, Spence, how're things going?" He offered his hand.

"Fine," Spence said. "Excuse my manners," he said to Yvette. "I didn't introduce you to my friends. Yvette and Lyle, this is Blake St. James and Lisa Burrows."

They interrupted their conversation to greet the couple. Lisa was instantly impressed. Newark or not, he was a fine brother: handsome, clean cut, but very sexy. She extended her hand, feeling a tingle as Lyle touched hers. "It's nice to meet you."

Spence chimed in. "Lisa runs Caché, the company that organized tonight's party."

"Oh, in that case, could you get me another glass of white wine? I'm dying of thirst," Yvette said.

Lisa looked at her as though she'd grown horns.

Blake bristled. "Lisa runs the company, *not* the bar."

"Never mind, I'll get it myself," Yvette hissed, and marched off.

Spence was embarrassed, and Lyle was shocked. He'd never seen Yvette act the way she'd been acting lately. Ever since they left his mom's house, it was as though he'd been dating a different person. She was constantly insulting waiters and doormen—just about everyone she considered "below" her. He turned to Lisa. "Can I get *you* a drink?"

She smiled at the gesture. "A sparkling water would be nice, but I'll get it myself. I really do have to get back to work."

Lyle wasn't letting go that easily, though. "I'll walk you to the bar. I could use something to drink myself."

They walked toward the long table covered in a white cloth. Lyle couldn't help noticing how pretty Lisa was. Although her evening dress was simpler than the couture all around him, she somehow looked more elegant than the society women. Maybe because she wasn't trying to show off.

After ordering from the bartender, Lyle turned to face her. "Nice event."

She smiled. "Thank you." She worked hard and long hours to make sure that a client was never disappointed.

"How long have you been in the business?"

"A little over a year now."

"Do you enjoy it?" He studied her closely and couldn't help but feel a connection to her. She was straightforward and down to earth—unlike some people he knew.

"Actually, I do. It's a lot of hard work, but worth every second of it. In fact, I can't think of anything else I'd rather be doing."

He took note of her sincerity. "You do it well," he said, raising his glass to her. In that moment, her eyes sparkled, and he stopped short, arrested by them.

"Thank you. Enjoy the rest of the evening," she said as she walked toward the front door to speak with Dakota Cantrell, who had walked in with her boyfriend, Phillip.

Interesting, Lyle thought, watching her very shapely behind head away. Most women would have had his name, rank and serial number by now, not to mention his W-2 stats, but Lisa hadn't asked him any of those questions. He rubbed his chin slowly as he watched her cross the room wearing not Dior, Gucci or Prada, but an air of dignity that was very becoming.

9

Unlike the Dow Jones Industrial and NASDAQ averages, the fake-bag business proved to be recession proof in the fashion mecca of the world. In fact, whenever money got a little tight for the style-conscious, voraciously consuming females in the Big Apple, they would stoically forgo the latest twelve-hundred-dollar Fendi bag, opting instead for its poor relation, the latest *fake* Fendi bag. Better that than being seen with last year's design. Besides, if the rest of their look was tight, then no one would ever suspect them of carrying a fraudulent handbag. And the fake designer bags that Jimmy traded in were the best of the best. In order to move product, he ordered his inventory from nimble-fingered copycats in Korea, as well as from other sources that tapped directly into the designer's factory. Even the designers themselves wouldn't recognize the difference from afar.

The only small problem with his thriving leather goods enterprise was that it was definitely illegal. It was cool with the cops if street vendors sold fake bags that were obvious fakes, like Goach instead of Coach, or Dolce and Cabana instead of Dolce & Gabbana, but when the product was a direct rip-off, that became a licensing issue. He decided that these were risks worth taking until he got his promotion.

But Jimmy was no fool, and he definitely did not want to wind up in the pokey again. Having toured through once on fraud charges, he could write his own chilling episodes of *Oz*. To mitigate the risks, he lined the "fake" fakes up on the sidewalk tables so that the common, undiscriminating customer—and the police—were free to peruse his array of Cucci, Kade Spade, and Louis Viton bags. In the small bodega behind him, though, hidden behind a fake wall, he housed his inventory of the "real" fakes. Like a wolf sniffing out prey, he'd lie in wait for a well-groomed, designer-clad dame to wander by and look at his table copies in disdain. Then he'd lure her inside the bodega, show her the good stuff and dare her to tell the difference between it and the real thing. This tactic always resulted in a quick sale, a happy customer, loads of referrals and repeat business.

He stood up from the rickety stool on which he was perched as a babe with a sweet tooth wandered toward his candy store. She was an uptown chick who was dressed from head to toe in couture. Though Jimmy didn't know a Chanel suit from a Christian Dior, he could smell the scent of money a mile away, and this one reeked like Fort Knox. She stopped to peruse his inventory of fake bags from behind a pair of large black Jackie O sunglasses. He knew his customers, so he surmised that either a nasty divorce was drying up her once-streaming cash flow, or the recent tumble in the stock market had come down hard on her portfolio. Either way, there she was looking down her surgically altered nose at his fake handbags. He'd seen this act time and time again. Even though she could no longer afford Madison Avenue prices, it was easy enough for her to maintain her snotty, upper-crust attitude of self-righteous entitlement.

"Can I help you find somethin'?" Jimmy asked, licking his lips, flashing his grille of badly capped teeth.

She looked at him as though she could not believe that he had the audacity to speak to her. "I don't think so." She began to move farther down the long table, avoiding his cheap cologne.

He leaned across the table, closer to her, so that he could lower his voice. "Well, if you don't find what you're looking for out here, I've got the real thing back there." He motioned his head toward the small storefront behind him.

Her curiosity and hunger for a good deal—both New York traits—got the best of her. She looked around to be sure that no one of importance would see her conversing with this lowlife. "What do you mean, the real thing?"

"Let's jest say, they look like the real thing." He held up his hands to show his palms and shrugged his scrawny shoulders. "I ain't sayin' thay's real, 'cause I cain't—that would be stealin'." He winked at her. "But I can guarantee ya that you'd neva know the difference. And I can tell *you* know the real thang." He looked her up and down, taking in her superior attitude and all the material things that fed it.

If she understood him correctly, what he was trying to say was that he had the real thing—bootleg, of course—and could sell her a "real" bag at a bargain price, which was exactly what he wanted implied. She looked around again, to make certain that she would not be spotted by one of the

Ladies Who Lunched. "Let me see what you've got," she whispered, making sure that her sunglasses were firmly in place.

"Come back here," he said, beckoning her behind the table into the little store where his private stash was hidden.

She reluctantly followed him, holding on tightly to her two-year-old Ferragamo in the process. She was living on the edge here. Who knew what dangers lurked in the small, dingy little hole-in-the-wall? Even so, the foray was worth it to snare a real designer bag for a steal. A new, expensive designer bag was just the thing she needed to staunch the nasty-but-true rumors that were circulating like free currency on Park Avenue. She was not stupid. She knew that all her so-called friends were gossiping about how her cheating soon-to-be ex-husband had run off with his strumpet mistress and left her barely scraping by while the lawyers sorted out the mess. This was the time that she had to keep up appearances, at all costs. So, at the risk of bodily harm—or worse, being seen by someone she knew—she crept behind the table and into the bodega, watching him as he pushed open a wall behind the store's counter and began pulling out a treasure trove of goodies.

In another minute, she was caressing a beautiful bag that she'd nearly drooled over just yesterday at the Gucci store on Fifty-seventh Street. The little bugger had been fifteen hundred dollars. Six months ago, she would have pulled out her American Express Black card like Quick Draw McGraw and begun to immediately inspect the matching wallet, but that was before Leland confused his penis with his brain.

But as the designer gods would have it, here it was, back

in her grip. She closely examined the stitching, the logo, the hardware, every thread and inch of the bag. She would have sworn on her Manolo Blahniks that this was the real thing. "How much is it?" she asked, her mouth watering.

"Three hundred," he said without batting an eye. He knew when he had a bite, and this one was hooked, line and sinker. The bag was not the real thing—it was just an excellent fake—and he'd paid only fifty dollars for it.

Without letting the bag out of her clutches, she fished her wallet from her shoulder bag and extracted three crisp hundred-dollar bills. She'd worry about paying her bills later. Jimmy took the notes and tried to shake her hand. "Come by next week. I'ma have some Pradas here."

She gave him only the tip of her immaculately manicured fingers to shake before grabbing the brown shopping bag from him so that she could quickly conceal her loot and make her getaway before being seen by a civilized person. Mission accomplished, she scampered away, quickly blending into the stream of pedestrians cruising down Broadway.

Jimmy couldn't help but snicker at the woman as she tottered away with her superiority over him, and most everyone else, still intact, even though she'd ventured—at least in her own mind—into the depths of degradation, purchasing hot designer goods from a street hoodlum. He reclaimed his perch on the metal stool and continued to keep a watch out for more prey. Soon the walkie-talkie on his hip buzzed. The "vendors" on the block used the remote transmitters to signal cop sightings.

" 'Zup?" He spoke quickly into the speaker, knowing it was probably bad news.

"Pack up now. The Man is coming," blurted out the vendor two booths away.

Jimmy's eyes darted to the right and to the left, but he didn't see any signs of trouble. "You sure?"

"Trust me—I ain't got time to talk. I'm out." *Click*.

As soon as Jimmy clipped the two-way radio back on his waistband, he saw a blue-and-white squad car round the corner. He nearly fell off his perch, scrambling to pack up his goods, ·but the cops were approaching too fast. He didn't have time to gather the "real" fakes in the back, so he grabbed the bags in front of him and fled down the street. He hated to leave his merchandise behind, but it was a small price to pay for his freedom. As he fled, he wondered how soon Tyrone was going to call about that four grand he owed.

Tyrone didn't know how long he could keep up this charade. Keeping Edmund at bay sexually had become an arduous task. During the last two weeks, his suitor had become relentless, insisting that intimacy was an important part of a relationship, and if they didn't consummate theirs soon, he would self-combust. Although Tyrone had satisfied Edmund orally, for obvious reasons he wouldn't let Edmund return the favor. He used the old "I want to take it slow" excuse—stringing Edmund along until he had ATM access to Edmund's money.

Tyrone was at the vanity, looking into a brightly lit magnifying mirror, plucking away at his thick, wiry eyebrows, when it suddenly occurred to him that he hadn't heard from Edmund all day, which was odd since he always called bright and early every morning.

So he decided to give him a call, even though he usually

waited for Edmund to initiate communication. He was also worried because lately it seemed that the calls were becoming more and more erratic.

"Good afternoon. Mr. DuBois' office. How may I help you?"

"It's Tess. Is he available?"

"Hold on please. I'll let him know you're on the line."

Tyrone held on for what seemed like five minutes. "I'm sorry, Ms. Aventura. He's not available at the moment."

"Oh, I see." Suspicion began to grow. *If he was out of the office, why did she tell me to hold on?* Tess thought. "Please tell him I called."

"That's strange," Tyrone mumbled when he hung up. "Edmund always takes my calls no matter how busy he is." His body heat began to rise as panic set in. He got up to open the window. A cool breeze blew through the room, providing him a little relief. He began to pace while his mind conjured up various scenarios. Maybe Edmund had met another woman who was sexing him up, or maybe he'd hired a private investigator and knew the entire story. Tyrone tiptoed back over to the open window and peeped out, expecting to see an undercover detective in a trench coat and fedora leaning against a light post, looking up into his apartment. But all he saw was the usual midday traffic. He shook his head to shake off his paranoia.

"Think, think," Tyrone said, and finally he sat back down at the vanity. "He probably just has a case of blue balls. Yeah, that's it. He's just mad 'cause I ain't gave him none." Satisfied with this reasonable explanation, Tyrone went back to extracting his unruly brows.

Yet by sunset, Edmund still hadn't called. Tyrone decided to call his house, prepared to bombard him with sweet nothings, but all he got was Edmund's answering machine. He didn't leave a message.

The next day, Tyrone put on a sexy dress, shoulder-length wig and spike heels. His plan was to stroll by Elsa's and get a read on how Edmund was feeling. He quickly donned a pair of dark shades as he stepped out of his apartment building as Tess and strutted down the street. As she approached the café, only a few blocks away, she could see that the outdoor patio was full to capacity. She slowed her stride to a leisurely pace and quickly scanned the tables, but no Edmund. Tess took off her shades and walked inside.

"*Bonjour,* Tess, *ça va?*" the handsome maître d' greeted her.

Tess returned the greeting with a kiss on both cheeks. "*Bonjour,* Jean Michele, *très bien,* and you?" After being seen with Edmund over the past few months, Tess was now on a first-name basis with Jean Michele.

"*Très bien, très bien.*" He returned the kiss. "Can I get you a table?"

Tess looked around the dining area for Edmund, then said, "No, just stopped by to say hello."

"Well, it's always a pleasure to see you."

Tess wanted to ask Jean Michele if he had seen Edmund, but she didn't want to imply that her man was MIA. "*Au revoir.*" Tess waved, and walked out.

Back in the apartment, Tyrone kicked off the pinching high heels, flinging them halfway across the room. Then he went straight to the answering machine. There were three mes-

sages. He breathed a sigh of relief; surely one of them was
from Edmund.

*Contessa Aventura, this is Alfred from La Petite Bou-
tique. Just called to tell you that your bill is sixty days past
due.* Tyrone had opened a house account and had been
charging dresses, shoes, purses and accessories with a complete disregard for the monthly bill.

*Man, it's Jimmy calling to see if you got your hands on the
cash yet. I almost got busted, so you can say I'm outta the
fake bag business. So I'ma need that cash back sooner than
later.*

The next message was a hang-up. "Damn, I bet that was
him," Tyrone said, pissed at missing the call. "I got to seal
this deal. I'm too close now to lose him. Plus my funds are
running low." Tyrone looked at the clock. "Edmund should
be home now. If he won't come to me, I'll go to him."

As he showered, Tyrone rehearsed the script in his mind.
Sniffing the money in the wind, he concocted a tear-jerking
story about needing money to save Tess' mother's estate in
Monaco from being sold for back taxes. Tonight would be
the performance of his life. If triumphant, he would walk
away with a hefty check. If not, he would be back to vogu-
ing for money at those cheesy transvestite pageants.

Tess took a taxi to Laval, a suburb on the south shore of
Lake Saint Lawrence. Edmund lived in a Tudor mansion
perched on a small hill. She admired the house as the taxi approached the circular driveway, and she imagined what it
must be like to live so well. The entire house was dark except
for a light that shone from the second floor. Tess paid the
driver, tightened the belt on her trench, walked up to the
front door and rang the bell. Her nerves were dancing

around like the Nicholas Brothers. She saw the hall light come on; then Edmund's face appeared in the window of the door.

"So, you *are* alive," Tess spat out the moment he opened the door.

Edmund looked surprised to see her, but quickly recovered and said, "Darling, come in, I—"

"No," Tess cut him off. "I just came by to check on you, since I haven't heard from you in two days. Now that I know you're fine, I'll be on my way." Tess turned around to leave, as if the taxi were still waiting.

Edmund caught her by the arm. "Where are you going?"

"I told the driver to wait, but obviously he left. If you'll be so kind as to call me a car, I'll be on my way," Tess said, crossing her arms dramatically in front of her chest.

"Tess, please don't go," he said, opening the door wider. "Please come in and let me explain."

Tess hesitated, as if seriously weighing whether to refuse his invitation, then slowly walked into the house and stood in the foyer, as if she had no intention of staying.

"Here, darling, let me take your coat," Edmund said, reaching for her raincoat.

"No, thank you." Tess pulled away. "Just call me a taxi, and I'll leave you to whatever it is you've been doing for the past two days."

"Tess, please let me explain. I've been—"

Tess put her hand up in protest. "You don't owe me anything—not an explanation and least of all your time," she said stoically.

Edmund walked closer to Tess and took her by the shoulders. "Stop interrupting me, please. I got your message yesterday, but I was rushing to catch the train. We had a crisis in our Ontario office, and I just got back thirty minutes ago. I rang your apartment, but obviously you were on your way here."

Tess willed tears, and within seconds they dutifully streamed down her rouged cheeks.

"Tess, what's wrong? Why are you crying?" Edmund asked, alarmed.

"I can't see you anymore," she said, now in full drama queen mode.

Edmund stepped back in shock. "What are you talking about?"

"I can't go on like this." She sniffled.

Edmund rushed to her side and embraced her tightly. "Like what? Tess, I love you," he implored, wiping away her tears. "I don't understand."

She had planned to tell him that she was going back to Monaco indefinitely to take care of family business. At that point, Edmund was supposed to ask what type of business, and she would spring the money issue on him. But now the conversation had taken a different twist.

"You love me?" Tess asked, surprised. She had been working her wiles on Edmund, but didn't expect him to confess his love to her so soon.

"Yes. I didn't think I could love again after Ella died, but then you walked into my life, and now I'm living again."

"You've been acting so distant lately. I thought you were upset because I've yet to make love to you," Tess said, pouring it on thick with full waterworks.

"Please, Tess, stop crying." Edmund hugged her close to his chest. "I can't stand to see a woman cry."

Most men can't, Tess thought, and cried even harder. If only Edmund had seen the accompanying smirk on her face, he would have known something was awry, but he was too busy comforting his "woman."

Tess broke away and walked over to the window. "Edmund, I don't want to lead you on. You know how I feel about casual sex. I think we should end this before somebody gets hurt," Tess announced abruptly, just in case Edmund was trying to use the "I love you" line to get her into bed.

"Aren't you listening to me? I love you, Tess," Edmund said, following her over to the window.

"And I love you too, but I can't offer myself to you. The last man who said he loved me used me as his bed warmer, then discarded me like a two-dollar whore once the sheets cooled off."

"Tess, I don't just want to sleep with you—I want to marry you," Edmund said, hugging Tess around her waist.

Her knees buckled, and she nearly fainted. She had planned to walk away with a fat check, not a marriage proposal. *Damn, I'm good*, she thought, and then spun around. She was overwhelmed. She was finally going to cash in for real. "Oh, Edmund, I love you so very much. I'll be the perfect wife."

Edmund smiled softly. "Is that a yes?"

"Yes, yes!" Tess gave Edmund a soft sensual kiss, sucking on his bottom lip, then whispered to him, "If I wasn't on my monthly, I'd make passionate love to you right now."

"Don't worry—I can wait. Now we'll have a lifetime to make love," he said, nibbling on the back of her neck.

10

One of the benefits of a two-parent home was having a pinch hitter always warmed up. That allowed one of life's small luxuries: an evening alone with a bubble bath, a glass of wine and your own thoughts. This wasn't a pleasure that Lisa had indulged since Justin was born, not until tonight. David had come by after dinner and taken their son to find a Halloween costume, and later they were going to check out the latest Harry Potter movie. After they left, Lisa had quickly gathered the necessary ingredients for a hot date with herself.

When she slipped into the steamy, sudsy water, the feeling was incredible, like sliding into a warm, snug cocoon. In one long breath, it relaxed her tired muscles and evaporated the stress that clung to her body. For her, it was truly a foreign experience to luxuriate in a bath rather than to rush through a shower. With a small child around, who had the time? She languidly reached a dripping, bubble-cloaked hand out of the warm water to pick up a glass of red wine. The full-bodied cabernet sauvignon relaxed her mind, along with the pleasing absence of all sound, another foreign experience for her. So, this was why those Park Avenue mothers with nannies could manage to look so damn good, she thought. Without the demands of a child twenty-four/seven, it was completely possible to exfoliate, wax, buff and tone.

After soaking up the blissful experience, Lisa stepped out of the lukewarm bathtub. She had at least another two hours of complete solitude. She patted herself dry with one of her good towels—the large, fluffy ones that had been housewarming gifts—before she padded to her bedroom with her wineglass. Sitting on the edge of the bed, she slowly massaged Dolce & Gabbana's rich perfumed body lotion into every inch of her skin. Normally she was lucky to have the extra few minutes it took to slap on baby oil. She even took a powder puff and layered the fragrance between her naturally full cleavage. Afterwards she stood in front of the full-length mirror that hung behind the door, appraising her voluptuous figure. She carefully cupped her breasts, enjoying their hefty weight in her hands. For a moment she remembered that investment banker—Lyle Johnson was his name. She'd seen how he looked at her the night of the museum party. She turned to the side, to check out the tautness of her stomach and the roundness of her derriere. Not bad at all, she thought, before slipping into a silk knee-length baby doll gown. Finishing off the last sip in her glass, she headed into the kitchen for a refill. It wasn't often that she had this opportunity.

"What now?" she wondered. She couldn't bear the thought of turning on the TV—why ruin the beautiful quiet? Instead, she grabbed one of the novels from a stack of titles she hadn't found the time to crack open. With book in hand, she turned on her bedside lamp and slid under the covers to lose herself in Tracie Howard and Danita Carter's latest dramatic tale.

Somewhere between their portrait of men, women and their many confounding issues, she drifted off into a deep sleep. She roused later to a sensual stirring between her legs. "Hmmmm," she purred, enjoying the building pleasure. She could almost picture Lyle Johnson's face beyond those wonderful fingers. It had to be a dream, was the thought that clung to her subconscious—at least until she heard another moan that wasn't her own. She turned over, and there was David in her bed, naked, his hands roaming all over her body.

"What are you doing?" she asked, startled.

"You feel so good, baby," he moaned, planting hot, wet kisses on her neck. She could feel his stiff erection poking urgently against her hip.

"Wait a minute. What are you doing?" she asked again, pulling away.

He held her close. "Lisa, I love you and our son. Please let me show you how much." His hand reached between her legs, his nimble fingers drawn to her pleasure center as he slowly rubbed his throbbing penis against her.

Lisa didn't remember the last time she'd had sex, so her body was responding in spite of what her mouth said. "I'm not ready," she panted.

This, however, was not the message her body was sending to him. David's hand was drenched with wet evidence to the contrary. And that was the only signal he needed. "Ohhh, baby, you are so wet." He quickly slithered down between her legs and tasted her sex, adding the wetness from his tongue to her own juices. He licked, sucked and probed until she was begging him *not* to stop.

She had ignored her sexual needs for so long. Now she was overwhelmed by the crashing waves of orgasms that came one behind the other, as she fought and succumbed to them in the same body-wrenching motion. When she was nearly breathless, with no warning, he pulled himself up onto her body and entered her in one long smooth stroke. Again, she felt compelled to protest, but the words were caught in her throat as her body focused all its energy on the sensuous invasion. She responded to him as eagerly and urgently as he gave it to her. Through sex-hazed eyes, she saw his lean, hard, muscled body as he held his weight up over her, allowing them both to see the pistonlike action in motion between them. His face was contoured into a grimace as his cheeks billowed in and out with the effort to sustain the rhythm they'd established.

"That's right, baby. Take this dick," he puffed.

"Ohhh, baby . . ." She was on the brink of total ecstasy.

The soaking bath, the wine, and now the hot sex all combined to stir an animalistic need in her to take every inch of his hardness. Stroke after stroke she chased the ultimate orgasm until it sneaked up and caught her, gripping her body like an sudden seizure. She savored the wave of contractions and David's urgent pumping as he released himself deep within her slick inner walls, before he collapsed on top of her, breathing deeply.

When the alarm snatched her back into reality the next

morning, she was stunned to see a slumbering David naked in her bed. "David, David, wake up," she whispered, shaking him urgently.

"What is it?" he asked groggily.

"What are you doing here?" Even as she asked the question, the answer came to her in snapshots of the night before, and in the feeling of remaining wetness between her legs.

He stretched deeply and rubbed his eyes. "I'm surprised you don't remember last night, since you really seemed to enjoy it then."

Lisa covered her eyes, trying to shut out reality. "This is not a good idea."

"That's not what you said then," he answered, reaching for her again.

She pulled away. "What about Justin?"

He rested on his side. "This is as much about Justin as it is about the two of us. Don't you think that he would love to see his parents together?" He reached for her once more, pulling her onto his chest. "I know you're probably scared, but don't be. We should be a family. And I meant what I said last night. I do love you."

Lisa searched his eyes for truth, praying that it was somewhere beneath his sincere expression.

"Don't worry. It'll be all right. I promise."

11

The gods were finally smiling down on Tess. Particularly, Aphrodite, the Greek goddess of love, who captured the heart of Ares, the god of war. She was no doubt giving Tess kudos for snaring Edmund. Tess' plan had been to get close enough to weasel some cash out of him, not to marry him. But now that Edmund had popped the question, she wasted no time planning a quaint wedding ceremony. They had their individual reasons for why the engagement should not be drawn out—Edmund because he wanted companionship in and out of the bedroom, and Tess because she wanted a solid commitment before he found out about her secret. She figured she would take five thousand dollars or so out of the generous wedding budget for herself, just in case Edmund was unable to stomach the truth about her hidden treasure. Hopefully things wouldn't come to that. In any case, Tess figured, she had nothing to lose. If Edmund was irate over her deception, he was certainly too high-profile in the community to make a big stink of it, a fact that Tyrone could use to extort even more money from the hapless man. Not wanting to dwell on that possibility, Tess reminded herself of the movie *The Crying Game*, starring Forest Whitaker, and how Dil, a cross-dresser, had managed to snag not one, but two men.

So she plowed ahead with the wedding plans, completing a guest list that was composed mainly of Edmund's business associates and a few of his close friends. Tess also fabricated a list of bogus friends, knowing that it would raise suspicion if she didn't make some contribution to the invitation list. But truth be told, besides Jimmy and his boyfriend, Anton, Tess had no one to invite, and those two surely didn't fit the image of the childhood friends she had concocted.

On the day of the wedding, the weather was made to order. The afternoon sun cast a warm glow over the garden at Edmund's estate, where the wedding was being held. The white trilliums, prairie lilies, arctic poppies and wild roses were all in full bloom. Forty wooden folding chairs covered in white linen with amethyst-colored bows tied around the backs of each were lined on either side of the white satin runner. An arch-shaped trellis laced with vibrant purple orchids framed the altar.

As Tess dressed in the upstairs master suite, she looked down out of the window facing the yard and marveled at the idyllic setting below. She watched as guests filed in and took their seats. Most of the women wore jewel-toned silk shantung luncheon suits with matching wide-brim hats. The men were dressed in their usual uniform—navy blue pin-striped suits, crisp starched shirts and the obligatory tie. When she saw the minister enter the garden in his white collar, her palms began to sweat. For the first time, she questioned whether she could really pull this off.

A knock at the door startled her back to reality. "Tess darling, are you almost ready?" It was Edmund.

"Just a few more seconds." In truth, she needed at least twenty more minutes. She had yet to wrap up her package. "I'll be down in a minute."

"Don't keep me waiting too long," he said through the door. "By the way, your maid of honor isn't here yet," he said with concern in his voice.

Tess had told Edmund that Sylvie, a childhood friend from Monaco, was flying in to be her maid of honor. "Uh, I forgot to tell you. She called last night and said her son came down with a severe case of chicken pox and that she didn't feel right leaving him alone with the nanny."

"What are we going to do now?" Edmund asked, sounding more like the nervous bride-to-be than she did.

Tess thought for a second. "Can you ask Walter's wife if she wouldn't mind standing up for me?" Walter Reed was Edmund's attorney and best man. The two met in college and had been best friends ever since.

"That's an excellent idea," Edmund called through the door. "I'm sure Edna wouldn't mind. I'll go ask her."

After Edmund left, Tess continued with her binding and padding until she felt confident that everything was tucked away in its proper place. She walked over to the door and inspected her girlish figure in the full-length mirror. Satisfied with the body-enhancing undergarments, Tess stepped into her wedding dress. The stark white gown was sleeveless with a conservative boat neck and a billowy silk organza skirt with tiny embroidered lavender flowers. Most people assumed that white was a symbol of virginity, when in actuality it signified the purity of love between the bride and groom. She wore a pair of white leather ballerina slippers, so as not to tower over her groom. Tess adjusted the clips of the veil on her hair, which was pinned back in a tight chignon and then flipped the chin-length netting over her face. Last, she slipped on a pair of white opera gloves. Admiring the finished product in the mirror, she had to admit that she was the epitome of the blushing bride. She picked up her bouquet of fresh white roses sprinkled with orchids and headed toward the door and her new life.

The minute she opened it, she was greeted by the overzealous wedding coordinator. "Ms. Aventura, I was just coming to check on you."

"Well, here I am," Tess said. She hadn't wanted a wedding coordinator peering over her shoulder, invading her privacy, but Edmund insisted, saying he didn't want Tess to be stressed out on their wedding day.

"Shall I signal the music to begin?" asked the coordinator, who was walking two steps ahead of Tess.

"Yes, I'm ready." Tess, who was normally as cool as an ocean breeze, was now a bundle of nerves. She hadn't expected the relationship to go this far. Suddenly another movie, *Boys Don't Cry*, flashed through her mind. That one was based on the true story of a girl who fooled everyone into thinking she was a boy, until her secret was revealed and she was killed. *Thankfully, Edmund's not the violent type*, she thought. But then again, who knew how he would react once he found out her dirty little secret.

Tess heard the beautiful voice of Andrea Bocelli singing his version of "Ave Maria," and she knew that was her cue to march in. From her vantage point, she could see Edmund standing at the altar, looking dapper in a white dinner jacket and tuxedo pants. Standing next to him was Walter in a black tuxedo, and directly across from them stood Edna, Walter's wife, in a mint green cocktail suit. Tess cringed at the color, which defied the lavender-and-white color scheme.

Once Tess reached the altar, the minister began his spiel on the holy sanctity of marriage. Tess basically zoned him out until he asked, "Can anyone here show just cause as to why these two should not be joined together in holy matrimony?"

She held her breath, half expecting someone to jump up and blurt out, " 'Cause she's a he!"

When no one did, the minister continued with the rest of the wedding vows. "Do you, Edmund Dubois, take Contessa Aventura to be your lawfully wedded wife?"

Edmund's eyes were blurry with tears as he said, "I do."

The minister then turned to Tess and repeated the same question. She hesitated a few seconds, thinking she should end this charade before someone got hurt, namely her. She quickly weighed her options—find another dead-end job or take her chances with Edmund. She chose the latter and said, "I do."

After a few more official-sounding words, the minister said, "I now pronounce you husband and wife."

Tess exhaled as she leaned in and hugged her husband. "I love you so much, Edmund," she whispered in his ear.

"I love you too, Mrs. Dubois."

Tess hoped that his understanding ran as deep as his love for her did. She held on to him tightly and prayed that the gods would continue to smile down on her.

The ceremony was followed by a catered reception in the

main dining room. Waiters served a dazzling array of beluga caviar, smoked salmon, goose liver pâté and lobster in a puff pastry. Champagne flowed freely as the handsome couple received well wishes from their guests.

"I can't wait to get you alone, Mrs. Dubois," Edmund whispered to her as she greeted a couple from his office.

Once the couple had walked away, Tess turned to her husband. "Once we get to Fiji, I'm all yours, Mr. Dubois."

"You're going to make me wait that long?" Edmund asked, sounding like a dejected child.

"Edmund, our flight is at eight o'clock in the morning. You know we have to be at the airport two hours in advance"—she kissed him on the cheek—"and if we start tonight, I'm afraid we'll miss the flight."

"I'll wait, on one condition."

Tess held her breath. "And what might that be?"

"Once we consummate our marriage, you'll never deny me again."

"I'll give you as much as you can take." Tess prayed that after the initial shock wore off, Edmund would overlook her *package*. After all, she was his wife now.

As the plane neared their honeymoon destination, Tess looked out at the azure lagoons and white sandy beaches of the Fiji islands. The moment it landed and she stepped out onto the tarmac, she could feel the tranquillity of the South Pacific paradise easing her anxiety. A chartered plane was waiting to whisk them away to the Vatulele Island Resort, an exclusive five-star romantic hideaway. After twenty-five minutes the puddle jumper touched down on the manicured grass runway. With only eighteen villas, Vatulele was a premier honeymoon locale for the rich and famous. The atmosphere of the island was extremely casual and friendly. As the guide led them to the Point, a secluded villa nestled in the hillside amongst lush island brush and tropical flowers, her trepidation began to mount again, building steadily like Mount Saint Helens hours before a volcanic eruption.

Once they reached the bilevel villa, they walked out onto the enormous terrace and took in the breathtaking view. Clear turquoise waters revealed coral reefs that surrounded the island. Palm trees swayed in the warm sultry breeze as the sun set, turning the sky a majestic blood orange.

"This *is* paradise," Edmund said, snuggling up behind Tess.

Here we go, she thought. "It is magnificent." She yawned, feigning fatigue, hoping to put him off. "What a long flight—I'm beat." She stretched her arms wide and yawned again.

"Come on, honey. Let's go to bed." He kissed her on the back of the neck, then took her by the hand and led her to the bedroom.

Edmund began to disrobe, until he was standing near the bed in his boxer shorts. Tess looked at his aged body. He had appeared fit in his tailored suits, but standing there nearly nude, he exposed the reality of his sixty-something body—sagging man breasts, varicose veins creeping down his thighs and a sadly protruding belly. Tess was instantly turned off. Trying to buy a little time, she said, "I have to freshen up." She picked up her tote bag and went into the adjoining bathroom.

She emerged twenty minutes later wearing a sheer black negligee, with the imprints of her fake nipples showing. A tight thong held her *package* in place. She sauntered over to the bed. Edmund was under the thin linen sheet, but she could see the swell of his engorged member. Her eyes caught sight of his boxers strewn on the floor. The sun had completely set, and she was grateful for the dimly lit room.

"You're beautiful," Edmund said, reaching over to turn on the bedside lamp.

Tess quickly walked over and put her hand on his. "Let's enjoy the moonlight."

"As you wish, my darling." He reached up, touching the rubber nipple.

Tess got in bed and straddled him. His sex pushed against the sheet that separated them. Tess could feel her own sex rising as they kissed passionately. She rose onto her knees, so that it wouldn't be revealed just yet. "Edmund"— she tried to say between kisses—"I need to tell you some—"

He stuck his tongue deeper into her mouth, stopping her midsentence. "I don't want to talk."

Tess knew the one thing that would buy her a few minutes, and that was a good old BJ. She tore back the sheet in one swift motion, slid down and covered his member with her warm wet mouth. She performed as if her life depended on it, and in a sense it did. She brought Edmund close to climax. Then to her surprise, he flipped her over and was on top before she could even react.

He reached down, stripped off her thong and headed south. "What the . . . ?"

"I can explain," Tess said urgently, pulling away.

Edmund stared in shock at the male anatomy of his bride. He blinked against the darkness. Thinking his eyes were deceiving him in the moonlit room, he reached out and in horror touched the rock-hard penis between his wife's legs.

Tess moved away in shame. "Edmund, let me explain."

He stared in disbelief. "You're a . . . you're a . . . man!" he stammered. His body jerked; then he toppled over and slumped to the floor.

12

Lyle snatched up his phone, stabbing at the keypad until Hilda picked up. "Get Paul and Michael in here—now." They were the firm's top sector analysts. The market was taking another nasty dive, and among the three of them, they had to quickly come up with an exit strategy that would minimize portfolio losses. Handling a market climate as tumultuous as this one was like sailing on choppy seas. If you sold your positions too soon, it was like waving a white flag. But if you held on too long, you ran the risk of trying to navigate the Pacific with that same white flag as your only sail.

While he sat pondering the obstacle course laid out before him, waiting for Paul and Michael, Hilda rang again.

"Yvette's returning your call. She's on line one."

He picked up the phone. "What time is dinner tonight?"

"Dinner?" She sounded puzzled.

"I have a dinner on the calendar for tonight with you and your dad."

"Oh, I'd completely forgotten about that," she said.

Stuttering, she added, "S-something came up, and Dad had to change his schedule. I'm sorry, but I forgot to tell you."

That was strange. The dinner had been scheduled weeks ago, and though they hadn't discussed it since, he'd assumed that it was still on. In fact, he'd had lunch with Senator Neuman and her father last week, and he'd confirmed dinner as they were leaving.

"No problem." Lyle hung up the phone with a frown. He'd been ignoring the fact that Yvette was pulling away from him. He found it hard to believe that the woman he loved—or at least thought he did—was shallow enough to end their relationship because of his family's lack of pedigree. He shook his head, determined not to believe the worst. There had to be another explanation. Even so, he had to admit, if he truly loved her, he'd care enough to find out what she was feeling.

Minutes later, Paul and Michael were gathered around his conference table, located in the corner of Lyle's spacious office with a view facing the Statue of Liberty. "Give me a quick sector analysis." He sat with his head resting on his hand, his elbow on the table, the muscles in his jaw taut with concentration.

Paul quickly referred to the notes that he brought in with him. He cleared his throat. "Financial services companies are taking a pounding, mostly due to the mistrust of accounting practices that are inflating earnings. For some reason, consumers feel that this sector is more likely to play the shell game than, say, biotech or utilities."

"That's not necessarily true. They all pretty much use the same firms and would benefit equally from some of their creative accounting practices," Michael said, rubbing his temple. Both men were feeling the strain. Their investors weren't the type to swallow big losses, even when chased with a really good excuse.

Lyle stood up from the table and began pacing. "It's not really important in the minds of investors what's true or what's false," he said, gesturing with both hands. "What matters to them is the perception. Right or wrong, they believe that if numbers are the problem, then those companies that deal in numbers day in and day out are more likely to be the bigger culprits." He paced the room as the wheels turned rapidly in his brain. "What's happening in retail?"

"Seems to be holding steady. The downturn in last quarter's unemployment numbers are reflected in last month's correction, and as long as interest rates maintain, it's likely that durable goods and consumer retail will both maintain their current positions, with little to no deviation."

After they had run through the primary sectors that drove the market, Lyle said, "This is what we do, boys. Take forty percent of our financial services common stock holdings, and buy up some key consumer retail stocks with a stop loss order on half. Look at the transportation sector, and consolidate within the top two airlines. I think that we've experienced the bottom of the September Eleventh effect on transportation. Also, take twenty percent of our total holdings, and place them in municipal bonds." He looked at his watch. "Then, let's meet back here at one o'clock for a reassessment."

After Paul and Michael had gathered their files, they headed off with their marching orders. Lyle sat back down behind his desk and pulled up the top ten accounts for a loss review.

His private line lit up with two short rings. It was Hilda. "Senator Neuman's office is on line one."

"Did they say what this is regarding?"

"I don't think bamboo sticks would have gotten it out of them," Hilda said, annoyed at the close-lipped politician. After all, it was her job to screen calls and gather information for Lyle, and she took it personally when she wasn't able to properly guard the gate.

"Put him through." Lyle leaned back in the chair. What was this all about? His lunch with the senator and Yvette's dad had seemed congenial enough, but he hadn't expected to become regular dining companions. "What can I do for you, Senator Neuman?"

"The real question is what I can do for you." The senator's deep Southern voice came cleanly through the phone line. Senator Neuman was a Yale alumnus who was from a prominent long-standing Democratic family in Atlanta, Georgia. His paternal grandfather had been a three-time congressman, and his grandfather on his mother's side was once the mayor of the Southern mecca. He was also married to a "suitable and respectable" woman with two adult children, and was the head of the Senate Finance Committee.

This man's answer took Lyle by surprise. He sat up in his chair. "Beg your pardon?"

"I'll just cut to the chase, Lyle. Confidentially, Chairman Washburn will be announcing his resignation from the SEC at the end of the week, and I, along with a group of colleagues up in the Senate, would like to sponsor you for his replacement as the chairman of the Securities and Exchange Commission."

Lyle was speechless. Never in a million years would he have imagined this.

"Lyle, my boy, are you still there?" the senator chuckled.

"I—I am, but I must say that I'm a bit taken aback. I mean, I'm honored." He stood up from his desk to help stimulate the circulation to his brain.

"And you should be. We've been watching you for a while now, and when Congressman Wesley tossed your name in the ring, I decided it was time to take a closer look. We think you're just the man we need right now to shore up investor confidence and help rebuild the economy."

"This is a surprise." Lyle was rubbing the back of his neck as he stood in front of his desk, still not quite believing what he was hearing.

"Let's not break out the champagne so quickly. As I said, we've been watching you, and we believe that you're our man, but as with everything that happens on Capitol Hill, there is a process. Assuming that everything checks out, we believe that with the right folks behind you, we can get you officially nominated and confirmed with no problem at all. But there's still a few little backdoor visits that have to be done, so I'll be in touch with you to set up our next steps."

It really was happening, Lyle realized. A smile spread on his face. "I'll look forward to it."

"Next time we'll have dinner. A nice juicy sirloin, medium rare."

"That sounds good, Senator Neuman."

When the phone clicked in his ear, Lyle didn't know

whether to pump his fist Tiger style, do an end-zone dance like Dion Sanders or to just jump up and down, but of course he did none of these. In typical cool Lyle fashion, he sat behind his desk and leaned way back with his hands clasped behind his head and did what he did best, a cost-benefit analysis. The only thing missing was a stout cigar and single-malt scotch, but he had a feeling that the good old senator would have those ready as after-dinner cordials come their next meeting.

Later that week, Lyle was again interrupted by a call. "Mr. Johnson, there's a gentleman here asking for you."

Lyle could tell by the condescending note in Peter's voice that his guest was anything but a gentleman.

"A Mr. Ernie Johnson. He says that he's your brother." This too was enunciated with apprehension and critical judgment.

Lyle could clearly imagine the scene unfolding in the marble-and-gold lobby of his fancy West Side apartment building. He was sure that the doorman, with his stiff upper lip, was eyeing Ernie sideways, as though he were a hoodlum who'd drifted too far south from Harlem.

Lyle shook his head, though he understood Peter's social prejudice, since he himself stood rightly accused at times. How often had he seen a bum on the street and walked by shaking his head? Even though Ernie had no one but himself to blame for his sad plight, it still hurt Lyle that his flesh and blood was on the receiving end of such disdain. "Send him up," Lyle said into the receiver.

"Yes, sir." Peter seemed surprised.

Lyle hung up the phone and rose from the chaise where

he'd been reclining while preparing for his upcoming meeting with the senator and some of his cohorts from the Senate Banking Committee. Though he'd been told that the dinner was merely a formality—a chance for them to get to know him personally—Lyle was no fool. He knew that they'd be checking him up one side and down the other, looking for any sign of warts, particularly any that might be contagious.

When he opened his door, there stood a sullen, angry Ernie, full of indignation. He walked past Lyle and into the apartment without saying a word.

"Hello to you too," Lyle said sarcastically over his shoulder to Ernie's retreating back. So much for the quiet evening that he had planned. Yet, as irritated as he was about Ernie's attitude, he was also curious. He couldn't imagine what his brother could possibly want to talk about—not enough to travel all the way from Newark to the Upper West Side of Manhattan.

He followed his older brother through the foyer and into the spacious living room, which presented a majestic eastward view from his twenty-fifth-floor view of the skyscrapers of Manhattan. It was just past dusk, so the cloak of impending darkness further enhanced the twinkling panoramic scene.

"So what's with the sudden appearance?" he asked, sitting down in one of the side chairs facing the sofa. He figured he'd get straight to the point. Maybe then he'd salvage a part of his night at home alone.

Ernie plopped down onto the Ultrasuede couch with his legs spread wide and his head hung low. "You really don't get it, do you?" He looked at Lyle as though he were clueless.

"Get what?" Lyle asked.

"You really believe that you did all of this yourself," he answered, looking around at the opulent creature comforts that came along with being Lyle Johnson.

"Nobody gave anything to me," Lyle huffed. "I've worked my ass off to get where I am."

"You would think that, wouldn't you?" Ernie shook his head in resignation as he rubbed two callused hands together. The sound was like sheets of coarse sandpaper being slid one over the other.

Lyle was getting pissed off. "Think it? I know it. In case you forgot, while you were hanging out on the corner with your sorry friends, smoking dope and drinking outta a brown paper bag, I was studying my ass off. That's how I got to where I am."

He stood up abruptly. As far as he was concerned, this little "meeting" was over. It was one thing to be forced to listen to this crap at his mother's house, but he'd be damned if he'd put up with it in his own.

"Do you think I wanted to be 'on the corner,' as you put it?"

"Obviously you did." He'd heard enough of Ernie's lame excuses to last a lifetime, and he wasn't in the mood for a remix of the same old sad songs.

"Did you ever stop to think that maybe I didn't have a choice?"

Lyle raised one eyebrow. "We all have choices. You've just always had an uncanny ability to pick the wrong one."

Ernie stood up himself and walked to within three inches of Lyle's face. "Don't you talk to me about choices." He squinted his eyes into a menacing glare. "Tell me, after Dad walked out, how do you think the lights were kept on so that you could keep your head buried in your precious books? And where do you think the money came from that kept the heat on and a roof over our heads?"

"Mom," Lyle said, as though it were obvious.

"Clearly your memory isn't as good as you'd like to think. Or maybe it's just more selective."

"What are you talking about?"

"Mom barely made enough money to buy groceries."

Was that true? Lyle turned to stare out the window, thinking back. When he was younger, he'd never thought about things like that, and since he'd joined Wall Street, he never had the time or inclination to bother.

"Do you think I wanted to be on the streets? I had no choice but to sell drugs. It was the only way I knew of to keep us from being kicked out of our house or, worse, separated." Ernie's voice lowered. His anger had long been spent. "After Dad left, I was the man of the house," he said with a stabbing motion to his chest. "So it was up to me to make sure that money came in, even though I was too young to legally work. So, I did what I had to so that we had a roof over our heads and food on the table." He glared at Lyle. "I won't make excuses about what came later. After a few visits through the system, it became impossible for me to get back on track."

For once in his life, Lyle was speechless. Though he'd known his brother to be many things, including a liar, he knew that he was telling the truth now. Suddenly it struck him: There was no way that their mother could have been the sole provider. His father had been the breadwinner. Why hadn't he thought of that before? The magnitude of it forced him back into the chair with his mouth ajar.

Ernie continued with his head hung low. "I did what I

had to do. It was that simple. And as far as drugs, the only thing I smoke now are squares."

"I had no idea." Lyle held his head in his hands as if he could hold steady the swirl of emotions. For as long as he could remember, he'd regarded his brother as a loser who was too weak to do the right thing. Now it appeared as though he had been courageous, given the choices.

Ernie remained silent, scowling. He'd sworn to himself that he would take that secret to his grave, never wanting to tell his little brother the truth. To him it was a cop-out, an excuse for how his life turned out, and he didn't want pity.

"Did Mom know?" Lyle had to ask.

"She never asked me where I got the money every month, and I never said. I simply put a wad in the tin container that she always kept in the pantry for grocery money."

Lyle remembered that container very well. He got up from the chair and joined Ernie on the sofa. "I am so sorry," he said, putting his arm over his brother's shoulder. The gesture felt foreign to him. They hadn't hugged, or even had a friendly conversation, for years. Lyle looked at him fully for the first time since they were young. He noticed the premature gray that covered his head of thick ungroomed hair, the rough hands with their ragged cuticles, and the deep lines that were permanently etched around his eyes, and the ones that ran rampant across his forehead. Lyle was ashamed. For the first time he felt burdened by the trappings of his own success.

"Don't feel sorry for me," Ernie warned. "That's not why I came here."

Lyle clasped his hands between his knees. "Why did you come?"

"I need a job. I've been beating the pavement since I got

home, but with no luck." He looked up at Lyle. "No one wants to hire an ex-con. Anyway, I was wondering if you knew of anything that was available."

Lyle thought for a moment. "You know, I have an idea. Why don't you come to work for me?"

Ernie looked at him as though he'd been smoking crack. "On Wall Street?"

"No." Lyle almost laughed. "I own a bar downtown."

Ernie's head swung toward him. "Really?"

"Yeah, I've owned it for a while now. I was thinking about selling it, but until I decide what to do, maybe you can help out." He'd just found out this week that his manager, Marc, was leaving, so a helping hand at Street Signs would be right on time.

"Doing what?"

"I don't know. Why don't we figure that out later? For now just say yes."

Ernie smiled again. "Okay, then, yes."

"Tell you what. Why don't we head out to grab a bite to eat?"

They headed down in the elevator, Ernie's arm around Lyle's shoulder. When they walked by the doorman, Ernie asked, "So what's it like to be rich?"

Lyle had never thought of himself that way, but he realized that in his brother's eyes he was Donald Trump. "I'm not gone lie and say, 'It's just okay,' but it is relative. Money doesn't make you happy—I know that sounds like a cliché—but it's true. After a while, it's just money."

They passed through the ornate revolving doors. "Easy for you to say. It might not buy happiness, but I'm sure it buys a lot of babes."

Lyle smiled slyly. "I won't deny that's one of the perks."

He directed them to a favorite neighborhood Italian place. When they were settled at their table, Ernie said, "So tell me about this Senate appointment that Mom's already been bragging to the whole world about."

Lyle shifted uncomfortably. "It's not done yet."

"Let her tell it, you'll be next in line for the White House."

Lyle shook his head. His mother had always been proud of him, and he'd always enjoyed being the recipient of that pride. Up until now. He suddenly felt like a fraud, as though he'd been masquerading all this time as the hero in the family, when in fact, Ernie was. He shook his head. *Just when you think you've got life all figured out,* he thought to himself, *it throws you a curveball.*

"How about we talk about Street Signs instead?"

13

The stately mahogany-paneled lobby of Walter Reed and Associates was intimidating, with its imposing marble columns and twenty-foot ceilings. Portraits of the Reed lineage in gilded frames lined the hunter green walls. The solemn eyes of the deceased barristers seemed to follow Tess as she walked toward the inner sanctum of the storied law firm, which felt more like a mausoleum to her. She was grateful for the plush burgundy carpeting that muffled the sound of her heels as she neared the reception area.

"Mrs. Contessa Aventura Dubois to see Mr. Reed," she announced to the receptionist. Walter Reed was a fifth-generation attorney, as well as Edmund's best friend.

"Have a seat, Mrs. Dubois. Mr. Reed will be right with you. His prior appointment is running a tad behind schedule." The matronly receptionist motioned to the tufted leather sofa to her left.

Tess sat down and nervously glanced through an outdated copy of *Field & Stream* as she waited. *Why don't they have better magazines in medical and law offices?* she thought,

while attempting to read an article on fly-fishing. Tess hadn't
seen Walter since the wedding, and she wondered how he was
taking the news of Edmund's untimely death. After uncovering Tess' shocking secret, Edmund had keeled over from a
massive stroke. Finding Walter's card in Edmund's wallet,
she'd called him with the bad news. Between wrenching
sobs, she told him how Edmund had complained of light-
headedness the night before the wedding, but that she'd
chalked it up to prewedding jitters. He'd seemed fine the day
of the wedding. She went on to describe her frantic attempt
to revive him—but to no avail. What she didn't bother to tell
him was that his friend's condition had been brought on by
the discovery of an unexpected body part on his new bride,
or that it took her fifteen minutes to finally call for help.

Tess wasn't able to concentrate on the article. She kept trying to imagine why Walter had summoned her to his office.
Maybe he knew the truth. Maybe Edmund had his doubts all
along and told Walter that if anything ever happened to him
to investigate her. Tess fumbled and nearly dropped the magazine on the floor as she put it back in the rack and picked up
another outdated title. While she thumbed through the peri-
odical, her mind continued to race, fueled by increasingly
paranoid thoughts. *Maybe Walter is meeting at this very moment with a private investigator and has pictures and supporting documentation to prove that I am an impostor.* Tess's
natural instinct was to get up and hightail it out of Dodge, but
her better judgment took over, and she stopped herself. *My
best bet is to come up with a counterlie,* she thought. *I can always deny any accusations, and if they have pictures, I'll simply say it isn't me.* Hell, if the police who were caught on
videotape beating Rodney King could say they weren't whip-

ping his ass, then surely she could deny a simple photograph. With her nerves momentarily soothed, Tess went back to skimming through the magazine.

Fifteen minutes later, the receptionist spoke and interrupted Tess' reading of "The Extinction of the Grizzly": "Mrs. Dubois, Mr. Reed will see you now."

Tess nearly fainted when the door to Walter's office opened and out walked a tall man in a tan trench coat with a thick tickler file tucked underneath his arm. Thinking her worst fears had come true, Tess' face turned beet red. The man brushed past her on his way out, barely glancing in her direction. It took all she had to walk into Walter's office. She just knew the guillotine was ready to drop down on her neck the second she stepped inside.

"Sorry to keep you waiting," Walter said as he greeted her at the door, "but my previous meeting ran over."

Tess tried to get a read on him, so that she could decide which angle to take, but it was hard since she didn't know him well. Walter led her by the arm to one of the leather chairs in front of his desk. She was glad for the support, because her knees nearly buckled under with each step. Once she was seated, Walter walked around his desk and took a seat. He looked every bit the distinguished attorney sitting behind the massive desk in his wing-back chair.

He folded his hands in front of him and began to speak slowly. "I'm so sorry, Tess." He dropped his head. "Edna and I were shocked when you called."

"Yes, it's all so tragic."

"As you know, I've been Edmund's attorney for over twenty years," he said, raising his head and peering directly into her eyes.

Here it comes, she thought. *He's gonna tell me the police are on their way up here to arrest me for perpetrating a fraud.* She nervously crossed and recrossed her long legs, waiting for him to continue.

"And with his tragic death, I've brought you here for the reading of his will." Walter retrieved a thin manila folder from the file cabinet behind his desk.

His will? Was that what this was all about? Tess wanted to clutch the faux Mikimotos that hung around her neck. A slight smile spread across her face as her emotions shifted seamlessly from the fear of being caught to the confidence that she had gotten away with her deception.

As Walter opened the folder and removed the will, he put on a pair of half-glasses and began to read. "Tess, as Edmund's wife and the primary beneficiary of his will, he has bequeathed to you the house and all of its contents, including the artwork"—Walter swallowed and cleared his throat before continuing—"as well as his pension, 401(k) and company stock options. His insurance policy was left to Margaret, his niece."

She couldn't care less about a policy. Who wanted to deal with a nosy insurance company anyway? Tess was as happy as a hog in shit. She'd finally reached the promised land, and the pastures were rolling in cash money green.

Walter continued. "This portion of the estate is valued at over two and a half million dollars."

Tess' ears began to ring. She couldn't believe what she was hearing. *Did he say two and a half million dollars?* She knew that as the president of Financier, Edmund was loaded, but she had no idea he was a multimillionaire.

Walter misread the expression on her face. "I know you

haven't been married long, and all of this may have come as a surprise to you, but Edmund came to see me shortly after your engagement and instructed me to change his will. Initially, he'd divided his assets between Margaret and the Alzheimer's Research Organization, but after he met and fell in love with you, he wanted to make sure that you were taken care of in the event of his death."

Tess wanted to jump up and do the Cabbage Patch. Finally, she could live the life of privilege she had always dreamed about. As Walter continued to speak his legalese, she zoned out, already planning how she would spend all that money. *First, I'll move into the house and redecorate it, and then I'll go on a major shopping spree. Maybe I'll even go on an extended European vacation and shop in London, Paris and Italy*, she thought. Tess touched the pearls around her neck. *Now I don't have to wear fake nothing. I can finally afford the best.* With her financial future secured at long last, Tess settled back into the chair with caviar dreams and champagne visions dancing through her head.

Since being scared straight, Jimmy had abandoned his lucrative side job, and he badly needed the four grand that Tyrone had promised. He and Anton were fed up with the roach-infested rattrap that they called home, and they needed the extra cash to move into a more desirable neighborhood. He had been calling Tyrone nonstop since lending him the money, and he'd finally gotten a call back. Jimmy was surprised to hear Tyrone so bubbly. The last time they'd spoken, he was extremely nervous about actually going through with the wedding. He didn't know how Edmund was going to take the news that he had married a man. But from the sound of Tyrone's voice, Jimmy assumed that Edmund had taken it very well. That is, until Tyrone went on to tell him that Edmund had died of shock on their honeymoon.

"Man, what you gonna do now?" Jimmy questioned.

"What you mean, what I'm gonna do?" Tyrone started laughing. "The question is, what ain't I gonna do?"

"What's so damn funny? The last time I talked to you, yo ass was 'bout to have a breakdown, worrying 'bout how Edmund was gonna take the news, and now that he's dead, it seems to me that you are back where you started."

"The big difference is," Tyrone said smugly, "now I ain't broke."

Jimmy didn't have a clue what Tyrone was talking about. "Man, what's wit' da riddles?"

"Can you spell *inheritance*? Jimmy, man, I done cashed in!" Tyrone screamed into the receiver. He went on to tell Jimmy that Edmund had changed his will and left him assets worth over two and a half million dollars.

At first Jimmy was speechless. He held the phone to his ear and mumbled, "Two and a half million dollars . . . ?" He couldn't believe it. Here he was trying to eke out a living selling fake purses and working as a file clerk, and his boy was sitting pretty on a few mil. After the initial shock wore off, he got pissed. "So when the hell was you gonna tell me yo ass had blown up?"

"Aw, don't get mad—I was gonna tell you," Tyrone said.

Jimmy's future suddenly looked a lot brighter too. "Now I know I'ma get my four grand, plus some."

"True dat, true dat. You know I'ma take care of my dawg. I'll overnight it tomorrow," Tyrone said with the confidence that came along with a hefty bank account.

"So what you been doing? I been calling you for a few days."

"I was buying furniture this afternoon to redecorate the house," he said grandly. "I'ma hook it up. Some of the stuff in there is nice, but most of it is so outdated." He was pumped to finally have a home all his own.

"You staying in Canada?" Jimmy had assumed that Tyrone would return to New York now that he could afford to live the high life.

"Yeah, I'm staying right here. I finally have a house. It ain't just a house, Jimmy. Man, it's a mansion with a circular driveway *and* a garden," Tyrone said proudly, as if he'd bought the house with his own hard-earned money.

"T, wit da kind of loot, you could do some serious damage here in the city," Jimmy said, envisioning his own shopping spree.

"Man, you know I can't come back to New York."

"They ain't lookin' for you no more. I told you—the heat done cooled off," Jimmy said convincingly. "Anyway, they was looking for Tyrone, not Tess."

Tyrone didn't understand what Jimmy was insinuating. "What you talkin' 'bout, man?"

"Think about it. You been dressing up like Tess, right?" Jimmy asked, warming to his sales pitch. The closer Tyrone was to him, the closer he was to Tyrone's money, and he wanted to be on a first-name basis with all those Benjamins.

"Yeah, so what's your point?" Tyrone asked, still not catching on.

"My point is, you could come back as Tess and rock it. Man, wit da kind of cash, you'd make them *Sex and the City* chicks look like rank amateurs," Jimmy said, stroking Tyrone's already overgrown ego.

Tyrone remained silent, contemplating Jimmy's words. "I hadn't thought about that." Which surprised even him.

"T, man, think about it. You fooled Edmund into thinking you was a chick." Jimmy was on a roll now. "You was so good, he married you *and* left you his money."

"True dat, true dat. And you're right. Nobody would know me as Tess," Tyrone said thoughtfully. "And I guess I could sell the house."

"After a while, you gonna git bored up there in da boondocks, all by yo' lonesome," Jimmy said. Then closing the sale, he added, "Now you can finally play wit' da high rollers in the Big Apple. Besides, man, success is the best revenge. Now that you got all that loot, you is definitely successful and can get some satisfaction on all them snooty-ass New Yorkers who looked down on you when you didn't have two cents to rub together."

Tyrone's lips firmed angrily at the memory. "You got a good point. I'll think about it."

"Yeah, think about it, but in the meantime send me my money."

"I'll put it in the mail tomorrow. I gotta go. I got an appointment with an interior designer. *Hola.*"

"*Hola* back," Jimmy said, and hung up. He was geeked. With Tyrone's stroke of fortune, he would no longer have to subsidize his income with undesirable odd jobs. He and Anton could finally move into that "deluxe apartment in the sky."

14

Caché's office was a hive of activity as Lisa and her three project managers and their assistants prepared for Ecstasy's big party. To anyone else, the scene seemed like unorganized chaos; to Lisa, it was business as usual. The thriving company now averaged at least two or three parties a week, so on any given day, the floors, tables and desks were strewn with sample floral arrangements, boxes full of invitations, and miscellaneous party favors. But even by Caché's hectic standards, the party they were planning now was one of the biggest of the year.

The much-lauded event was to celebrate the release of the group's new album, *Love of Money*. Their last two CDs had gone double platinum, so this party was a hot ticket for hip young New Yorkers. It was being held on the floor of the New York Stock Exchange, which was no small coup for Caché, but with Sound Entertainment's deep pockets, and the even deeper connections of Dr. St. James, most things were possible.

The VIP list was an impressive compilation of the boldest names in urban entertainment, so every last detail was triple-checked, as was the media list, which was just as comprehensive. Demonstrating their trademark cleverness, Caché designed invitations that were replicas of hundred-dollar bills with a portrait of the three singers replacing that of Benjamin Franklin.

"So how's it going?" Morgan asked when Lisa finally made it past mounds of boxes to reach the telephone.

"Do you really want to know?" Lisa answered, plopping down on the sofa that sat across from her desk. Though she occasionally played up the drama, Lisa and Morgan both knew that everything was under control. Lisa ran the office with the efficiency of a drill sergeant.

"Since I know Miles will ask me when he walks through the door tonight, I guess I do." Morgan's husband, Miles Nelson, was the president of Sound Entertainment, the record label for the group.

"I don't want to get in the way of pillow talk, so I guess I'd better give you an update," she laughed, while getting comfortable on the couch. "First of all, believe it or not, everything is on track. Even the rare coins have been delivered by Kenny Smaltz, the coins dealer that I mentioned."

"Was he able to get enough?"

"For the VIPs, yes. Everyone else will get chocolate coins in gold foil wrappers with Ecstasy embossed on them. And of course, they'll be tied together in mesh, with a gold ribbon."

"That sounds great."

"It should be, if I live to see it."

"Okay, so what's the bad news?"

"Nothing really. It's just that the stipulations for having the party at the Exchange are never-ending, since they've never done anything like this before."

"Just make sure that the security is extra-tight. Who's in charge of it?" Dr. St. James had tugged on some heavy strings to get the chairman to agree to let them have a party there. The last thing they needed was an incident with security, or bad press.

"I've hired Century Protectors. They have an impressive background in personal and crowd security, so I'm not really worried about that."

"As long as they can keep some of the more gangster of the rappers in line, we should be okay. In fact, Dr. St. James and I are counting on that."

"This place looks incredible!" Morgan said. She did a complete 360 to take in the elaborate decor for Ecstasy's party. The floor of the Exchange was cleverly transformed into a Monte Carlo casino. Blackjack, roulette and crap tables occupied the perimeter, circling the core of the large room. An elevated dance floor rose in the middle, and stripper poles were scattered throughout the cavernous space.

Lisa scanned the elaborately decorated room too, but instead of props, she was searching for something else altogether. It occurred to her that Lyle Johnson might be here. Since the Studio Museum party, she'd thought of him often—and of his elitist girlfriend. He was too down-to-earth for someone like that. He was better suited for . . . someone like her. She dismissed the thought for the hundredth time—guys like him always went for girls like Yvette, not ex-strippers with out-of-wedlock children. "Yeah, it turned out nicely," Lisa agreed, nodding her head, returning from her trip to fantasyland.

Morgan wrapped an arm around Lisa's shoulder, hugging

her closer. "Oh, stop being so modest. You've done an incredible job. I don't know what I'd do without you."

Lisa smiled, enjoying the praise. "Given what you did for Justin, I could say the same for you."

She turned to face Lisa. "So how are you?"

"I'm really good," Lisa answered, smiling.

Morgan stepped back to take a fuller look at her. "That sounds like an understatement, judging by the glow on your face." She hadn't noticed it initially. In fact she'd never seen Lisa look like that before. It was assuredly the look of a woman who was being satisfied in the bedroom.

"Me? Glowing?" Lisa replied coyly.

"Either you're getting good sex, or you hit Lotto and forgot to tell me." After living through Dakota's ups and downs in the man department over the years, Morgan could spot the signs of orgasms a mile away. Lisa couldn't be more obvious if she had worn a neon marquee on her forehead.

Lisa folded her arms lightly across her chest. "I wouldn't say that I was in love."

Morgan mimicked her stance. "What exactly would you say?"

"Let's just call it a case of lust." A sly smile spread across her face, lighting up her smooth, even features. Even though she still didn't trust David where an emotional relationship was concerned, there was no doubt about his ability between the sheets.

Morgan was happy to see Lisa so alive—a far cry from the dour girl she'd met not long ago. She realized that being a single mother definitely didn't leave a lot of time for self-satisfaction, which made Lisa's joy even sweeter. "So tell me, who is the lucky guy?"

Lisa braced herself for Morgan's disapproval. "David," she said.

Morgan almost visibly bit her tongue. "Oh," she finally managed.

Before she could say another word, Lisa said, "I know how you feel about him, but he has changed. Besides, I'm not making any commitments. Right now, it's really about Justin."

Riiight! Morgan thought, but she decided it was best not to share all her opinions. "Just be careful."

"He's really been great with him. In fact, having David around has been like having a real family. I've never seen Justin happier."

"And what about child support?" Morgan asked, cutting to the chase.

"Child support?"

"Yeah, you know, what most real fathers do for their kids." Morgan didn't trust the fact that David happened to show up on Lisa's doorstep now that she was financially comfortable. She had heard all about guys like him, who go from their mother's house directly to another woman's, spending their whole lives having females take care of them. He sounded just like the type to her.

"Morgan, why don't you give the man a chance before you condemn him?"

Morgan waved her hand. "I don't have to give him a chance. After all, I'm not the one sleeping with him."

"Just wait until you meet him tonight," Lisa said, though she wasn't by any means sure if that was such a good idea. David was too unpredictable to trust with anything. Especially her heart. "You'll like him—I'm sure of it."

"Okay." Morgan said, taking a deep breath.

Lisa dropped the subject fast. "Good. Now let's run through the checklist."

The two women took a stroll through the room, checking on the chef, the DJ, the lighting technician, as well as security. Everything was ready to go.

By ten thirty, a caravan of Hummers, Navigators and Town Cars had deposited a stream of New York's hottest young trendsetters. They filled the cavernous room from wall to wall. Gone were the three-piece suits and button-down collars that ran the world economy during the day, replaced by tight tube tops, baggy jeans, lots of skin and the latest designer status symbols.

The lighting was dimmed with the exception of the pin lights on the gaming tables and scattered across the dance floor. Cristal, Belvedere, and Courvoisier flowed freely, along with the hot tracks mixed smoothly by Frank Ski. Instead of trade tickets strewn on the trading floor, fake dollar bills with Ecstasy's picture in the center floated from the ceiling like confetti. The energy was hot and sexy, just the way Miles wanted it. Even though Ecstasy's debut and sophomore albums had been huge successes, he knew how fickle the urban market could be. Just ask Sisqó, Macy Gray, and Toni Braxton. One minute, you're hot like fire; the next second, you're lukewarm. It was that simple. The only way to avoid it, Miles believed, was to stay current, trendsetting, and not be bogged down by the weight of success.

Morgan, Miles and Phillip, Miles' V.P. of A&R, watched the action from a glass-enclosed VIP booth high above the trading floor. "Great job," Miles said to Morgan before planting a kiss on her forehead.

"Thank you, or I should say, 'Thank Lisa.'" She raised her chin to kiss him full on the lips.

"Now that's customer service," Phillip teased.

"I hope all your clients don't get this kinda treatment," Miles added.

"Only the tall, dark and handsome ones," she teased back.

"In that case, I hope Lisa's handling customer service too."

"Lisa is handling everything."

As proof, Lisa walked into the room, checking her watch. "Are the girls ready?" she asked. At eleven thirty, they were to make their grand entrance and perform their single, "Mo' Money, Mo' Honey."

"They're finishing up their wardrobe change, and should be ready in five."

"Great." Lisa stepped away and began talking into her head mic, coordinating the DJ, the lighting, sound and special-effects technicians.

"So this is where all the non-hip-hop people are. I was almost turned away at the door for not having my navel showing," Dakota joked as she hugged Morgan, Miles and Lisa.

Phillip greeted her with a hug and a light kiss. They'd been dating for a year now, and the best odds in the house were on a wedding by year's end.

A few minutes later, Lisa spoke into the tiny microphone. "Everything's set. Start the track in two minutes."

On cue, the lighting dimmed further. A giant plasma screen was lowered from the rafters, and Frank mixed in the first bars of the hit single. The crowd went wild when the girls rose through the elevated stage wearing tight-fitted three-piece suits with thick European ties and spats. Each of them wielded a long, fat cigar and a thick wad of cash, while their images were duplicated on the wide flat screen behind them. As they sang the hit song, the card dealers, who doubled as dancers, joined them on stage for a sexy, well-choreographed performance that brought the house down. Exotic dancers worked the poles, and every head was nodding while many in the crowd sang the hook. At the end of the performance, bags of Ecstasy cash floated from the ceiling, and the girls bowed to rousing applause.

"That was off the hook!" Phillip said, pleased with the way things were going. Just then, he was pulled away by a group of industry executives congratulating him on Ecstasy's success.

"Yeah, it was awesome! Good job, Lisa," Morgan said.

"Thanks." Lisa was staring down at the floor, her lips pinched together.

"Are you okay?" Even though everybody else was charged after the performance, Lisa seemed subdued.

It then occurred to Morgan why she seemed so tense. "Is David here yet?"

"No." She turned away quickly. She'd checked her cell phone and called home for messages, but hadn't heard anything from David. She was really looking forward to his coming tonight. She wanted him to see her work, and she wanted him to meet Morgan, Miles and Dakota. For once, it would have been nice to be out with a date, even though she was working. Morgan had Miles, Dakota had Phillip, and she was tired of always being the fifth wheel.

Morgan touched her shoulder. "Don't worry, something must have come up."

Lisa wasn't into being coddled. "I'm okay."

Miles' assistant Lauren walked over to greet the group of women.

"Where did Phillip and Miles go?" Dakota asked.

"They were attacked by a band of hoochies near the crap tables. I tried to save them, but there was nothing I could do," Lauren teased.

"I'd better go rescue my man," Dakota said, feigning concern.

To her retreating form, Lauren said, "You'd better take some backup!"

"It's that bad out there, huh?"

"Trust me," Lauren said, "the titty committee is out in full force tonight."

Morgan, Lisa and Lauren stood along the opening, looking down at the throng of undulating flesh and bravado below. The women were all over the men like extras in a Jay-Z video. A few were even slithering down the stripper poles, holding the bar between their breasts. Lauren was right: it was like Sodom and Gomorrah down there.

"Check out that scene," Morgan said, pointing in the direction of a guy who was sitting on a chair at the blackjack table with a bikini-clad honey giving him a lap dance that might be outlawed at Scores, the infamous strip club in Manhattan. Though his back was to them, you could see by his movements that he was thoroughly enjoying it.

"Now they need to get a hotel—" The next word stuck in Lisa's throat as the man in question turned to a friend who stood nearby, witnessing the attention.

It was David.

Morgan and Lauren turned to Lisa and saw the mortified expression on her face. Though she'd never met David, Morgan knew immediately who John Doe was.

"Lisa, you can't let this get to you."

Lisa pulled away and ran out of the room.

*   *   *

Though the party had been a huge success, Lisa couldn't wait for it to come to an end. She'd been hurt by David's lewd and insensitive behavior, especially after she had extolled his nonexistent virtues to her boss, and was further humiliated that Morgan had to see it herself.

After witnessing the lap dance, Lisa left the VIP booth and headed downstairs—mainly so that she wouldn't have to continue to face Morgan. She bumped into David near the crap tables, along with a scantily clad blonde with black roots who was draped over him like the sheen on a cheap suit. Upon seeing her, he made a feeble attempt to disengage from the tawdry woman, but it was too late. He pleaded with Lisa to talk to him, that the girl meant nothing, but Lisa abruptly turned and hurried in the opposite direction. In doing so, she nearly bumped into a tall, handsome man. It was Lyle! How much had he seen? He held Lisa by her shoulders to steady her.

"Are you okay?" he asked.

She closed her eyes and shook her head back and forth, trying to erase the sordid vision of David from her mind. It didn't work. "I'm fine," she lied, trying to pull away. In his eyes was concern. She realized he had seen everything.

"Are you sure?"

She was so embarrassed she wanted to disappear through the floor. "Yes, I'm sure."

"Is that man important to you?"

She couldn't explain. It was too complicated. "Not anymore," she said quietly.

"A fool like that doesn't deserve a beautiful woman like you."

She was touched that he bothered to say that. "I'm really fine. It was nothing." With that, she fled from him.

Later, while sitting in the backseat of the taxi as it headed up the West Side Highway, she continued to agonize over what had happened. Why was it impossible for her to have a meaningful relationship with a decent man? Didn't she deserve one? Or were the likes of David all that she had coming her way? How did it feel, she wondered, to be able to count on a man to take care of her? So far, Lisa had never known that feeling, not even from her father, who left when Lisa was only four years old. Was she destined to be with men who were losers?

Burdened as she was by the awful night, she dismissed it the minute she saw Justin's smiling face as he ran to greet her just inside the apartment door. He'd stayed up way past his bedtime.

"Mommy, Mommy! Guess what I did today." He smiled, proudly displaying the gap in the middle of his front teeth. He was the perfect little boy age, young enough to still want to snoodle with his mom, but old enough to make little attempts at independence.

Lisa stooped down to be eye to eye with the true love of her life. "I don't know," she said, faking seriousness.

"Guess," he implored, still smiling broadly.

"Let's see." She put her hand to her chin as though she were deep in thought. "Did you build your mom a new house?"

His brow furrowed. "No, silly—that would have taken at least three days."

"Oh, okay. Well, did you buy us a new car?" she teased, tickling his tummy.

He squealed with laughter. When he caught his breath,

he said, "I don't have my dwiver's license yet." As though that would have been the only thing in the way of him and four wheels.

"Okay, then. I give up." She tossed her hands in the air.

"I pulled another toof for the toof fairy. See," he said, pulling the small bloody evidence from his pajama pocket.

"Wow, that's a big one too," she said, rumpling his hair. "If you keep that up, you won't have any left."

"How much is this one worth?" he asked, now all business.

She stood up. "Not sure. I'll have to consult with the tooth fairy about that."

"I think it should be twice as much as these." He pointed to the gap off to the left side.

"Oh, really?"

"Yeah, it's bigger. See." He was right—it was a molar.

"We'll see." She took off her coat and draped it over the sofa.

"Dad said that it should be worth more too."

She nearly froze in her tracks. It suddenly dawned on her that David wouldn't be as easy to erase from her life as she might want. She now had to consider his growing relationship with Justin as well. "Oh, really?"

The little boy stood taller, undoubtedly influenced by the words of his dad, who could do no wrong in his eyes. "He said that I'm a big boy now."

She hid the anger from her voice. "When did he say all of this?"

"He came by school today."

Lisa felt a knot form in her gut. "Go wash up for bed. We'll deal with the tooth fairy later."

After he'd scampered away, Lisa paid the baby-sitter and headed to her own room to prepare for bed. Now her mood was even worse than it had been before. How dare David show up at Justin's school like that, as though he had parental rights? After slipping on a cotton nightgown, removing all traces of makeup and brushing her teeth, Lisa peeked in on Justin. He was already sound asleep, no doubt dreaming of the money the tooth fairy was obliged to leave him.

She sat on the edge of the bed, smiling despite a bad day. She couldn't help but be happy whenever she saw that precious little face. She leaned over to lightly kiss his smooth dimpled cheek before slipping a five-dollar bill under his pillow and quietly pulling the tooth away. After carefully tucking the covers snugly around him, Lisa kissed his sweet face again and tiptoed out of the room.

Traces of memories from the day swirled through her mind. Flashes of David and his bimbo made her cringe. Alternating with them was the concerned face of Lyle Johnson. How could David do that to her? She wanted to bury her head under the pillow and never come out.

Eventually she drifted off to sleep. She dreamed of Justin running through a field of daisies, searching the ground for his missing tooth, while David looked on from the sidelines, pointing him in one direction after the other. When the child was near exhaustion, she ran to him, shouting, "It's not there! It's not there!" while David continued to point from one end of the field to the other.

As she twisted and turned in her sleep, she felt the presence of someone else in her bed. Startled, she jumped up. David was sitting on the side of the bed with his shirt off.

"What are you doing here?"

"What do you mean? I'm going to bed," he slurred. She smelled the stench of alcohol on his breath.

"Not here you aren't."

He looked genuinely surprised. "Wh-why not?" He reached over for her, no doubt thinking that he could sweet-talk his way under the covers.

With his closeness came the lingering scent of cheap perfume. She yanked away from him and switched on the bedside lamp. He looked as wretched as he smelled. His eyes were bloodshot, and he held his head in the stiff manner that drunks do in a vain effort to emulate sobriety. There was even lipstick smeared across his mouth. "I want you out of my bed!"

"Wh-wh-what did I do?" He frowned, as though he really had no idea.

"Let's start with humiliating me in front of everybody, by hanging all over any female that would let you."

"I wasn't hanging on them," he protested. "They were hanging on me." As though that made any difference.

"I certainly didn't see you pushing them away."

"So that's what this is about? You're jealous." He tried his mack-daddy smile, followed by a sad attempt at seduction by licking his lips.

"Don't flatter yourself. I'm just finally realizing that I deserve a lot better than you."

"Oh, just because you got a little job don't mean nothin'."

"It's more than you got." For the last two months, he'd been claiming to look for work, but deep down, Lisa knew he didn't really want to work. It was much easier for him to live off her instead.

"That's what's wrong with black women. Always beatin' a brother down," he said indignantly.

She'd heard this sorry song before.

She threw the covers aside and hopped out of bed. "Well, in that case, I'd strongly suggest that you slither back downtown and crawl into bed with one of the scrawny tryin'-to-be-black chicks I saw you with earlier."

"Wait a minute, baby." He stood up, and his pants dropped around his feet. He stumbled to raise them while trying to catch up with her as she headed to the doorway.

"I want you out of here," she demanded.

"What about Justin?" he asked. He'd finally realized that she was serious.

She stood firm, with her hands on her hips. "What about him?"

"I'm not leaving without my son."

"Nigga, you must be crazy. You don't have a pot to piss in or a window to throw it out of, yet you're talking about taking 'your' son, who you've never given a cent of child support to."

He played the only card he had. "I'm his father."

"Well, why don't you act like it and get a job to support him? Meanwhile, I won't hold my breath," she said sarcastically. She went to the side of the bed, picked up his shirt, along with the cordless phone. "If you aren't out of here in five minutes, I'm calling the police." She threw the shirt at him and headed out the bedroom door.

Two minutes later, he walked by, still tucking the shirt into his pants. "You haven't heard the last of this," he threatened as he sulked past her and out the door.

15

Tess felt like Julia Roberts playing the hooker who romped up and down Rodeo Drive in Beverly Hills, bearing armloads of shopping bags in the movie *Pretty Woman*. Only in Tess' version, she raided the ritzy designer stores along Madison and Fifth avenues in New York City. She waltzed into Gucci and wasted no time at all buying a fifteen-hundred-dollar black GG shoulder bag, along with the matching three-hundred-dollar wallet. Her next stop was the Prada boutique, where she purchased two suits: one with trousers and the other with a slim straight skirt. She chose the New York color of choice—black—for both. Her next stop was Barneys, the FAO Schwarz for adults. It was an emporium full of American and European designer labels made to order for style-conscious trendsetters. Tess made a beeline up the escalator, heading straight to the latest couture collections, in search of evening wear to round out her growing wardrobe. Now that she was in New York, it was only a matter of time until she was included on the social roster of the city's elite, and she had to look the part. She spotted a beautiful black silken-wool floor-length evening dress on display, and without so much as glancing at the price tag, she summoned the saleswoman.

"I would like this in a size six."

"Shall I put the dress in the fitting room while you look around?" asked the snooty saleswoman.

Tess was meeting with a Realtor for lunch and didn't have time to go into the dressing room and try it on. "No, thank you. You can wrap it," she said, and whipped out her AmEx card. Edmund had also been generous and thoughtful enough to add her name to his account before the wedding.

The saleswoman looked surprised, as if she were expecting to work a little harder for her commission. "Are you taking it with you, or should I send it to your home?"

"You can send it to the St. Regis." Tess had been staying at the luxurious five-star hotel since arriving in New York. She decided on the stately landmark property instead of one of the trendy boutique hotels because she wanted to lie low until she was completely settled in a place of her own.

She dashed out of the store and strolled down Madison Avenue on her way to Tao, a restaurant on Fifty-eighth Street that combined the cuisine of Japan, China and Thailand into artful gastronomical treats. She was having lunch with a Realtor who was known to have the best listings in the city. She arrived before he did and was seated upstairs opposite the gigantic gold Buddha that protected the room.

"Contessa Aventura?" asked a handsome, well-dressed man.

Tess looked up and appraised him from head to toe. He was dressed in a black suit with a notched collar and black knit mock turtleneck.

"Call me Tess. You must be Spence?"

Spence Ellis was considered a celebrity real-estate broker, partially because of his hefty commissions and partially because of his leading-man good looks and magnetic personality. He was almost as famous as his elite clientele of athletes, actors and old-money mavens. Tess had read an article on him in *Gotham,* the hot magazine that highlighted the happenings in and around New York City. She had been intrigued by the smooth-shaven chocolate face in the picture that accompanied the article. She promptly called his office and made an appointment. When she told Spence her criteria for an apartment—something in the million-dollar range— he immediately set up a luncheon meeting.

"Nice to meet you," he said, sitting down.

After they ordered, Spence went into his spiel. "I have a quaint one-bedroom with a terrace on Park Avenue."

After knocking around Manhattan for years, Tess knew that in New York real-estate speak, *quaint* meant "closet-sized." "Actually, I was looking for something a bit larger than quaint." Tess leaned in and gazed into his sable brown eyes. She could tell by his speech and mannerisms that he was gay and not the least bit interested in her. She had to remind herself that she was a different person now and not to slip back into the familiar. As Tyrone, she would have had Spence on a platter for dessert, but as Tess, she had to maintain a distant composure.

"I also have a three-bedroom duplex with a roof garden on Fifth Avenue. It faces Central Park. It's a tad expensive, but worth every square inch."

"That sounds delicious," Tess said, slightly licking her lips. "When can I . . . ?" She was going to ask when she could see the apartment, but then thought about the location. In her former life as Tyrone, he had lived on the Upper East Side with his mother, Mattie, the maid to the St. James family. Tess didn't want to move too close to the old stomping grounds.

"Excuse me?"

Tess quickly switched gears. "Do you have anything downtown?"

"As a matter of fact, I have a fabulous loft in SoHo. It's two thousand square feet with a gym and laundry room. But unfortunately, no terrace or balcony."

"Well, a girl can't have everything."

After lunch, they took a taxi downtown. The loft was located on Broome Street near West Broadway. The building had originally been an old factory, as were most of the buildings in the area, with cast-iron columns in front. The ground floor was occupied by a trendy boutique that catered to men; next door was a hip-looking bar. They walked inside the building and took a private elevator to the fifth floor. When the door opened, Tess nearly gasped. It opened right inside a spacious loft, with twenty-foot ceilings and blond hardwood floors. Floor-to-ceiling windows lined the far wall. Tess walked in and instantly felt at home.

"Let me show you around," Spence said, walking ahead down a long hallway. Entering a large bedroom with a marble bathroom inside, he waved his arms and announced, "This is the master suite."

Tess didn't show any of the excitement she felt. She knew how to play hardball and act as if she didn't particularly care for the space. If there was any room for negotiation, she could blow it by appearing overzealous. So she simply nodded as Spence explained the amenities of the loft.

"This is the gym," he said, showing her a room adjacent

to the bedroom. "It's a little small, but has state-of-the-art workout equipment, from a treadmill to Pilates apparatus."

Tess wanted to scream. This was just what she was looking for. "How long has this loft been on the market?" She knew that since 9/11, the real-estate market downtown had suffered, and she hoped that it was still a buyers' market.

"Actually, this loft isn't even listed yet. But I'm sure it won't last long once it's on the market."

Obviously the sellers were once again reigning. She walked through the loft a second time, this time envisioning herself perched on the window seat sipping a cup of herbal tea. "What's the asking price?"

"It's going to list for one-point-eight, but if you make me an offer, I'm sure I can get the owner to come down to one-point-five," Spence said, eager to close the deal.

Damn, a million and a half, Tess said to herself. She had money now, but at the rate she was spending, it wouldn't last long. "How about one-point-two?"

"I'm sure he'll agree to one-point-three, especially in cash," Spence said, negotiating up.

Sensing that $1.3 million was his final offer, Tess thought about it for a minute. Knowing that prime real estate in Manhattan didn't last long, she said, "I'll take it."

"Excellent!" Spence said, pleased, and Tess wondered if she shouldn't have bargained harder. "Come back to my office, and I'll draw up the papers."

"Yes, I'd like to do that."

Tess couldn't believe that after all the years of scraping by in and out of seedy transient dives, she was finally going to possess her very own "piece of the rock."

16

"**D**on't go up in there actin' ugly," Jimmy instructed Anton as they rode in the back of a taxi. They had finally gotten the call from Tyrone to come over to his new place and pick up the rest of their money. While he was in Montreal, he had bothered to send only the initial loan amount of two grand.

"You ain't got to tell me how to act," Anton spat. He was still upset at Tyrone for not sending the entire four thousand to begin with. "I just don't git why he made us wait all dis time fo' the rest of our money."

"It's only been a few weeks," Jimmy reasoned. He was also irritated at Tyrone for making them wait, but he didn't want to walk in with an attitude and risk pissing him off. His plan was to play nice. Now that Tyrone had money, Jimmy wanted to get his share of it. "Besides, we got to play it cool until we cash in." Smiling, Jimmy looked over at Anton. "*Ka-ching!*"

"Word," Anton responded with a sly grin, and slapped Jimmy a high five.

When the taxi pulled up in front of a nondescript building, Anton said, "This is it?" He scrunched up his face as he got out of the taxi. He knew in New York that you couldn't read a building by its exterior; in most cases it was all about the interior. But with Tyrone's grandiose taste, Anton expected to see a building with all the trimmings—a uniformed doorman and a plush door-to-curb runner, all under an elaborate awning.

Jimmy took a crumpled piece of paper out of his pocket and read the address he had scribbled down. "Yep, this is it." They walked over to the black metal door. Jimmy quickly scanned the panel of doorbells with corresponding names looking for Tyrone N. Thomas, but didn't see it. Then it dawned on him that the apartment would be listed under Tess' name. He ran his finger down the short list of names, and sure enough, C. Aventura Dubois was listed in bold letters. Jimmy pressed 5B, and within a few seconds a buzzer sounded. He pulled open the door, and they stepped inside. Painted a dull gray, the lobby wasn't impressive in the least. There were two elevators, an old cage-type and a smaller one a few feet away with a key insert, which appeared to be private. They stepped inside the waiting elevator and clanged the cage door shut. The elevator slowly jerked up toward the fifth floor. It came to an abrupt halt when it reached its destination.

"Wit' his money, I'd think he'd be livin' large," Anton said, eyeing the chipped paint on the ceiling.

Jimmy didn't comment on the condition of the building, because he had seen far worse. When he reached apartment 5B, he rang the bell and impatiently waited for an answer.

"Well, it's about time."

"Excuse me?" Jimmy asked the woman who greeted them. "Uh, uh, I must have the wrong apartment," he stammered, and stared. Standing before him was over six feet of beauty. Her rich auburn hair was blunt cut and dusted her shoulder blades; her makeup was flawless, enhancing sculptured features, making the overall effect—magnificent. *If I were straight, I'd be all over her,* Jimmy thought. He then turned to walk away.

"Hey, where are you going?" asked the woman.

Jimmy looked perplexed. "Is this apartment 5B?"

"Yeah, fool, get in here. It's me."

Jimmy's jaw nearly dropped to the floor as he and Anton said in unison, "Tyrone?"

"In the flesh," he said. "I'd like to introduce you to Contessa Aventura Dubois," he laughed, spinning around so that they could get the full effect of Her Highness.

Anton and Jimmy walked into the loft in a state of disbelief. Of course they knew about Tess, but seeing her up close and personal was shocking. There were no traces of Tyrone, not even a hint of testosterone. He was all Tess. "Damn, I got to give it to you." Jimmy slapped him five. "You all that and some cream."

"Glad you approve," Tyrone said, leading them into the loft.

As Anton was busy checking out the decor, Jimmy was checking out Tyrone's transformed body. "Man, where'd you put the beefcake?" he asked, noticing there were no traces of Tyrone's manhood poking through the black jumpsuit he wore.

"It's tucked away in a safe place," he chuckled.

Anton slowly walked around the room in amazement. Tyrone was indeed living large. Everything from the drapes to the furniture seemed to be custom made; his initial sentiments about the shabby building quickly dissolved as he surveyed the well-appointed loft. "Is this silk?" Anton asked, fingering the throw on the back of the sofa.

"Hundred percent, imported from Bali," Tyrone said with arrogance oozing from every syllable. "So you must be Anton?" His disapproval was barely hidden.

Sensing the hairs rising on the back of Anton's neck, Jimmy walked over and put his arm around his boyfriend's waist. "Tyrone, this is my new man."

"Charmed, I'm sure," Tyrone said, sinking into the cushions of the sofa and crossing his long legs.

Jimmy sat across from him on one of two oversized chintz ottomans as Anton continued his inspection. "What this set you back?" he asked, referring to the Bang & Olufsen stereo system mounted to the wall.

"You don't even want to know," Tyrone said, evading the question.

"I bet it was more than four Gs," Anton said with disdain, "and speaking of four Gs, where's our money?" Tact never had been his MO.

Tyrone patted an envelope on the cocktail table. "Your two thousand dollars is right here."

Jimmy reached for the package. "What about that bonus we talked about?" he asked, thumbing through the bills.

"Oh, that's right. I completely forgot." After liquidating

Edmund's assets, Tyrone had promised to give Jimmy an extra bonus for helping him create Tess to begin with. After all, if it weren't for the hormones that he'd stolen from the doctor's office, she wouldn't have been around to collect all those millions.

"I just bet you did," Anton hissed.

He rolled his eyes so hard, Jimmy was afraid they'd roll right out the sockets. He shot Anton a look to play it cool. "No problem, I know you good for it," Jimmy said.

"I don't have much cash in the house. Can I . . . ?"

Anton bristled and was set to pounce. "Why don't you take yo' a—"

But Jimmy stopped him short. "It's cool, man—we can wait until tomorrow." Jimmy didn't have to face Anton to know that he was giving him a menacing look behind his back. Jimmy didn't want to wait any more than Anton did, but what choice did they have? "I can go to the bank with you in the morning," Jimmy offered.

This time it was Tyrone who bristled. "Who said I'm going to the bank?"

Anton butted in, "You just said you didn't have any money in here."

"Before you cut me off, I was going to offer you a check."

"We ain't takin' no check. We want cash." Anton crossed his arms tightly in front of his chest. He wasn't budging.

Tyrone dug deep into his pocket and threw a few crumpled bills on the table. "Here's your damn cash," he sneered.

Jimmy looked at the money and counted three hundred dollars. This wasn't what he had in mind. The bonus he envisioned came with a few more zeros than that. "Come on, y'all. We ain't goin' argue over no money. We'll take a check"—he gave Tyrone a knowing look—"but you know cash'll be better."

Tyrone cut his eyes at Anton, then turned his attention back to Jimmy. "Call me tomorrow, Jimmy, and I'll give *you* cash." He stood up. "I gotta run." Then he walked to the door.

Jimmy followed closely behind, but Anton lingered, reluctantly trailing them. "Okay, I'll see you tomorrow," Jimmy said.

"I know one thing, Jimmy, better check that Negro," Tyrone said to himself once they had gone. "Coming in here eyeballing my shit and demanding *my* money." He slid the wig off and fanned it in the air. "I need a drink after all that drama."

Tess did a quick change out of the catsuit and into a black leather dress with billowy bell shelves and a pair of Robert Clergerie shin-high boots.

Her initial thought was to visit one of Tyrone's old haunts, but she didn't want to chance running into any of his former cronies. Looking out the window, she noticed the bar located on the ground floor of her building. Tess decided to pop in and have a drink or three.

The second she walked in, she felt right at home. It was called Street Signs and had a cozy feel to it, reminding her of The Backroom, a bar Tyrone had once managed when he was impersonating Blake St. James. That was how he ran the scam on Morgan and Dakota in the first place. Tess scanned the room, but didn't see any familiar faces, only beautiful ones. "The pretty people are in the house tonight," she mused. There was an eclectic mix of Euro trash, model types, Wall Street boys and a sprinkling of wannabes. *I think I just found a new watering hole. I'll fit in just fine.* She smiled at the possibilities.

She selected a choice booth near the back. She scooted into the plush velvet nook and positioned herself so that she had an unobstructed view of everyone that crossed the threshold. Ensconced on her throne, Tess felt every bit the queen awaiting the arrival of her subjects.

"Would you care for a drink?" asked the waiter who appeared at her side with tray in hand.

Tess pondered the question for a second, then replied, "I think I'll have a sidecar." She'd been having a love affair with the ancient martini, which was making a resurgence these days.

"Would you like a sugar rim?"

"Yes, please."

Within a few minutes, the waiter reappeared with her drink. Tess leaned back into the velvet cocoon and languidly sipped the amber-colored liquid, waiting for the show to begin.

"If the stars are aligned tonight, maybe I'll meet another benefactor," she mused, keeping her eyes peeled for an Edmund Dubois type—obscenely rich and desperately lonely.

Tess watched as a trio of blondes from Generation Next came in, saddled up to the bar and ordered cosmos. *Don't they know that drink is played?* she thought, as always the expert on drinks.

The bartender swiftly swiped a slender, frosted bottle of Belvedere and a stout, chestnut-colored bottle of Cointreau from the well-stocked shelf. She poured the spirits into a polished shaker, added a splash of cranberry juice for color and a few squirts of fresh lime juice before wrapping the shaker in a bar towel, plopping in four ice cubes, and shaking it vigorously. Tess counted at least fifty shakes. The bartender then took three martini glasses out of the cooler and as if on stage, with a dramatic flair poured the ruby-colored cocktail into the waiting Y-shaped glasses. The performance was reminiscent of Tom Cruise's in the movie *Cocktail*, where the patrons came to witness the theatrics of the bartenders as they concocted one exciting elixir after the other.

The trio sipped their trendy cocktails and chatted idly among themselves. Occasionally, as if on silent cue, the three flipped their blond tresses—which ranged in color from ash to honey to strawberry—in unison.

Slowly people began to trickle in until the bar area was buzzing with after-work chatter. Tess soon noticed a large disparity, three to one in the ratio of women to men. With batting eyes and beckoning breasts, the trolling trio attempted to hook a lone Wall Streeter. He took one glance in their direction and walked to the opposite end of the bar: he was too smart to be snapped up by such blatant bait. *If this is my competition*, Tess thought, glancing at the trio, *then call me Tyson, because I'm gonna knock them out in the first round*. If there was one subject Tess knew, it was how to woo a man. The only problem was, tonight there was no one in the bar worth wooing. She stifled a yawn and signaled the waiter.

"I'll have another sidecar."

"You got it," he said, and retreated to the bar.

Tess put her elbows on the table, interlocked her fingers and rested her chin atop her hand. Pursing her lips, she brooded. *If this scene doesn't pick up soon, I'm going to have to find another preyground to stalk.*

Sipping her second drink, Tess watched the same scene—designer-clad desperadoes on the hunt for a cash cow—unfold a half dozen times. "I'm outta here," she said finally, taking one last sip.

As she began to ease out of the booth, the velvet drapes that covered the front door blew open, and in walked a tall drink of chocolate milk. He was beefcake-calendar handsome, a cross between Michael Jordan and LL Cool J. Tall, bald and fine. Tess quickly eased back into the booth and resumed her *I Spy* role. The hunk breezed through the bar, stopping every few feet to plant kisses on waiting cheeks. The women all seemed to know him; even the extremely efficient bartender greeted him warmly. Clearly he was the catch of the day.

At least he knows how to dodge a bullet, she thought, admiring how he slid through the slippery fingers of the gold diggers.

He walked to the end of the bar and scanned the room. His eyes stopped dead on Tess. His piercing stare made her fidget with nerves. She smoothed her hair and remembered that she was Contessa Aventura Dubois, a woman of substantial means with no need to panic. He summoned the waiter and whispered something into his ear. The waiter immediately made his way toward Tess.

"Uh"—he looked down at his hands sheepishly, then back at Tess—"I'm going to have to ask you to move." It was his responsibility to place the reserved sign on Lyle's table each evening, and he'd forgotten to do so tonight.

"Excuse me?" Tess looked up with questioning eyes.

"This is Mr. Johnson's private booth."

"Who?" She was not accustomed to being dismissed.

He begin to shift his weight nervously from one leg to the

other. "Look, I'm new here and I forgot that this was his private booth. He's offered to buy you a drink at the bar instead."

"You tell this Mr. Johnson, whoever he is, that he can join me right here in the booth and I'll buy *him* a drink," Tess said, and leaned back farther, crossing her legs and showing no intention of moving.

The waiter returned to the Jordan Cool J look-alike and whispered in his ear. In an LL-type gesture, Mr. Tall Dark And Luscious licked his full lips and stuck his hands in his pockets before proceeding slowly toward the booth.

"Hello, there," he said, his voice deep and smooth. "May I introduce myself?" He extended his well-manicured hand. "I'm Lyle Johnson, the owner of Street Signs."

Tess fanned out her arms in a welcoming gesture. "Please join me," she offered as if *she* were the owner.

"My pleasure." He flashed an Ultra Brite smile and slid into the booth.

Tess quickly sized him up, from his buffed crocodile loafers and gabardine slacks to the slender antique Rolex on his wrist. Lyle Johnson was the genuine article; he reeked of class and plenty of cash. Tess tried to sniff out any scent of bisexuality, but all she smelled was straight-up unadulterated male. She thought about turning up the charm and putting the moves on him, but decided against it. From the fawning women at the bar, she could tell that Lyle was a ladies' man, and unlike Edmund, he would expect more than a peck on the cheek at the end of a date. It wasn't worth the risk of exposure to flirt with him. Besides, Tess had another plan in mind for Mr. Lyle Johnson.

"Tell me"—she scooted close to him—"what's it like owning a bar?"

17

Being the assistant manager for Street Signs would be the first legal job that Ernie'd ever held. Not once had he filled out an application for employment or a W-2 form, or been offered a benefits package. Sure, he'd made plenty of money—often losing it just as swiftly—as either a dealer, a hustler of stolen auto parts or a neighborhood numbers runner. He found it strangely ironic that Lyle named his bar Street Signs, given the fact that his little brother didn't know a damn thing about the streets. Luckily for Lyle, Ernie was a master of street life, because whether Lyle knew it or not, running a bar was about as far from white collar as you could get, especially considering all the cash that flowed through.

As much as he looked forward to this new opportunity, Ernie was also nervous. Though he'd never admit it, he was eager to prove to his brother, to his mother and to himself that he'd grown beyond his troubled past.

His mother had been as thrilled by Lyle's job offer as Ernie was. To her it symbolized the mending of a fence that she'd feared was forever broken. She cried tears of joy after hearing about the reconciliation between her two sons. She had no idea what had precipitated the miracle, nor did she care. The most important thing was that the two boys would now be brothers again.

"Don't you look spiffy," she said, smiling warmly at Ernie as he slid his arms into a light overcoat.

"Thanks, Ma."

She reached up and took his face in her hands. "I am so proud of you."

Anxious to avoid an outburst of emotions, Ernie quickly said, "I haven't done anything yet."

"But I know that you will do a great job." She kissed him and finished buttoning his coat, as though he were still her five-year-old son.

After taking the PATH train to Christopher Street, he took a taxi to TriBeCa, stepping out right in front of his new place of employment. This was the first time he'd ever even seen the bar, since chichi Manhattan nightspots weren't exactly his watering holes. He couldn't help but be impressed. The outside boasted a swanky burgundy awning, a velvet rope and even a bouncer. The door was heavy oak with a brass handle, and an imitation street sign had the name of the bar on either side.

"Can I help you?" the bouncer asked, taking in Ernie's creased but dated corduroys and the shirt whose collar looked to be hand-pressed. Ernie's wardrobe was not exactly par for the course at Street Signs.

"I'm Ernie, Lyle's"—he paused—"new assistant manager." He'd come close to telling the bouncer that he was Lyle's brother, but quickly remembered that he'd convinced Lyle not to let anyone know. The other employees would figure he'd got the job solely because of their relationship. With a common last name like Johnson, there was no reason that they'd ever know the two were brothers.

He walked inside the bar and was further impressed by its cool, hip decor. Even though it was early, only three o'clock, he could feel the vibe of the place. Everything from the velvet lounge chairs to the custom upholstered booths to the all-oak bar and the crystal glassware was top shelf. Not to mention the exotic array of alcohol, which Ernie also took note of.

"You must be Ernie?"

He turned to face a young woman sporting a mass of cinnamon-colored dreads. "I am. And you are . . . ?"

"I'm Jeanine, the bartender." She eyed him cautiously.

He nodded. "Lyle mentioned you. He said that you'd show me the ropes." Ernie reached out to shake her hand.

"Hope you're a quick study, because I don't have all day to teach."

Ernie didn't want to start off with a strike on the first day, so he bit his tongue and followed her to the back office, which was located down a narrow hall, past the lavatories. Once inside, Jeanine took Ernie through the various operating procedures, which included those for the bar itself, light food service, coat check, valet parking, accounting, security, city and state regulations, inventory, cleaning, et cetera. By the time they emerged two hours later, Ernie's head was spinning like that of the little girl in *The Exorcist*.

She noticed that he seemed flustered. "What bars have you worked in before?"

Ernie didn't want anyone snooping into his background. "Why? Is this an interview?"

"No," she snapped. "You just seem a little overwhelmed. Are you sure you can handle this?" she challenged.

He bristled. For two hours, Jeanine had been treating him like a busboy, instead of a manager. "Piece of cake," he said with a lot more confidence than he actually felt.

"In that case, I'm back at the bar." She left with a toss of her long dreads.

Driving her away may have been a mistake, Ernie thought. After all, he needed as much help as he could get. He called after her: "I do have a few more questions."

She swung back around with a look of mock amazement. "With all your experience, I'm sure that you could run this place without my help," she said sarcastically.

Ernie stuck his hands down into his front pockets, shuffling from side to side. Jeanine's quick jabs unnerved and attracted him at the same time. This was a real woman, no fluff. "I didn't say all that."

She cocked her head to one side, sizing him up. "Okay. I'll show you how things work here."

Taking him behind the bar, she explained how their specialty drinks were one of the keys to the bar's success. And the waitresses, she said, were very popular with the male customers, but they had to be watched, because this didn't always go over well with the female customers, who had their own scores to keep. It was also important that he kept the light-fare chef, Paul, stroked, or he'd simply feel ignored and not show up. He was as temperamental as a woman, Jeanine confided.

Throughout her spiel, Ernie was intrigued by Jeanine's smarts and easy confidence. "Where are you from?" he interrupted her to ask.

She looked at him strangely. "I'm from D.C. Why?"

"Just curious. So what brought you to New York?"

A little annoyed, she said, "School."

"What school? What are you studying?"

"What is this, an interview?" she asked. They both laughed. "NYU," she finally answered. "I'm getting a master's in photography."

Ernie was impressed. She was not the sort of chick he was accustomed to being around. "Photography, huh?"

As they'd been talking, the place had started to fill up with a light Wall Street crowd and the feeder fish that kept them satisfied. Ernie marveled at the exotic combination of women who swarmed about. They were white, black, Asian, Hispanic, Indian; they came in all colors, and *very* little clothing. Every chick here looked as if she'd spent the whole day at Mario Badescu or the Red Door, getting done up for this very night. *No blemishes, broken nails, cracked polish or split ends here*, he thought. He glanced at Jeanine, who was expertly shaking a Grey Goose apple martini. This was shaping up to be a very interesting gig.

18

Tyrone spent the day romping around Chelsea, the Village, TriBeCa and SoHo clad casually in jeans, a T-shirt that read HOCKEY—CANADA'S OTHER RELIGION and a leather jacket. He also wore a baseball cap with the brim broken so far down on his forehead that it touched the top of his dark aviator shades, concealing the upper portion of his face. He began his outing with four thousand dollars bulging out of his billfold, but after browsing around the boutiques in lower Manhattan and picking up a little somethin'-somethin' in just about every store, his wallet was now significantly slimmer. Tyrone loved the high from buying an expensive item without weighing the price. It was euphoric. He now understood the phrase, "If you have to ask the price, you can't afford it." It was excursions like this one that he had dreamed of as he watched his mother Mattie, receive and unwrap packages for the St. James family from the three Bs—Bergdorf, Barneys and Bendel. Mrs. St. James would shop the stores along Fifth Avenue with no regard to the hefty price tags that hung from the items. She would have her purchases delivered to the penthouse, and Mattie would plow through layers upon layers of tissue paper before uncovering the latest treasure. He could remember his mother being flabbergasted at the cost of the Bob Mackie gowns and Chanel suits as she clipped the price tags and hung the garments in Mrs. St. James' vault of a closet.

Though he had been back in New York for a while, he had not seen his mother. It was too risky. Still, once a week, a courier delivered a package to her containing ten crisp Benjamins, with a note that read:

Spend it all in one place! Love, T

But knowing his mother, she would stash the bills away for a rainy day.

Tyrone shifted the shopping bags in his hands as he strolled past Street Signs on his way home. He slowed his stroll and peered into the plate-glass window. There, surrounded by a bevy of beauties, was Lyle. Once again the ratio was lopsided, with just a smattering of men. "What that bar needs is someone to attract the bees to the honey," he chuckled, "and that someone is Tess. She'll know how to bring in the big spenders. Besides, Tess needs something else to do besides shop." Tyrone picked up his pace and rushed upstairs to change before Lyle left for the evening.

"I have just the right outfit," Tyrone said once he was inside the loft. He emptied the contents of the shopping bags onto the bed, and rummaged through the tissue paper until he uncovered a slinky flesh-tone Roberto Cavalli spaghetti-strap number. The dress had strategically placed cutouts and was revealing in all the right places—the small of the back, high on the thigh, across the clavicle. Tyrone showered and made his transformation into Tess in record time. He slipped on a pair of Ron Donovan strappy sandals and teetered toward the private elevator.

When Tess sauntered into Street Signs, she discreetly glanced around the room for Lyle, but he was nowhere in sight. She took a seat at the bar, deciding that her performance would play out better perched on the edge of a bar stool instead of secluded inside a booth.

"What can I get you?" asked Jeanine in a friendly way, as she did with all repeat customers.

Tess wanted a sidecar, but champagne would be a better accomplice. "I'll have a glass of Veuve." Before giving an unforgettable performance, she needed to ensure she had the proper audience, so she leaned in and nearly whispered, "Is Mr. Johnson in tonight?"

"He was here a minute ago." Jeanine looked around the bar. "He's probably in the office. Did you need to see him?"

"No," Tess said. *As long as he sees me*, she thought.

The bartender seemed nice enough, so she decided to get the 411 on Mr. Lyle Johnson. "Is that all he does, run the place?"

Jeanine shrugged, not willing to reveal much. "No."

"Oh, where else does he work?"

"On Wall Street," was all Jeanine said as she twisted the cork off a bottle of champagne.

"Oh, yeah," Tess leaned in closer. "What does he do?"

"I couldn't say." Jeanine continued filling the glass with the effervescent liquid and placed it in front of Tess. Then she walked to the opposite end of the bar to serve another customer.

Couldn't or wouldn't? Tess thought. The heifer probably didn't want to give up any information because she wanted him all to herself.

Never mind that. Tess peered over the rim of the champagne flute as she took a sip, looking for a patsy. And sure enough, at the end of the bar was a bland-looking man in a bland-looking suit, drinking a bland-looking drink. Tess stared in his direction, willing him to acknowledge her. He seemed lost in thought, but she didn't let up until he slowly raised his head. *That's right, that's right*, she chanted silently. *Look this way.*

Then as if on cue he looked directly into her eyes. Tess gave a slight wink and a smile. He swiveled around on the stool, looking behind him, and nearly lost his balance, but no one was there. Sheepishly gazing at Tess, he pointed his index finger into his chest and mouthed, *Are you talking to me?*

She did a sexy shoulder pivot, slightly licked her bottom lip and nodded yes. She could tell by his awkwardness that he wasn't accustomed to getting hit on by a beautiful woman. Tess watched as he turned up the glass, no doubt trying to find a little courage in the bottom of his drink. He gathered his briefcase and shambled toward Tess.

"Uh"—he coughed nervously—"is anyone sitting here?"

"You are now," Tess said, fanning her manicured hand in the direction of the empty bar stool.

He nearly tripped over the legs of the stool as he plopped down. "I'm Barney Robinson," he said, grinning.

Tess extended her hand. "Contessa Aventura Dubois, but you can call me Tess."

"Nice to meet you, Tess," he gushed.

Wish I could say the same, she thought. "And you . . ."

She flashed a big phony smile. "You must be a bodybuilder."
She ran her hand up his scrawny arm.

"Don't I wish." He grinned. "No, I'm an accountant for
Deloitte Touche."

She picked up her half-empty glass, putting the flute on
the bar nearly in front of him.

"Would you care for another drink?"

She smiled, then said, "Only if you'll join me."

"I would love to." He scooted the bar stool a tad closer
to her. "What are we drinking?"

"Champagne."

He signaled the bartender and boomed like the last of the
big spenders, "I'd like to order a bottle of bubbly."

Jeanine looked unimpressed. "We have Dom, Veuve,
Piper and Cristal by the bottle. Which 'bubbly' do you
want?"

His smile dissipated; he didn't have a clue which brand to
order. He looked over at Tess for a hint.

"We'll have the Piper," she said.

Over champagne, Tess entertained him with one amusing
story after the other, often using her arms to make dramatic
gestures. "Then there was the time when I was upstate at a
polo match and turned over what I thought was a divot, but
to my surprise it wasn't a divot—it was—"

"Dung!" chimed in a tall, attractive man.

Tess feigned a shy, embarrassed laugh. "How did you
guess?"

"I used to play on the circuit. I've watched many a pretty
lady make the same unfortunate mistake." He extended his
hand and smiled broadly. "I'm Doug."

"Doug, this is Barney"—she motioned toward her patsy—"and I'm Tess. Nice to meet you."

He looked down at her long shapely legs, giving her a quick once-over. "The pleasure is all mine."

Before long Tess was surrounded by a multitude of males. Her witty stories, some with sexual overtones, drew the men like moths to a flame. She reveled in the attention as they ordered bottles of champagne to fuel her fire.

"Nobody invited me to the party."

Tess peeked through the crowd, trying to find the man behind the voice. Now that the show was revved up and in full gear, she only hoped Lyle saw her commanding performance. She smiled, seeing Lyle's face coming closer. "I didn't think you needed an invitation, since you do own the joint."

"What's the occasion?" he asked, looking down the bar at the various champagne buckets.

"No occasion, just celebrating life."

He gave her an approving smile. "Well, you can celebrate here anytime you like."

Knowing he was a numbers man, Tess could practically see him tallying the hefty tab she had brought in. "I'll just consider Street Signs my home away from home."

He bowed. *Mi casa es su casa.*

"I'm going to hold you to that," she shot back.

"Lovely ladies are always welcomed"—he glanced at her waiting court of men—"especially those with an entourage. You guys have fun. See you later. I've gotta run."

Little did he know, Tess thought, that he would be seeing her much sooner than later.

*   *   *

"Good morning, Hilda. What's my schedule for the day?" Lyle asked as he breezed into the office.

She peered over the half-glasses balanced on the tip of her keen nose. "You have a ten o'clock with the Syndicate Team from Warburg Dillon Reed. A twelve thirty lunch with a Ms. Dubois. A three o'clock conference call with the San Francisco office. Drinks at five thirty at the Four Seasons with O'Neal Morgan from Deutsche Bank, followed by dinner. The Four Seasons restaurant on Fifty-second between Park and Lexington, not the Four Seasons Hotel on Fifty-seventh." She rattled off his appointments from memory without batting an eyelash or referring to her calendar. "There's a printed schedule on your desk, so I won't have to update you every hour on the hour," she said in a slightly overbearing voice.

Lyle was accustomed to her haughtiness and didn't flinch at her tone. "Thanks," he said before turning to walk into his office. Then he stopped midstride. "But I'm still going to bug you," he teased.

"What else is new?" she said, returning her attention to the stack of mail on her desk.

Lyle hung his head and chuckled. As much as he hated to admit it, he loved their verbal jousting. It kept him on his toes. Once inside his office, he removed his suit jacket and hung it on the back of the door. Settling in behind his desk, Lyle picked up the printed version of his schedule and quickly perused the day's appointments. He crumbled the paper into a ball and tossed it into the trash. Hilda would be calling before each one of them anyway. Picking up the phone's headset, he began to adjust the silver band onto his head, but stopped and stared at the wastebasket. Lyle suddenly retrieved the schedule and smoothed out the paper on his desk. After rereading it, he buzzed Hilda.

"What took you so long?" came the clipped response.

Lyle ignored her sarcasm. "Who is Ms. Dubois?" He met at least a half dozen women on any given day, but didn't recall this one.

"Shouldn't you ask yourself that question?"

"Come on, Hilda," he said. "Didn't she leave a first name?" Lyle asked. "Besides, I thought I was having lunch with Senator Neuman today."

"The senator had to reschedule. He had an emergency meeting in Washington. And yes, she left her entire name—" She paused for effect. Normally she didn't book miscellaneous women into his lunch schedule, but Ms. Dubois had the refined tone of someone of substance.

He waited a few seconds. "Well?"

"Contessa 'Tess' Aventura Dubois. She assumed, correctly, that you would need more than a name. So she said to tell you, '*Mi casa es su casa.*' "

Hearing the phrase he had spoken just last night instantly jogged his memory. "Oh, sure. Tess." He didn't know her well, but he liked her style. More important, he liked the business she'd brought in.

Lyle retreated back into his office, rolled up his sleeves and got down to work. His large office suite was equipped with four flat-screen overhead monitors facing him and three smaller ones set around the perimeter of his massive desk. Lyle soon was tapping the tip of a Mont Blanc against his bottom teeth, watching one of his pet stocks lose its market share. "Damn it," he said to the screen of red stock symbols. The market was once again taking a roller-coaster ride. He knew better than to jump the gun and panic sell; the day wasn't over yet.

"Lyle," Hilda called through the intercom, "Yvette's on line one."

Lyle exhaled and picked up the receiver. "Hey, what's up?"

"Hey, baby." She was back to cooing. "Are we still on for dinner tonight?" Over the last week, her attitude had taken a drastic about-face. She had even picked up the talk of marriage again. It was all a little too coincidental for Lyle, since it happened to coincide with the senator's public announcement that Lyle was his nominee for the chairmanship of the SEC. When Lyle asked about her change in attitude, she told him that she had simply not been feeling well before.

"Where do you want to go?"

"I know this very romantic place that's really cozy. You'll love it."

"Where is it?"

She lowered her voice. "My place," she purred, "and you don't need a reservation."

"Ah, I'm really tied up. It looks like a late dinner meeting."

"What?" she cried, outraged. "Tied up? Did you hear what I said?"

"I heard," Lyle said calmly, thinking about her father, the congressman, and his ties to the senator. He tried to smooth it over. "Why don't we talk this weekend?"

"I'm busy this weekend." *Click.*

After he hung up, an image of Lisa Burrows popped into

his head. He recalled how upset she had been at the Ecstasy party, how much he'd wanted to comfort her. It was odd, because he'd never felt that way toward Yvette.

Frowning, he buzzed Hilda. "Where am I meeting Tess for lunch?"

"Klein's. It's a new restaurant downtown."

"I'm on my way." He rose from his desk, leaving the bleeding screens behind, along with his trepidation about Yvette.

Tess arrived at the restaurant first. Standing at the podium, waiting for the hostess, she took in the scene. It was the perfect combination of old-world charm meets New World chic. Located in a former turn-of-the-nineteenth-century bank, it had the original beveled molding and cashier cages intact. Ivory leather booths, floor-to-ceiling organza sheers and pinpoint overhead lighting gave the room a modern feel.

"Your name?" asked the hostess who stepped up to the podium.

"The reservation is under Johnson, for two," Tess said, pleased at the choice of restaurant. Initially she'd been reluctant to have his bossy assistant pick a place, but the woman insisted.

"Would you care for a table or a booth?"

"A booth, please."

"Follow me," said the well-dressed hostess as she led the way.

Tess settled into the comfortable booth and ordered a bottle of San Pellegrino. She decided against an alcoholic beverage because she wanted her mind clear when she pitched her idea to Lyle.

Soon her mark appeared at the door. Smiling as he approached the table, Lyle greeted Tess. "We meet again, and in a booth, no less," he remarked, referring to their first encounter at Street Signs.

"I know you're partial to them," she teased back.

He unbuttoned his jacket and eased onto the leather cushions across from her. "So, Tess, I was surprised to see you on my calendar today, though I did enjoy your performance last night. And I must admit, it was quite a show. You had those guys springing for the expensive stuff."

"Well, that's exactly what I wanted to talk to you about."

Before Tess could launch into her pitch, the waitress came by with menus. "Today's catch is butter fish over a creamy lemon rosemary risotto. We also have a succulent free-range chicken served with tender spring vegetables. Do you need a few minutes?"

"No," Tess said hastily. "I'll have the butter fish."

"I'll have the same, thank you."

Tess cleared her throat. "I noticed that Street Signs has a predominantly female clientele, which isn't necessarily a bad thing, providing you can bring in the sponsors to pick up their tabs."

"You mean, like you did," he said, quickly catching on.

"Exactly, because you know as well as I do that we women will buy one, maybe two drinks, and spend the rest of the time nursing the second drink, looking for someone else to buy another round."

"Tess, you're not telling me anything I don't know. Street Signs just doesn't seem to attract a large male clientele anymore, with the stock market plummeting. Don't get me wrong. We get our share of men, but not on a daily basis."

"Trust me. That's not entirely it. The women flock into Street Signs for a piece of the charismatic Lyle Johnson"—she winked—"while the men have to rely on the babes that are not focused on you to stroke their fragile egos. And that's where I come in."

Lyle put an elbow on the table. "What did you have in mind?"

From his body language Tess could tell that he was all ears. "I'd like to propose a partnership between us. Street Signs needs more than just an on-site manager."

Lyle asked bluntly, "Do you have any experience running a bar?"

"As a matter of fact, I do. Years ago, I managed a cigar bar on the Upper West Side and single-handedly turned the business around within a matter of months. I also have extensive experience running bistros in Paris as well as Canada."

Lyle was impressed. "To be honest with you, Tess, I'm considering selling the bar. It's been losing money lately, and I've been too preoccupied to focus on ramping up business."

"In that case, this partnership would be perfect. Not only can I bring in the hefty receipts, as I proved last night"—she paused and watched him digest the idea—"but I'm also willing to buy a share of Street Signs," she added, significantly.

Lyle had never entertained the idea of having a partner, but he liked the sound of it, especially a partner with experience. "How much of a share are we talking?"

"As much as two hundred thousand will buy."

"It'll buy you a twenty percent share in the business," he said sternly, as if there wasn't any room for negotiation.

Extending her hand before he had a chance to rescind the offer, Tess said, "Lyle, you've got yourself a partner."

"I'll have my lawyer, Denise Brown, contact you."

"I'll look forward to her call."

Tess knew her inheritance wasn't going to last forever, especially with her lavish sprees and expensive taste. And being broke again definitely wasn't on her agenda, so she saw this as a smart investment to help secure her financial future.

Besides, having access to a loaded cash register was always advantageous.

19

It had been raining for three straight days and nights. It felt like the beginning of the second coming of the Flood. It was pouring so hard that even Noah would have battened down the hatches. Jimmy sat on the hard cold seat, soaked from head to toe; his five-dollar street umbrella had blown inside out as he ran to catch the bus. He watched the rain seep through the rubber seams of the large windows. He was on his way home from Alphabet City, where he had tried in vain to get the deposit refunded on the apartment they'd had their sights set on. They had handed the money over the day before meeting with Tyrone, assuming that the "bonus" he was giving would be substantial enough to help finance a new life for them too. But the following day, when Jimmy met Tyrone, he'd been extremely disappointed to get only another five hundred dollars rather than the thousands that they were counting on.

Without the extra money, their funds were disappearing faster than contestants on *American Idol*. So Jimmy was more than a little steamed when the building manager told him that the deposit had been forfeited. Jimmy pleaded with him to give them a few more days to come up with the rest of the money, but the shyster manager insisted he couldn't hold the apartment indefinitely and that the deposit was without a doubt nonrefundable, no exceptions. As the bus slowly made its way uptown, Jimmy couldn't help but think of Tyrone cruising around the city in the back of a luxury Town Car. While his butt numbed to the hard plastic seat, Tyrone's was probably warm and cushy, sitting on butter-soft leather. And to make matters worse, Tyrone hadn't returned any of his phone calls. It seemed that Mr. Millionaire was trying to distance himself quick, fast and in a serious hurry. *He gonna make me act ugly*, Jimmy thought.

The synchronized rotation of the wheels lulled Jimmy into a light sleep. As he nodded, he dreamed of cashing in on Tyrone's jackpot. His eyes popped open when, through his slumber, he felt his stop coming up. He looked out of the window on the off chance that it had stopped raining, but the monsoon was still raging. Without an umbrella, he glanced around, hoping someone had left one behind. No such luck, but on the seat next to him was a copy of the *New York Gazette*. He quickly grabbed it and rushed toward the rear exit. Outside, Jimmy opened the newspaper and held it over his head for temporary shelter from the elements. He ran from the bus stop to his building, trying to dodge thumb-sized raindrops along the way. By the time he reached the apartment, he was soaked to the bone. He dropped the waterlogged newspaper on the floor and peeled off his clothes, leaving a trail of soaking wet jeans and soggy sneakers on his way to the bathroom. After being pelted by cold rainwater, Jimmy craved the comfort of a warm shower.

Stepping out of the stall and feeling refreshed, he looked on the rack for a towel but remembered Anton was at the Laundromat, doing the wash. "Guess I'll have to air-dry," he said. As he walked into the bedroom, beads of water dripped down his limbs onto the bare floor. Opening the top drawer of their secondhand bureau, he took out a pair of Joe Boxers and slipped them on.

Anton was such a neat freak, doing the laundry and scouring the place clean as if they lived in a hospital ward. They were the modern-day *Odd Couple,* the black Felix and Oscar. Jimmy went into the living room to pick up his clothes before Anton came in and pitched a hissy fit. He took them to the bathroom and slung them over the shower rod to dry.

"I hope Anton didn't drink the last forty," he mumbled, heading to the kitchen. Opening the refrigerator, he found a half-empty bottle of malt liquor. "Well, I guess a twenty is better than nothing at all." He chuckled, and walked back into the living room.

"Oh, shit," he said, looking at the partially dried newspaper lying by the front door. "Don't let Mighty Maid come in here and see that paper on the floor." He bent down to pick it up—and nearly fell over in shock at the picture staring up at him.

"What the . . . ?" he mumbled, taking the newspaper to the couch and sitting down.

There in the "Talk of the Town" section of the *Gazette* was a picture of Tyrone dolled up as Tess and grinning like a hyena with a strikingly good-looking man at her side. In shock Jimmy read:

The Tycoon and the Contessa

Lyle Johnson, the handsome Wall Street hunk, has taken on a partner for his cozy TriBeCa lounge, STREET SIGNS. Contessa "Tess" Aventura DuBois, a wealthy widow from Montreal, has joined forces to resuscitate the flatlining watering hole. Sources say that Ms. DuBois has invested a few hundred grand to keep the bar off life support. And from the hordes of people lining up to sample their ingenious martinis, it appears that Street Signs is indeed on the fast track to recovery.

Jimmy threw the article on the cocktail table. "Ain't that a bitch. No wonder he can barely squeeze out a few grand for an old friend. He's busy breaking off a few hundred grand for some damn stranger."

He stood up and began pacing back and forth, shaking his head and mumbling, "That's why he ain't been returning my calls. He too damn busy showboating at that bar." He was incensed. It was high time Tyrone was brought back down to reality. Becoming an instant millionaire had definitely gone to his head, giving him a case of selective amnesia. He had conveniently forgotten whence he came.

As Jimmy paced the floor, a bud of an idea began to take bloom. He suddenly stopped midstride. "I wonder what Tess's new business partner would think if he knew about Tyrone?" Jimmy smiled crookedly. "I bet he would gladly pay a few hundred grand to keep that little secret buried in the closet."

Like a wolf in couture clothing, Tyrone lay sprawled in the lap of luxury. His size elevens casually dangled off the edge of the expensive longue, clad in purple silk slippers with poofy marabou tops. He languidly sipped an extra dry martini. He was happier than a termite in a lumberyard. Finally he was living the life he'd felt entitled to: Baccarat crystal stemware in the latest designs, vintage French champagne chillin' in the Sub-Zero and a female mink throw elegantly tossed across his hand-embroidered chaise longue.

He remembered all too well the many shopping trips he'd taken in and out of the tony shops along Madison Avenue with his friend/nemesis Blake St. James. Or more accurately, Blake shopped and Tyrone simply went drooling along, living vicariously through his friend's array of no-limit credit cards. Nor could he ever forget the luxurious way the St. Jameses lived in their grand Fifth Avenue penthouse, while he and his mother simply existed for the purpose of their continued comfort. Well, those days were over, Tyrone declared as he downed the last of his cocktail and admired the exquisite five-carat diamond ring that he'd had designed in the shape of a T. He'd just picked it up earlier today. And it looked remarkable on his long slender finger, even if he had to say so himself. Which he did, since no one else was there to share it all with.

That was the only wrinkle in his perfectly appointed life. He lay there, pouting at his inability to flaunt his newfound wealth. The only person he knew in New York that he could be himself around was Jimmy, but now he was in a relationship and Tyrone didn't want to be bothered with that loser Anton. And making new friends as Tyrone was dicey, since there was still an arrest warrant out there with his name on it. The only way he could make new friends as Tyrone, rather than Tess, would be to meet people who were new to town and had no knowledge of his previous life. Also, he'd have to come up with yet another alias. How did life become so complicated?

As much as he loved playing the role of the glamorous and incorrigible Tess, it would be even more fun to prance up and down Christopher Street in a pair of tight jeans and a designer wife-beater, working the boys into a slippery lather with every step. The thought of it gave him an excellent idea. Why not dress in disguise—maybe a pair of dark shades and a hat would do—and hit some of the gay clubs tonight? He deserved a little fun. He'd earned it. Taken with the idea, he hopped off the chaise and headed into his bedroom to prepare for his first night out as Tyrone.

Forty-five minutes later, he sauntered out of the service entrance of his building dressed in a pair of flat-front Fendi slacks that hugged his round rear, a Dolce & Gabbana cotton sweater with a deep V-neck, square-toed loafers and Armani light-tinted sunglasses. He topped it all off with a New York Yankees baseball cap, which he pulled down low over the shades. Once he was safely on the next block, he switched from the Tess twist to the Tyrone strut, calling full attention to his six-foot-two-inch frame. When a vacant taxi came up the block, he stuck out his hand with his pointing finger delicately arched. "Come to Momma," he crooned as the car drifted to a stop curbside. "The East Village." He figured he'd cruise around the old neighborhood a bit before deciding which club to hit. After all, it'd been a long time since he'd done the New York gay scene.

After scoping out a few places in Alphabet City, he decided on an innocuous-looking spot that he'd heard Jimmy mention a few times. It was called the Manhole. A small cobalt blue sign hung just above the rusted metal door. There were no hours posted, credit-card-accepted signs or even a bouncer in sight, but there was a doorbell, which Tyrone gingerly pushed.

A window slid open in the center of the door. "May I help you?" a faceless voice asked.

"I imagine so," Tyrone said in his best diva voice. "I'm a little thirsty tonight. Can a girl get a drink?"

The door opened at once. "I think you'll find plenty to choose from here." The voice belonged to a six-foot Adonis. He was a copper-colored god, or goddess, Tyrone thought. His head was clean-shaved, calling attention to his flawless features, which included a set of pecs that appeared to be carved out of Shona stone.

"I'm sure I will," Tyrone said, winking at the piece of male perfection. He then strutted purposefully past the dreamboat, knowing that the man's eyes were locked like heat-seeking missiles on his undulating buttocks.

Once past the dimly lit entrance hall, a burly specimen with no facial expression whatsoever opened another doorway. The man reminded Tyrone of the guards posted outside the Royal Palace in London. He was tempted to tease the poor man until he responded, but he figured he'd best try to keep a low profile tonight. As if that were possible.

Once inside the sultry nightclub, he was pleasantly surprised to see a bevy of fine specimens lounging throughout the place. They came in every size, shape and color. Feeling like a starved man at an all-you-can-eat buffet, Tyrone coolly approached the bar as if he were working a catwalk, his narrow hips thrust forward. "I need something warm and wet," he cooed to the bartender.

"I can think of a few things," the young Asian boy-toy responded, "but why don't we start with Courvoisier?"

"I wouldn't have it any other way."

Many of the patrons had checked out Tyrone's dramatic entrance, as well as his spicy repartee with the bartender, taking copious note of the tall, handsome man who seemed to suck the very air from the room. Upon closer inspection, they appraised the exquisite ring on his right hand, the pricey designer gear and the expensive sunglasses. The boy reeked of cash and was drenched in style. Tyrone could feel the array of eyes prying. Fortunately, he didn't see any familiar faces.

Once the bartender had returned with his drink, Tyrone retreated from the bar, content to take a further look around. The room was full of overstuffed chairs, cozy nooks, somber lighting. He saw another door in the back through which a gaggle of boys had just disappeared. With his drink in hand, pinkie properly extended, Tyrone headed in the same direction. Once through the door, it was as if he'd woken up in another dream. The windowless room was completely dark with the exception of blue lights, which cast a mysterious, eerie but sexy glow over the packed room of revelers. The overall effect was surreal, particularly when combined with the surround sounds of Madonna oozing through the in-wall speakers.

Men were everywhere, wall to wall, in pairs, trios, groups and gangs. All danced mindlessly to the thumping beat, hips thrusting, butts undulating, heads thrown back in the heat of bliss. Tyrone blended right in, swaying rhythmically to the beat, while sipping his drink and scoping out the talent.

He felt a tap on his shoulder. "Can I buy you a drink?"

"I already have one." Tyrone turned around to face Morris Chestnut's body double. "But if you stick around, I'll be sure to have another."

"I'm Kendall." The boy gave Tyrone a brilliant Colgate smile, every tooth bright white and perfectly straight.

"I'm T-Timothy," he finally said, remembering his new alias.

Four drinks later, the two men were wrapped tightly in a heated embrace in yet another hidden room, whose only furnishings were of the kind that reclined. There was a separate charge of one hundred dollars to enter, which Tyrone gladly forked over, further impressing his young stud. To repay Tyrone's kindness, Kendall gently pushed him back onto a long chaise and kissed him deep and hard, while rubbing his erection against Tyrone's. The delicious friction heated Tyrone's loins in a way that petting sessions as Tess never could. Besides, the boy had skills. He released Tyrone's penis and caressed its length smoothly, cupping his balls tenderly, while Tyrone arched his back to provide easy access to every inch.

Sensing Tyrone's urgency, Kendall slid down his long

lean body, stopping halfway to take Tyrone's organ into his mouth. He licked and sucked as though he'd just pulled up to a table for his last meal. For Tyrone, the sensation was euphoric. He held Kendall's head and lost himself in the boy's mouth, enjoying every ounce of his release. So did Kendall, who didn't let a drop go unswallowed.

"Let's go somewhere else for a nightcap," Tyrone said, after catching his breath.

"If you don't mind, I'd like another order of the same."

"In that case, I know just the place," Tyrone said, buckling up his pants.

As they left hand in hand, a pair of eyes followed them every step of the way.

20

Dakota's man was on the road with Ecstasy, so she decided to call Lyle's office on the off chance that he was available for an after-work drink. Though she'd run into him at Ecstasy's party at the Stock Exchange, they really hadn't had a chance to catch up recently. "Hello, Hilda. It's Dakota Cantrell, over at SBI."

"Oh, yes—hello, Dakota. How are you?" Hilda asked.

"I'm good, thanks. I was calling to get on Lyle's calendar for an after-work libation."

Hilda paused for a second as if checking his calendar. "You're in luck—his five thirty just canceled for today. How docs that sound?"

"Excellent. Where?" Dakota knew that Hilda took pride in choosing venues for her boss.

"The World Bar across from the United Nations."

"That sounds great. Thanks, Hilda."

"You're quite welcome, Dakota. Take care."

The World Bar was located on Forty-eighth Street and First Avenue, in the Trump World Tower. It was an intimate bilevel lounge and the perfect hideaway for UN diplomats who wanted a cocktail or two before heading off to destinations unknown.

"Hey, girl," Dakota said, greeting Monica, the beautiful hostess, who knew everyone by name as well as by drink preferences.

"Dakota Cantrell, how have you been?" Monica asked, embracing her in a warm hug.

It was amazing, Dakota thought. She hadn't seen Monica in quite a while and still the other woman knew not only her first name, but also her last. "Really good."

"You haven't been by lately. What's new?" Monica asked as she showed Dakota to a choice window seat.

Dakota beamed as she thought about her sweetie. "Phillip Anderson!" It came out like a testimonial. She hadn't meant to shout, but she definitely could testify about the virtues of her man.

Monica looked confused. "Who?"

"Phillip, my new man." The words rolled off her tongue with ease. "Well, the relationship isn't exactly new anymore. We've been going out now for about a year now."

"A year?" Monica didn't know Dakota well, but she knew her track record, based on the many nights she spent sitting solo at the bar. "Do I see a broom in your future?" She raised her perfectly arched eyebrow.

Now it was Dakota that looked confused. "A broom?"

"Yeah, as in jumpin' da broom."

They both began to laugh; then Dakota said, "Let's just say, for the moment he's definitely sweeping me off my feet."

"What's so funny?" Lyle asked, walking up.

"Girl talk," Dakota said, greeting him with a kiss on the cheek.

"Lyle Johnson." Monica greeted him in the same manner. "Congratulations on your nomination. I read about it in the *Gazette*. They did a great spread on you."

"It was all right," he said modestly.

"Good seeing you two again," Monica said, leaving them to their privacy.

Once she left, Dakota turned to Lyle. "The article was more than all right, Mr. Cool, Calm, and Collected. Now tell me, when was the last time the Securities and Exchange Commission nominated a brother for the top position?" She looked him squarely in the eye. "I'll tell you when—never, that's when."

Lyle threw his hands up in mock defense. "Maybe so, but still, I'm trying not to get ahead of the game. I don't have the appointment yet."

"Well, you don't have anything to worry about. You're a perfect fit"—Dakota squinted her eyes—"unless you have a few bodies lying around."

Lyle laughed. "None that they can find," he said, continuing to crack up. "No, seriously, my U4 is as clean as the Board of Health," he said, referring to the industry's regulatory background check, which goes through the Federal Bureau of Investigation. "You're right—I shouldn't be paranoid. There's nothing in my past that would prevent me from getting the appointment."

"Now that's the spirit!"

Beaming with pride, he said, "Thanks for the pep talk, D."

"You don't need a pep talk—you need a party. A huge party to celebrate the appointment—and I know just the company to handle all the details. How about Caché?" Dakota had noticed a spark between Lyle and Lisa at the Stock Exchange party. She was good at reading people and could detect the slightest attraction if they were in the same room together. Besides, she knew Lyle's girlfriend, and Yvette was a stuck-up debutante. He deserved better than that.

"Whoa, slow down. Let's wait until I get the nod before we go planning a party." Still, he grinned, contemplating the idea. He would not mind discussing it if Caché—or more important, Lisa—was involved with the planning. After all, the party had been a huge success at the Stock Exchange, not to mention he'd found Lisa extremely attractive.

Dakota took her cell phone out of her purse and quickly dialed Caché before Lyle had a chance to object. "Hey there, Lisa. Dakota here. Do you have time to meet with a prospective client?" She looked at her watch. "I know it's late in the day, but if you could meet with him briefly this evening, I would really appreciate it. Great! Thanks, Lisa—we'll be right over."

Lyle felt himself blushing at the thought of seeing Lisa again. He didn't quite know what it was about her that he found so alluring. Maybe it was the vulnerability he witnessed at the Exchange party. Whatever it was, he felt a connection with her. "I take it we're going to meet with Lisa," he said with a twinkle in his eye.

"Yep." Dakota stood up. "Let's get a move on it. She's leaving in an hour."

*   *   *

They snagged a taxi outside the World Bar and headed uptown. Traffic on First Avenue was light, and movement
crosstown was swift. What would normally have been a
thirty-minute cab ride sailed by in half the time. They got
out in front of a handsome Harlem brownstone. Lyle was
unaccountably nervous, switching his briefcase from one
hand to the other, as Dakota rang the bell.

"Hey, there. Come on in," Lisa said, appearing at the
door. Her hair was pinned up in a loose ponytail, with the
ends spiked at the top. She wore a capped-sleeve shell that
hugged her ample bosom, and a pair of slacks.

"You remember Lyle?" Dakota asked, knowing full well
that she did.

Lisa smiled. "Of course," she said, and extended her
hand. "How are you, Lyle?"

"I'm good," he said, taking her hand and shaking it
longer than necessary. The soft touch of her skin sent an unexpected charge through his veins. He stared into her eyes
for a few seconds, trying to detect whether or not she felt the
same voltage.

"Mission accomplished," Dakota said to herself. Watching Lyle and Lisa standing in the middle of the foyer holding
hands told her what she suspected all along—they had the
hots for each another. Dakota cleared her throat, disturbing
their trance.

Lisa dropped her hand, breaking their connection.
"Come into the office, and tell me what type of event you
have in mind."

Once seated, Dakota took charge. "I think we should

start planning Lyle's confirmation party. His appointment is practically in the bag, and there's no need to delay the inevitable."

Lyle interjected, "I don't want anything elaborate, maybe a select group of colleagues and friends at Street Signs."

Lisa couldn't help but smile at his modesty. He was the first black man nominated to head the prestigious Security and Exchange Commission, yet he wanted to downplay his congratulatory party. Most men would want to pump their fists and let the whole world in on an accomplishment of this stature. "A small party at Street Signs is doable," she said mildly. "What date are you looking at?"

Lyle took an appointment book out of his briefcase and thumbed through a couple of pages, then looked up at Lisa. "How about six weeks from Friday, on the tenth? The following Monday is the confirmation hearing, so that might work." The senator had assured him that if nothing derogatory came up the week before, then his appointment was assured.

Lisa checked her desk calendar to make sure the date was open. "You're in luck. We don't have anything scheduled for that day."

During the rest of the meeting, they discussed numerous ideas, such as sending cigars along with the invitations and having the wait staff dress like 1920s-era cigarette girls. Lyle agreed with every single suggestion. An hour later, the party was completely planned down to the Thurgood Marshall stamps that were to be used on the invitations. Since Marshall was the first black person appointed to the Supreme Court, Lisa thought it was befitting of Lyle's nomination.

"Well, guys, I think we've covered everything," Lisa said, putting her pen aside. "I hate to cut this short, but I have to leave."

Lyle stood up and extended his hand, wanting to touch her soft skin again. "Thank you for your time and your ideas. I'm sure the party will be perfect."

Feeling the chemistry between them, Lisa flushed with embarrassment. She didn't even know this man, but she felt a serious attraction that couldn't be denied. "I'll do my best."

Dakota headed on out. "Thanks, Lisa, for seeing us on such short notice."

"Anytime. I'll speak with you soon," Lisa said, leading them to the foyer.

Just before leaving, Lyle turned around to Lisa, took a business card out of his breast pocket and said in a deep, sexy voice, "Call me if the need arises."

Lisa liked that. "If the need arises, don't worry. I'll call," she said in a seductive voice of her own.

Once they left, Lisa leaned against the closed door to catch her breath. She couldn't believe someone as polished and successful as Lyle could possibly be interested in her. "It's probably just my imagination," she told herself as a defensive mechanism against his charm.

21

Owning a piece of Street Signs had turned out to be a better opportunity than Tess had initially imagined. What started out as an impulse was now proving to be sheer genius. Not only was she the proud co-owner of a hot bar in downtown Manhattan, but she was also perfectly poised to nab her next prey—or shall we say husband. Besides, the work was easy. She could do it in her sleep. The only minor annoyance was the assistant manager, Ernie, who was always hanging around, asking stupid questions. She certainly knew his type, straight from the street, but she was also more than capable of dealing with him. But for now, she'd let her legendary élan keep him in his place.

Kicking off her four-inch Christian Louboutins, she flopped down onto her canopy bed, massaging her fake breasts with perfectly manicured hands. Though the 36Cs weren't hers naturally, the friction did arouse the pert breasts that lay beneath. Maybe, she thought, it was time for her to go for the boob job. She'd gotten an excellent referral, and it could only help in her quest for the next benefactor. After all,

Edmund's money wouldn't last forever. At her burn rate, she'd be lucky to have a positive balance in her bank account come next year. She'd have to really put herself on a budget. No more trips to Harry Winston, Cartier or even Barneys. The boob job she considered an investment. It would cost only seven grand—surely she could afford that. The real question was whether she was ready to go that extra, permanent step. The downside was that they would be pretty awkward to explain to the boys at the club when she partied as Timothy. Right now she had the best of both worlds, so why rock the boat? Tess continued to argue back and forth. Then again, she thought, those boy-toys at the club were doing nothing to sustain her lifestyle. Only real men did that. Even if she did find a bisexual sugar daddy who'd sprinkle some cash toward a good-looking guy, it was always such a precarious arrangement, subject to his ability to deal with his own guilty conscience. No, Tess realized, the safer way to financial security was as Tess, not as Tyrone. Tyrone was strictly for fun.

Shimmying out of her tight pencil skirt, Tess rolled down her panty hose and unleashed her manhood. She wasn't sure that she could ever part with that, and she rubbed it sensuously. Her plan would be similar to the one she used before. She'd seduce the pigeon down the aisle, then worry about what to do with him later. So maybe she would get a breast implant, nothing too large that she couldn't flatten out for Timothy's benefit, but enough to entice any red-blooded man.

Continuing his transformation, Tyrone removed the lipstick, mascara and makeup before slipping into a silk kimono. It was late, so a delivery would have to do. He ordered Thai from a local joint and picked up the stack of mail that he'd brought in after work. Along with the usual suspects, from Barneys, American Express, MasterCard, and invoices from Harry Winston, his interior designer and his wine purveyor, there was another, strange-looking piece of mail. It was a cheap envelope with no return address. The name and street address were handwritten in an elemental scrawl. Remembering the anthrax scare after 9/11, Tyrone almost didn't open it, but his curiosity got the better of him. He slid an onyx letter opener along the seal and carefully peered inside. He saw a single sheet of paper folded over three times, which didn't seem too ominous, so he pulled it free and laid it flat onto the top of the Italian marble counter.

Along with a copy of the picture that ran of him and Lyle in the "Talk of the Town" was a note written in a childish scrawl that was obviously an attempt to disguise the sender's handwriting. It said

Don't you two look cozy? But my guess is that your new partner might have second thoughts if he knew his co-owner was a he rather than a she. The real question is this: How much is my silence worth to you? To save you the trouble, I'd guess in the neighborhood of $25,000. (It's always best to work in round numbers.)

> *Ta-ta,*
> *Your friend and*
> *admirer*

P.S.: Send payment to P.O. Box 6969, New York, NY 10010, no later than Friday—or you won't need a PR person to have your mug (minus the wig) splashed all over the New York papers, and specifically the "Talk of the Town."

Tyrone's head began to swim. He felt dizzy and faint as he backed toward the lounge chair near the window with the back of his hand pressed against his temple. He couldn't believe this was happening to him. Now, of all times.

It had to be Jimmy. Who else knew of his cross-dressing? He'd kill that ungrateful son of a bitch. How dare he, after all that he'd done for that loser. After the wave of nausea passed, his first impulse was to head uptown and kick his scrawny little ass. He picked up the telephone instead.

"You punk-ass mothafucker," Tyrone spat into the phone.

"Who the hell is this?" Jimmy shrieked.

"Who the fuck do you think it is? Or do you have a whole list of mothafuckers you tryin' to blackmail? I oughta come uptown and open a can of whup-ass on you."

"Tyrone?"

"Don't play like you don't know who this is, you sorry piece of shit." By now all of the street was coming outta Tyrone.

"Listen, man, I don't know what the fuck you talkin' about, but I'm not about to sit on this phone lisnin' to this crazy bullshit."

"You know damn well what I'm talking about. You sent me a blackmail letter. How could you?" He abruptly broke out crying at the thought of all of his hard work being outed. It just wasn't fair.

"Listen to me, Tyrone," Jimmy said, losing patience. "I did not send you a blackmail note. You got that? And by the way, I'm sick of your diva-ass bullshit!" His pent-up frustration took over. "Ever since you got your hands on that damn money, you bin actin' like yo' shit don't stank, but let me tell you, it's smellin' to high heavens. And I ain't got to put up with this bullshit, so unless you can try to be a friend, like before, then we ain't got shit to talk about."

Tyrone was silent. He was taken aback by Jimmy's anger. Maybe he had been a dick.

Jimmy continued. "And now you call me with some blackmail bullshit. I don't know what you talkin' about, because I didn't do it."

"Then who did?" Tyrone started to cry again.

"I have no idea. Why don't you calm down and tell me exactly what happened?"

After he'd taken Jimmy through the note, word by word, Jimmy said, "Are you sure that no one else knows that you are a dude?"

"No one besides your buddy Anton," Tyrone said. "He probably did it. I saw the way he was lookin' around here, countin' my money."

"Anton didn't do it. I woulda known. Are you sure no one else knows?"

Tyrone squeezed his temples, trying to stave off an intense headache that was closing in on him. "I did go out with this one guy, but he doesn't know anything about Tess."

"How do you know that he doesn't know? Did you bring him home?"

In a small voice, Tyrone answered, "Yeah."

"That was pretty stupid. With your address, there are any number of ways for him to figure it out."

"What should I do?"

"I suggest you pay him and hope that he goes away quickly."

"I don't have that kind of money sittin' around."

"I thought you got close to three million dollars from Ed-mund."

"I did, but that shit don't last forever. How do you think I got this apartment? The little money that I've got left is tied up in money market funds, and if I take it out, I lose some of it."

"I don't know nothin' about no money market accounts, but I do suggest you figure out where to get your hands on some money, and quick. The last thing you need is that kind of publicity."

"You're right." He pulled himself together. "I'll find the money."

"I think that's a real good idea."

22

Ernie was really getting into the swing of working as the manager at Street Signs. He was usually the first person there in the early afternoon, taking stock of inventory and supplies, reviewing orders, checking payroll, and fine-tuning scheduling, and he was usually the last to leave, only after securing the cash receipts, reconciling the register, and making sure that the bar was properly cleaned up for the following day. By then it was usually well after four a.m. But he had no complaints. As far as Ernie was concerned, this was the easiest sixty grand a year he'd ever made. No undercover police to tiptoe around or street gangs to worry about. Who knew that going straight could be so easy and rewarding?

Though he and Lyle were careful not to let other employees know of their relationship, another benefit of the gig was that the two brothers had grown closer. On most nights, Lyle insisted that he stay in the second bedroom of his tony Upper West Side apartment rather than commuting all the way to Newark at such late hours. Every time Ernie walked past that snotty doorman, he was again tempted to make a snide remark, but he was trying to become a bigger person.

The job wasn't easy, though, especially since he had to deal with Miss Tess every day. There was something about that woman that bothered him, but of course, according to Lyle, she walked on water, even in four-inch stilettos. He had to admit that she did keep the place packed night after night, but other than drink free champagne and chat up customers, she didn't do much else. Tess usually showed up a little after seven, just minutes before Lyle would stroll in, and she'd leave just after midnight, regardless of what condition the bar was in. Instead of acting like a co-owner, she was more like a regular customer. She wasn't his concern, though. If Lyle wanted to be partners with some aristocratic dame with a gift for gab, that was his business.

Ernie did ask him why he'd chosen to go into business with her, and his answer was, "Appearances are everything, and she has the style and wit that draws a certain type of clientele, with money to burn, and that's just the kind of customer that we need. Plus," he added, "she's rich and has lots of experience in the business."

Tess had given him a list of references, but they were all in France. She said that the owners of the bar that she once worked at on the Upper West Side were no longer around, and she had no idea how to reach them. Though Denise, Lyle's attorney, had called the Parisian contacts, the conversations weren't that helpful since she spoke no French and the references (whoever they were) spoke little to no English.

"Speaking of appearances," Lyle said, "we need to take you shopping."

Ernie held his worn ten-year-old leather bomber jacket open. "What? You tryin' to say I don't look good?"

Lyle laughed. "Let's just say that you're not exactly a fashion plate."

Looking away, Ernie said, "I really can't afford the kind of designer duds that you Wall Street cats wear."

"My treat," Lyle said, putting his arm around Ernie's shoulder. "Consider it an investment in the bar. I can't have my manager looking less than fly."

Ernie gave him an amused sideways glance. "I didn't know that looking fly was in my job description."

"When you run a bar, it's fifty percent drawing people," Lyle explained.

"I thought Ms. Tess' job was to sit around and entertain the guys."

"Yeah, but somebody's gotta keep an eye on the ladies." Lyle winked at his brother, and they laughed.

Two hours later, they walked out of Barneys with shopping bags full of clothes. Ernie had to agree with whoever said that clothes made the man, because he felt like a million and change when he walked into the bar later that night.

After checking on things in front, he retreated to the back office to pore over the invoices of goods received. Though he never finished high school, he was as astute with numbers as his acclaimed brother. It ran in the family.

"What, pray tell, are you doing?" Tess drawled in the condescending tone that she reserved for those who didn't match her lofty station in life. She stood over him with a frown.

Ernie didn't bother to look up from the column of numbers. "I'm balancing the books."

"You really don't have to do that," Tess said, sliding the accounting ledger from under his nose.

Ernie raised his head, looking up at the towering six-two woman, and for a moment he felt as though he were seeing a caricature of a female. He shook the vision aside and said, "As manager, that's my responsibility."

"Not anymore." The cloying charm that she usually oozed was gone, replaced by a dry, very matter-of-fact tone. "I'm taking over those duties."

"Since when?" Ernie had never known Tess to do anything other than lift a champagne flute.

"Excuse me?" She looked at him as though he'd grown horns.

Ernie was undaunted by her attitude. He'd seen much worse. "I said, since when?"

She put her hands on her narrow hips. "Listen, honey, the last time I checked, I was a co-owner here, and you were simply a paid employee." She shifted her weight from one foot to the other. "I don't plan to go anywhere, and unless you're ready for a career change, I strongly suggest that you refrain from questioning your boss." She snatched the rest of the financial reports from the desk, made a dramatic turn and left the room.

Ernie leaned back in his chair, slowly stroking his goatee. *Something is definitely up with home girl*, he thought.

"What's wrong with queen bee?" Jeanine had just walked in the door, and she was looking over her shoulder at Tess.

"That's a really good question," Ernie answered.

Jeanine noticed his thoughtful expression. Though she'd

originally been skeptical of Ernie, he'd proved to be reliable, fair and a very nice guy. "Is it me or is she a piece of work?" Jeanine reached for one of her bartending aprons that were stocked on the office shelves and slid it over her head, shaking the dreads free.

"I haven't quite figured her out . . . yet, but something is definitely up with honey."

"Try telling that to Lyle." She remembered the twenty-one questions that Tess had asked about Lyle as she sat at the bar, before they became partners, so Jeanine didn't trust the woman one bit.

"I did," he said.

Jeanine walked past him and into the stockroom and climbed on a footstool to check the inventory of the house wine. She was stepping down with a case firmly in her grasp when her foot slipped. Ernie had been watching her—for all the wrong reasons—and luckily he saw her lose her balance. Quickly he stepped forward to catch the heavy box of wine in one arm, while stopping her fall with the other. It all happened so quickly that neither was prepared when she ended up against his muscular chest.

"Are you okay?"

She was staring up at him, near speechless. "I–I'm fine. Thank you," she finally said.

Thank you, he wanted to say. "No problem," he said instead. "Are you sure your ankle is okay?" He put the case down on the floor.

She put a little weight on it and winced.

"Here," he said, ushering her into the office and to the desk chair. He placed another chair in front of it and lifted her foot onto the seat. "Wait here, and I'll get some ice."

While he was playing Mr. Nightingale tending to her ankle, Jeanine was thinking more about her hormones than about her foot. Being in his arms just now was quite unsettling. Those rippling muscles oozed bad-boy sex appeal, and the unexpected appearance of this sensitive side of him equaled a dangerous combination. One thing for sure, she decided, she'd best stay away from him—at least while in small quarters.

When Ernie came back in, soaking towel in hand, she noticed how much he filled the doorway.

"Does it really hurt?" he asked, hurrying forward.

"No, it's not that bad," she replied, feeling hot and bothered. She gasped as he wrapped the ice-cold towel around her leg. If only, she thought, she could cool down her emotions so easily. "That's a lot better. Thanks."

Later, when the crowd showed up, Ernie made his rounds of the floor while Tess did what she did best, hold court in one of the prime booths, making exaggerated gestures as she weaved a long witty tale about hanging out with Mick Jagger and Donatella Versace at her apartment along the Champs-Élysées. The gullible group of men hung on her every word. She wrapped up the tale by explaining how she'd inherited the apartment and her contessa title by marrying the Count of Winscott in a lovely ceremony in the middle of his thousand acres of vineyard in the Bordeaux countryside. Which, she explained, was how she became such a connoisseur of wines.

"I can take one sip of wine and tell you the year it was harvested, as well as the soil, sun, and rain conditions that same year."

Of course, this boast led to a betting game. "Prove it," one of her many admirers dared her.

By this time, Lyle had walked in and joined her court. She slowly twirled a lock of her hair. "I'll tell you what. If I guess correctly—and I can assure you that I will—you buy the champagne of my choosing for the house."

"And if you don't?"

"Then I'll buy a round of your choosing for the house."

Lyle held his breath. This little gambit could prove to be very expensive. He tried to give Tess a questioning look, but she refused to glance in his direction.

There was no way that this master of the universe would back away from what he was sure would be a sure win, especially now that everyone in the bar was in on the fun. "As long as I get to pick the bottle."

Tess gave him her brightest smile. "I'd have it no other way."

"You've got a deal, little lady."

Without turning to look at him, Tess said, "Ernie dear, would you mind escorting the gentleman through our wine cellar?"

Before leaving with the preening customer, Ernie threw a sidelong look at Lyle. After the two were gone, Tess called over to Jeanine, "I suggest that you put ten bottles of Cristal on ice. Also pick up the European almanac from the back office while you're at it."

Lyle began to do the math in his head. If Tess lost and the guy chose Cristal, which was three hundred a bottle, they could be out of three thousand. He felt a little queasy at the prospect, and began loosening his tie.

Tess wasn't the least bit nervous. She continued to make small talk with a cadre of customers who were drawn to the epicenter of the excitement.

Ten minutes later, the master of the universe parted the crowd around her, followed by a frowning Jeanine, who was holding a silver tray with a glass of red wine in its center.

Making a show, Tess swallowed a gulp of water and moved it about her mouth. "Just cleansing the palate," she explained to an expectant audience. When she was sure that she had everyone's rapt attention, she took hold of the wineglass by the stem and swirled it several times to release its bouquet. Like a true aficionado, Tess allowed her keen nose to tilt into the bowl of the glass to inhale the aromatic properties of the elixir, before tipping the glass back to take in a mouthful. She swished the liquid around, as though gargling, while wearing a look of extreme concentration on her face. The room was dead silent.

After she swallowed the wine, she sat with her eyes lightly closed, as though still in deep thought.

Seeing a bet won already, the master of the universe said, "Well?"

Tess opened her eyes as though she were being awakened from a trance. "Those grapes were undoubtedly from the Rhône River valley."

"The what?"

"From Côtes du Rhône, a one hundred and forty–mile stretch between Lyons and Avignon. It borders Provence in the south of France," she explained with indisputable authority.

Not sold on her geographical discourse, the master of the universe pushed forth. "So what's the name of the wine, and what were the soil conditions?" He crossed his arms as though waiting for an answer that he didn't expect to get.

"That part is easy," Tess said, taking a sip of water. "It's a 1973 bottle of Châteauneuf-du-Pape."

He was shocked. Although he couldn't pronounce the name that he'd seen on the bottle, he knew that was it. To attempt saving face, he asked, "Weather conditions?"

"Also a cinch. That particular year I happened to summer between Saint-Tropez and Provence. I remember glorious sunshine, just about every day, with only a mild amount of rain, which of course kept the fungus down, as well as the acidity. Which is why this bottle is superb. Can I see?"

Lyle presented the bottle to Tess before showing the rest of the gathered crowd. *Oohs* and *ahs* filled the room. Everyone was notably impressed, even Mr. Big Bucks, who couldn't help but admire the lady who'd just unloaded him of three grand.

Tess raised a finger. "Jeanine, you can start uncorking those bottles now."

23

Lisa was hard at work the next day when Morgan sauntered into the office, as if she'd left only the day before. "Surprise!"

"What are you doing here?" Lisa dropped the stack of paperwork that she was poring over back onto her desk.

"Good evening to you too." Morgan smiled and slowly turned around, taking in every detail of her office. "Wow, it feels good to be back. Where is everybody?"

"Stephen took the day off, Nan is meeting with a client, and Marjorie is at the printers putting in the order for Lyle's invitations."

"So we're all alone?"

"Yeah . . . Morgan, what are you up to?" She noticed the stealthy expression on her friend's face.

In answer, Morgan reached into the canvas tote that she'd brought in over her shoulder and pulled out a bottle of Dom Pérignon and two champagne glasses.

Lisa gave her a worried look. "Are you feeling okay?"

"Of course. Can't I stop by and have a glass of champagne

with my new business partner? Where's the champagne bucket?" Morgan asked, looking around the office.

"It's in the pantry." Lisa went into the kitchen and returned with an ice-filled crystal bucket. She was reaching for the bottle when Morgan's words registered in her brain. Her hand froze in midair. "Did you say partner?" She pointed her index finger at her chest. "Me?"

"Congratulations!" Morgan rushed over and gave Lisa a big hug.

"Are you sure?" Lisa was dumbfounded. It had never occurred to her that Morgan would give her a piece of the company.

After popping the cork and pouring two glasses, Morgan handed one to Lisa. "It's my company, isn't it? Well, technically, it's mine and Dr. St. James', but he's in wholehearted agreement with this decision, which, by the way, gives you fifteen percent ownership of Caché."

"I can't believe it."

"Cheers!" Morgan raised her glass to meet Lisa's.

Lisa could barely contain her euphoria, as tears streamed down her face.

"You're going to have to stop that crying, you know. Tears just flatten the champagne. And we can't have that," Morgan teased.

Lisa wiped her cheeks with the back of her hands. "I don't know what to say."

"You don't have to say a thing. Your work has said it all over the last year. I couldn't have done a better job myself."

"Caché's success means the world to me, and you can be assured that I'll do everything in my power to make sure we continue to soar."

Morgan raised her glass again. "To reaching the stars."

"To reaching the stars," Lisa repeated.

"I hate to drink and run"—Morgan took one last sip— "but I'm meeting Miles for dinner. Tonight's date night for Mommy and Daddy. I'll talk to you tomorrow."

Lisa hugged Morgan good-bye. "Thanks again, partner."

Once Morgan had gone, Lisa went back into work mode. The slight buzz from the bubbly had her feeling mellow as she coordinated color swatches for an upcoming event. An hour later, she still couldn't decide which shade of pink to choose for the baby shower of an Upper East Side socialite. The expectant mother was having a girl, and wanted pink but not *pink* pink. With Justin at a midweek sleepover, she didn't have to rush home, which gave her more time to ponder the pink dilemma. "I think another glass of champagne will help." Filling her flute, she sat on the sofa, leaned her head back and took a sip. After sitting in the ice for a few hours, the champagne was chilled to perfection. She shivered slightly as the cold effervescent bubbles tickled her throat. "That's so good," she said, kicking off her shoes, shifting from work mode to relax mode.

As she was savoring the return of her buzz, the doorbell rang. She looked at her watch: it was after eight o'clock. *Who could that be?* she thought, putting the glass on the table before answering the door. She peeped through the small square window on the door and nearly passed out. He was the last person she expected to see. Her heart began to race. She tugged at the belt around her waist to tighten it and smoothed the front of her dress before opening the door.

"What brings you to this neck of the woods?"

"I was at a fund-raiser at the Schomburg Center and

decided to drop by to see how things are going with the party," Lyle said. "I hope it's not too late. I saw the light on and just took a chance that you'd still be here."

"No, not at all," she said, stepping aside. "Come on in." Lisa suddenly realized that she didn't have on any shoes. She felt uncomfortable and exposed as Lyle walked closely behind her and into the office.

Spotting the champagne bucket on the cocktail table, and her half-full flute, Lyle asked, "What's the occasion?"

"Morgan offered me a partnership today," Lisa said, beaming with pride.

"Congratulations," he said, reaching out to hug her.

Thrown off balance, Lisa fell into his embrace. It must have been the combination of the alcohol and lack of shoes that sent her equilibrium off kilter. Standing nearly cheek to cheek with him, she could smell the intoxicating scent of his cologne, which drew her in like an aphrodisiac. With his arms wrapped around her, she felt safe and secure. A feeling she never had with David. "Excuse me," she said taking a half step back, but still in his embrace.

"For what?" he asked with his arms firmly around her waist.

She could feel the blood rushing to her face. "For stumbling into you. It seems I lost my balance."

"And I thought you were just glad to see me," he chuckled.

The closeness between them was almost too much to bear. Lisa wanted to kiss his full lips but didn't want to make a fool of herself in case she was reading him wrong.

Besides, he was a client and she was a professional. She glanced down at her feet and thought, *A professional sans shoes*. She released herself from his grip. "Would you care for a glass of champagne?" she offered.

"I would love one."

She disappeared into the kitchen and brought back a fresh flute. When she returned, Lyle was seated on the sofa with his suit jacket unbuttoned and tie loosened. Lisa poured him a glass and topped off her own. She walked over to her desk and retrieved his file before joining him on the sofa.

"This is a mock-up of the invitation, which I messengered to your office a few days ago. Since we didn't hear back from you, I assumed you didn't have any changes."

He took the posterboard from her, then studied it long and hard. "Looks great."

"Good, because we've already gone to press. The invitations will be addressed and mailed within the next few days."

"You don't waste any time," he teased.

"Time is the one thing in life you can't get back," she said retrospectively.

How well Lyle knew that. He had spent nearly a year with a woman who he thought was going to be his wife and the mother of his children. Though she denied it, Yvette was clearly horrified that he'd grown up in Newark. It was clear she had no plans of crossing the Hudson again anytime soon, and he knew that was not a very promising sign for the future.

Lisa raised her glass, took a sip and peered at Lyle over the rim. Up close and personal in the dim light of the office, he appeared even more handsome than before—his face had that fresh-shaved look, even at this hour. It was so silky smooth that she wanted to run her hand up and down his cheeks.

Shaking off the temptation, she took another document out of the folder, bringing her thoughts back to the party. "This is an itemized list of expenditures." She handed him the paper. "As you can see, we're staying within the budget. I found a great champagne that's comparable in taste to Dom, but is half the price. I don't believe in paying a higher price just because of a name. Besides, most people couldn't tell the difference between a two-hundred-dollar bottle of champagne and a forty-dollar bottle."

He smiled and nodded his head in agreement. "You're a rare breed," he said, looking longingly at her.

She felt prickles run up the back of her neck. "What do you mean by that?"

"Most women, given the opportunity, would spend money as if it magically replenished itself overnight."

She pinned him with a no-nonsense look. "I'm not most women."

He gave her an appraising once-over, took the last sip of champagne and said, "I can see that." What he needed in his life, Lyle realized, was a woman like Lisa—beautiful, smart, and down to earth—not a superficial status monger like Yvette, who was ready to dump him because he didn't hail from a prestigious zip code. Feeling an overwhelming urge, he leaned in and passionately kissed Lisa.

The instant their lips touched, a fiery lust erupted that caught them both by surprise. They hungrily devoured each other's tongues as if this kiss were way overdue. Lyle's hand found its way to Lisa's breast, and instead of pulling away, she pressed her body even closer to his. Unhooking her bra, he caressed her nipples lovingly, something he had been longing to do. His mouth watered for her taste. Trailing his tongue from her mouth downward, he sucked them until she moaned with pleasure.

With her eyes closed in ecstasy, Lisa reached to unbuckle his pants. Slipping her hands inside, she felt his rock-hard erection and gasped at its girth. Her panties were beyond wet at the thought of it deep inside her. Lyle must have read her thoughts, because he reached under her dress, slid off her panties, and eased her back onto the sofa. Standing up, he dropped his pants to the floor and removed his silk briefs, unleashing the biggest penis she had ever seen in her life. She wanted every inch. Leaning back against the sofa, she reached for him, inviting him. Lyle hovered above her, slowly lowering his body on top of hers, until the tip of his penis was kissing her slippery clitoris. Lisa's mind was reeling with pleasure as he teased her mercilessly. She couldn't take it any longer and crooned, "Please let me have it."

"Whatever you want, baby," he whispered.

"Oh, Lyle," she panted.

Lyle lost himself deep inside her core. She met him with her hips, matching him thrust for thrust. Their timing was kismet, as if they were longtime lovers, their bodies meshing together into one.

"I'm coming, I'm coming," Lyle cried as he withdrew from her.

Lisa quickly reached down and helped him toward release.

Breathless, Lyle collapsed on top of her and held her tight. As they lay silent in the afterglow, Lisa wondered what she had just done.

24

Time to make the doughnuts, Tess mused as she got ready for work. Well, it wasn't exactly work—it was more like playacting, and she had the role of a lifetime. *I'm glad he's off today,* she thought.

Everything would have been perfect if Ernie hadn't come on the scene, since Lyle was preoccupied with work and the SEC nomination. But Ernie was looking after the bar with the utmost attention to detail. A little too much detail, as far as Tess was concerned.

I don't know where he got off taking control of managing my books, she tsked as she applied a thin layer of gloss. *I'm just going to have to talk to Lyle about cutting Mr. Ernie's hours.* She thought about it for a minute. *Then again, maybe not. Lyle has formed such an attachment to that lowlife. I'll just cut his hours myself. As a matter of fact, I'll call him at home tonight and tell him not to come in for the rest of the week.* Tess blew a kiss in the mirror at herself. *You're so smart.*

As she was on her way to the door, the telephone rang. "Hellooo," she sang into the receiver.

"Hey, man, whatsup?"

Tess dropped the high register. "Hey, Jimmy, whatsup?"

"Uh, uh, I was just calling to see if you got another one of them letters," he stuttered.

Tess looked over at the pile of unopened mail on the pedestal near the door. "Probably," she said, now unconcerned.

"What you mean, probably?"

"I mean, I didn't open the mail today."

"So you didn't pay up from the last time?" Jimmy asked, referring to the initial blackmail note.

"Yeah, I paid up." Tess looked at her watch. "Look, man, I gotta go—I'm running late for work."

"Hold up, hold up," Jimmy said with urgency. "What if that wacko sends you another letter? Whatcha gonna do then?"

"Don't worry. I'm already thinking ahead. Like I told you, most of my funds are tied up, but I got an aqueduct that flows directly into a sea of cash," Tess said coolly, as if she wasn't worried about a thing.

"What? You got a what?" Jimmy asked, puzzled.

"Let's just say I got everything under control. Now I really have to run. I'll talk to you later."

Tess hung up the phone, grabbed her purse and keys, and headed out the door. When she got to Street Signs, she greeted the bouncer with an air kiss. "And how are you this evening?" she asked, but didn't wait for a response. "More important, how's the crowd tonight?"

"It's kickin'," was all the side of beef could manage.

It's a good thing you've got muscles, because your brain hasn't had a workout in years, she thought. Tess nodded and strolled toward the entrance, then turned around. "You haven't seen Ernie tonight, have you?"

"Naw."

She knew he was off, but just wanted to double-check and make sure he wasn't lurking around. Confident that she wouldn't have to deal with Ernie looking over her shoulder, she strolled into the bar.

"Tess, there you are," said one of the regulars.

"Hello, Charlie. How are you?" she said, giving him her signature air kisses.

"I'm better now that you're here." He looked around. "These girls here can't hold a candle to a real woman like you."

Tess had to chuckle. *If he only knew.* "Thank you, Charlie. You're so sweet." She pinched his cherry red cheeks one at a time.

"Have a drink with me, Tess?" he asked, almost pleading.

"I'd love nothing more than to have a drink with you, but I have a ton of paperwork to do. Tell you what. Let me buy you a drink, and if I get finished early, you can buy me one," Tess said, always the diplomat.

"Well, okay."

Tess had dodged one bullet and was making her way back to the office when she felt a large hand on her butt. "Hey, sexy, where're you rushing off to?"

She was caught off guard for a moment, until she spun around and recognized the man attached to the hand. "Tom, please remove your hand," she said sternly, looking into his handsomely rugged face.

"Why? You know you want it," he slurred in her ear,

putting his other hand around her waist and pulling her into him.

Tess could feel his growing sex on her rear. She wanted to pull away, but her body instantly responded. Tom was just the type of man that Tyrone loved best—straight, strong and sexy—the type whom he cruised the gay bars for, a straight man who was bi-curious, who wanted a little taste of the other side. Tom began to grind deeper into her, running his massive hand up her thigh. Tess began grinding back—it felt so good. She was going with the flow until her nature began to rise and she remembered that Tyrone wasn't out tonight. She had too much to lose over a quick feel, so she quickly snapped out of her lust-induced trance.

"I'm flattered, Tom, but I don't date customers," she said, peeling his grip, finger by finger, from around her waist and stepping away.

Tom stumbled forward. "Come on, Tess. Don't tease me. You know you want this." He cupped his crouch.

"Go get a cup of coffee and tell Jeanine it's on the house," she barked, and scurried to the office before being accosted by another unwanted advance.

Within the confines of the office, she was finally able to breathe a sigh of relief. "Now where's that checkbook?" She opened several desk drawers, but didn't find it. Tess spun around in the swivel chair and attacked the filing cabinet. She pulled the top drawer open so hard, the entire cabinet nearly fell forward on her. After steadying it, she riffled through the drawers frantically, but still no checkbook. Then Tess remembered that it was probably in the safe. She walked over to the far wall and swung open the Erte painting that was hinged on one side, allowing the other side to open freely. "What's the damn combination?" Her heart was racing so fast that she couldn't think straight. "Just calm down." After a few seconds, she recalled the magical numbers that opened the safe. And sure enough, there it was. "Eureka!" she said in satisfaction. She took the oversized leather-bound checkbook out of the safe and walked back to the desk.

Tess sat down and proceeded to read each check stub, examining to whom each check was made out.

After she'd figured out the pattern—how often checks were paid to which vendors—she nodded her head. "Perfect," she said under her breath. She then took a pen out of the top drawer, wrote a check, and tore it out of the book. She was slipping it into her bra when she heard a loud voice: "What are you doing?"

Startled, Tess jerked her head up and immediately slammed the checkbook shut. "Excuse me?"

"I spoke to Lyle about it," Ernie said firmly, walking toward the desk, "and he said that I should continue taking care of the books."

Tess leaned back in the chair, pissed that he would run to Lyle about decisions that she made. She'd take that up later. For now, the mission was to get the hell out of the office with the check in hand. "Well, you forgot to pay one of our vendors who's been calling for his money," she said in a condescending tone, as if he were incompetent. "Anyway, aren't you supposed to be off tonight? What are you trying to do? Milk us for overtime?"

"It is my night off, and I ain't trying to milk nobody for

nothin'.'" Ernie was dressed in a knitted cream V-neck pullover and a pair of black gabardine slacks, looking as if he were ready to step out on the town.

"Listen, the next time I tell you something, I'd appreciate it if you didn't run behind my back to Lyle." She casually folded the check in her palm. "Decisions about delegation are between the owners"—she pointed the pen at her chest—"and that would be myself and Lyle."

"Lyle's my br—" He stopped short.

"What? What are you babbling about?" she asked, discreetly slipping the check in her hip pocket.

"Lyle's my boss, and I tell him everything."

Tess stood up to leave. "But I'm his partner." She walked to the door, then spun around. "And don't you forget it!"

Once outside the office, she smiled, patted her pocket and strutted back to the noisy bar area. "I need that drink now," she exhaled, looking for Charlie.

"What a bitch," Ernie mumbled in Tess' wake. He walked behind the desk, took a seat and flipped open the checkbook that she had forgotten to return to the safe. "I just don't trust her," he said out loud.

"Me neither," agreed another voice.

Ernie looked up to see Jeanine standing in the doorway. Her dreads were swept up in a loose ponytail, with a few strays framing her face. Ernie loved the way she styled her copper locks, one day wearing them cascading down around her shoulders and the next in one huge braid hanging midway down her back. "There's something about that woman that I just can't put my finger on," he said.

"I know." She walked into the office and took a seat across from him. "The first day I laid eyes on her, I knew something was strange." Jeanine had a keen eye from years of looking through a viewfinder. "But like you said, I just can't put my finger on it." She twirled a dread. "Don't worry, though—I will. Anyway, enough about Ms. Thang. I thought you had the night off."

"I do. I just came in to, uh . . ." Ernie stalled for a second, trying to find an excuse for dropping by. "I was in the neighborhood," he said lamely. Actually, he had come by to ask Jeanine to his new place for dinner.

She gave him an appraising glance. She had never seen him dressed so nice. He usually wore loose shirts, not form-fitting sweaters. She could see his well-defined biceps and pecs through the thin fabric. "Well, you sure do clean up nicely."

Ernie blushed at the compliment. "Thanks."

She became all business again. "I'd hate for you to mess up that nice sweater, but I need some help with a new shipment of vodka that came in this afternoon. The delivery guy stacked a few cases of champagne on top of it. I thought we had enough vodka behind the bar, but they're drinking cosmos like water tonight."

"No problem," he said, pushing the chair back. He came out from behind the desk to help her. "Uh, uh"—Ernie cleared his throat, gearing up for the big question—"Jeanine, what are you doing on your night off?" he asked nervously.

"Certainly not coming in here." She gave him a wry look. "Unlike some people, I could use a night off."

"I just moved into the city, and I was wondering if you'd like to come by my new apartment for dinner, say around eight o'clock? You know, like a housewarming," he rambled.

Jeanine didn't say a word. Instead the corners of her mouth turned up into a huge smile, telling him all he needed to know. "Yeah, that'll be cool," she said nonchalantly, trying to disguise her excitement.

Pleased that he had accomplished his mission, Ernie turned the lights off and locked the door behind him. With his mind preoccupied with thoughts of their upcoming night out, he forgot all about checking the records for the unpaid vendor Tess had somehow found.

25

Tess nearly beat the tellers to the bank, she was there so early. She had urgent business to take care of, and didn't have a moment to spare. She rushed out of the apartment so fast that she didn't have time to don one of her famous wigs. Instead she settled on a black fedora with a broken-down brim.

After bolting through the revolving doors, she learned that her personal banker was off for the day, so she had to settle for a trainee.

"Good morning, ma'am. How can I help you?" asked the underling.

Tess sat down in one of the chairs in front of his desk. "I need to transfer some funds," she said, skipping the pleasantries.

"Okay, ma'am." He pushed his oversized glasses farther up on his nose. "Just swipe your . . ." He pointed to the electronic black box at the end of his desk.

Tess was a step ahead of him. Before he completed the

sentence, she had already swiped the card and returned it to her wallet.

The young associate tapped his pen on the edge of the desk as he waited for the information to appear on the screen. "I guess the system is still asleep." He chuckled, making a weak, and unappreciated, attempt at humor.

Tess didn't crack a smile; she wasn't in a laughing mood. She just wanted to complete the transaction and get on with her day.

"Voilà." He raised his pen in midair like a maestro conducting an orchestra.

"I take it the system is up?" Tess smirked, unimpressed with his theatrics.

"Yes, it is. Now, what can I help you with?"

"I want to transfer twenty thousand dollars out of my money-market fund and into checking," she instructed, getting down to business.

He looked at the screen for a few seconds. "Are you sure?"

"Excuse me?" she asked, glaring at him. "What do you mean, am I sure? Of course I'm sure," she said, her voice spiking in range with every word.

Flustered, he tried to defuse a brewing altercation. "I'm so sorry. I didn't mean to imply that you were uncertain," he said apologetically. "It's just that you're going to lose a significant amount of interest if you transfer a large amount like that into a low-interest-bearing checking account."

She rolled her eyes. "I don't care about the interest. Just transfer the funds," she demanded.

He didn't say another word, but typed a few strokes on

the keyboard and waited for the transaction to be completed. Once the money was transferred, he asked hesitantly, "Is there anything else I can help you with?"

"As a matter of fact, there is." She took a folded check out of her purse. "I need to deposit this into checking."

"Sure thing." He took the check from her, barely looking at it. He did as instructed.

Standing curbside outside the bank, Tess breathed in a deep sigh of relief. She was confident that the blackmail situation was under control. Hailing an approaching taxi, she hopped in and headed home to recuperate before giving another performance at Street Signs.

Tess was laid out on the sofa, drooling like a baby, when the shrill sound of the buzzer jolted her back to consciousness.

She blinked her eyes open and wiped the spit from the corners of her mouth. "Who the hell is that?"

Stretching her long limbs along the cushions, she reluctantly rose and ambled toward the intercom. "Who is it?"

"FedEx," announced a gruff voice through the speaker.

Tess wasn't expecting a package; then she remembered she had ordered a half dozen specially designed human hair wigs from California. "Come on up," she yelled into the intercom and hit the door open button.

"Sign here," said the Federal Express guy once he reached the loft door.

Tess hesitated and looked down at the package. It wasn't a box, as she had expected, but a nine-by-twelve-inch next-day express envelope. She had a sneaking suspicion that it was a love letter from her elusive blackmailer.

"You gonna sign or what? I don't have all day," he said curtly.

She snapped out of her fog and scribbled her signature on the electronic confirmation pad, took the package and closed the door on the rude deliveryman. Tess wanted to toss the envelope in the garbage along with the other trash, but decided it would be to her benefit to read it instead.

Her body felt heavy with despair as she lowered herself back onto the sofa. Tess scrutinized the outside of the envelope for any possible clues, but the typed label didn't yield any evidence to the identity of the perpetrator. When the first letter came, with crude childlike writing on the envelope, she had automatically assumed it was Jimmy and his sidekick, Anton. But Jimmy assured her in no uncertain terms that they were not behind this scheme to out Tyrone. Tess turned the situation over and over in her mind, trying to think of who else would gain from exposing her, but she kept coming back to Jimmy and Anton. After all, they had come into some extra cash lately, evidenced by a trip to Jamaica they were planning. Jimmy said it was from his resurrected fake purse business, but Tess wasn't so sure. "I might as well get it over with." She ripped the tab, opening the cardboard envelope.

She peeked inside. "What the . . . ?"

Her breath caught in her chest. Using two fingers, she gingerly removed the contents and laid them on the cocktail table. She stared in disbelief. Staring back at her in black-and-white was a copy of Tyrone's rap sheet. The arrest report detailed every single crime that he had ever committed. Tess cringed as she read the grim details. Living the life of Riley in a million-dollar loft, wearing designer duds, and sporting a twenty-thousand-dollar ring, she had conveniently forgotten about Tyrone's criminal past. But she was quickly brought up to speed as she rattled off a laundry list of various charges: petty theft, forgery, grand larceny, breaking and entering.

Tess stopped reading. "Breaking and entering?" she asked aloud, puzzled. "I know Tyrone did a lot of shit, but I don't remember breaking and entering." She continued to peruse the list and discovered that some of the trumped-up charges didn't belong to Tyrone at all. *I bet they got his rap sheet mixed up with someone else's,* she thought. *Well, it's not like I can hire a lawyer to expunge the charges.* She threw the pages back on the table and picked up the note that came along with it:

Not only is "Tess" a tacky cross-dressing fraud, but she's also wanted by the police! All a little birdie has to do is sing a song and the police will swoop down and carry her off (kicking and screaming, no doubt) to the nearest state penitentiary. That is, unless you drop off $50,000 in cold hard cash (I told you round numbers work best) to P.O. Box 6969, New York, New York 10010.

Ta-ta, until next time . . .

P.S. Don't delay, or else the police will be on their way!

"Fifty thousand dollars!" Tess yelled into the open space. Jumping up, she flailed the note, sending it sailing into the air. "First it was twenty-five grand—now it's fifty! What's next? My firstborn?"

As Tess raged, the phone rang. She stared at the ringing

phone, afraid to pick it up. Thinking that the blackmailer may have resorted to harassing phone calls, she tipped over and peeked at the caller ID. It was Lyle.

"Hellooo," she said, carefully disguising her fear.

"Tess, it's Lyle."

"Hey, there. How's it going?"

"Not too good," he said, his voice stern.

Tess' palms instantly began to sweat, and she could feel moisture forming in the creases underneath her arms. She had never heard this tone before. Maybe Ernie had told him about her office visit last night. No, that couldn't be it. Besides, Ernie didn't see anything out of the ordinary. All he saw was her sitting at the desk going through the checkbook, which was her right as co-owner.

"What's the problem, Lyle?" she asked reluctantly.

"Here's the thing . . ." he began

Here it comes, she thought. *My gig is up—he knows.*

"Well, I have to go out of town next week, and I know I told you Ernie will be working with Lisa on the party. But I was wondering if you could lend your expertise if need be?"

Tess was relieved. This she could handle, as long as Morgan wasn't involved. But she could survive that too. After all, it was Tyrone who had swindled her, not Tess.

"Don't worry, Lyle. Consider it done." She grinned into the phone. Her secret was still safe.

"See, that's the thing, Tess. I am worried. It's getting down to the wire, and I just want everything to go smoothly."

"Don't you worry about a thing. I've got everything under control."

26

Life couldn't get any better for Ernie. Not only were he and Lyle closer than they had ever been, but his job was a dream, and he had a woman on the horizon. To complete his new life, he had finally moved into his own place. He'd gone from his momma's house to the big house upstate, and after his stint, back to momma's house. A home of his own always seemed an impossible dream—until now. With the help of Spence Ellis, Lyle's real estate broker, he'd found a one-bedroom apartment two short blocks from Lyle's condo. Though Ernie was only renting, he felt like a proud homeowner the moment he turned the key in the lock.

As he walked in carrying a small bag of groceries from the gourmet shop around the corner, he could still smell the vapors from the freshly painted walls. Ernie inhaled deeply and smiled. He loved the smell of fresh paint; it reminded him of new beginnings. Before their father had disappeared like mist in a fog, he would paint their small frame house every spring, saying that a fresh coat would liven up the old place.

He went into the kitchen and placed the bag on the faux-marble countertop. The apartment couldn't hold a candle to his baby brother's; there were no Sub-Zero appliances in a modern kitchen, only Kenmore's finest. No panoramic views of the city's illustrious skyline, only views of the fire escape on the building next door. And the bedroom was so small that Ernie could stand in the middle of the floor, stretch out his arms and nearly touch the walls. No, this wasn't a Donald Trump penthouse, but it was his, and Ernie was pleased to call it home. He hummed an upbeat tune as he put sugar in a decanter that he had bought from Bed Bath & Beyond. Lyle had told him about the superstore on Sixth Avenue that was one-stop shopping for every household need. After a few hours of wandering through the aisles in awe, Ernie came out with four shopping bags brimming with a good portion of their inventory.

Ernie's culinary skills were sketchy at best, so when Lyle told him about Gourmet on the Go, with prepackaged, partially cooked meals, his fear of burning dinner was laid to rest. He reached in the bag and took out trays of grilled salmon with lemon risotto and beef tenderloin on a bed of steamed spinach, just in case she was a meat-eating kind of girl. For dessert, he had bought key-lime pie with a raspberry sauce. He read the instruction labels which said to remove and slowly heat at 325, so he turned on the oven, plated up the food, and discarded the Styrofoam evidence. He took two flutes out of the cupboard and put them in the freezer to chill. The small dinette table was set with one of his mother's lace tablecloths and a pair of antique pewter candle holders, both housewarming gifts from Mom.

Ernie went into the tiny bathroom to shower and shave.

Standing underneath the new Water Pik head, he let the hot spray bead down on his head, saturating his hair. He shampooed and conditioned his woolly head with extra care. Tonight was special, so he took the time to scour every inch of his muscular body.

Thirty minutes later, he was standing in front of the bureau mirror in his bedroom, appraising his outfit. He wanted a casual at-home kind of look, so he wore a pair of drawstring pants which he tightened around his taut stomach and a white sleeveless muscle shirt. He winked in the mirror, pleased that the ensemble accentuated his solid physique. One of the benefits of being on lock had been pumping iron every day, a ritual he'd kept up. Remembering Jeanine's stolen glances at him, he mused, *Now she can see these muscles unwrapped, in the flesh.* Ernie looked at the digital clock-radio on the dresser: 7:42. He slapped a handful of aftershave on his cheeks, turned off the light, and went into the kitchen.

He put the plates in the preheated oven, then went into the living room and loaded the five-disc CD player with all Barry White tunes and turned the music down low. If the master of love couldn't get her into the mood, then nobody could. Just as he lit the candles, the doorbell buzzed. Ernie shook out the match and tossed it in the trash before answering the door. Suddenly his casual demeanor faded. *What if she ain't interested?* he thought. *Then I'll look like a fool.* He started to flick on the lights and put Barry on mute, but the bell buzzed again, forcing him to answer it. He looked through the peephole, and there she was, holding an arrangement of wild ginger and birds of paradise.

"Welcome to my palace," he greeted her, opening the door.

"And these are for the king," she chuckled, handing him the bouquet.

He took the flowers. "Thanks. Come on in." His heart began to beat wildly at the sight of her. Gone was her typical bar attire of slacks and a top, replaced by a black jersey miniskirt showcasing her calves and a plunging V-neck sweater exposing her deep cleavage.

"Nice place," she said, looking around.

"Thanks. Would you care for a glass of champagne?" Ernie asked, eager to take the edge off.

"I would love a glass." She followed him to the kitchen and, talking a deep whiff, said, "Something sure smells good. Ernie, I didn't know you could cook."

"I'm a man of many talents." He winked, putting the vibrant tropical flowers on the counter.

"I just bet you are."

Turning his back, Ernie took a bottle of Moët & Chandon White Star out of the refrigerator. When he turned around, he caught Jeanie staring at his arms. For her benefit, he flexed ever so slightly as he popped the cork. Retrieving the chilled flutes, he poured them each a glass.

"Umm, that's good," she said, taking a sip. "White Star is the perfect blend." She took another sip to taste. "It's smooth with a hint of sweetness, without being overbearing." Spoken like a true bartender.

Ernie put the glass to his lips and took a big gulp to ease his nerves. "It's good, all right. Dinner'll be ready in a few. Let's go into the living room." As she led the way, his eyes zeroed in like lasers on her round tight buttocks. Watching the fluid fabric move sensually around her thighs aroused him, another byproduct of being on lockdown. He could feel an erection coming on, and he took another hurried swig of bubbly to calm himself down.

There was an awkward silence as they sat on the sofa and sipped champagne. Ernie didn't know what to say, so he pointed the remote at the stereo, increasing the volume. If he didn't have the words, maybe Barry would, and sure enough, as if on cue, the maestro of love began to croon "Secret Garden." Noticing Jeanine grooving to the sexy lyrics, Ernie extended his hand. "Let's dance."

Putting the flutes on the cocktail table, they stood up at the same time, both eager to be closer together. Ernie wrapped his arms around her waist, gently pulling her close, and she instinctively reached up, and put her arms around his thick neck. At first their steps were uncoordinated, as they stumbled clumsily together, but before long they found a synchronized rhythm and began swaying as one to the music. Ernie tightened his grasp around her waist, bringing her body closer to his. He nuzzled his nose in her neck, and took a whiff of her perfume. "You smell so good," he whispered.

"So do you." She leaned in even closer.

Ernie could feel his sex growing and obviously so could she, because she began to work her hips against it. Standing in the middle of the floor, they did a slow sensual grind, until he was rock hard. He slowly moved his hands down her thighs and underneath her skirt, taking a handful of her full, ripe behind.

Jeanine let out a moan, as she savored his strong yet gentle touch. She was already moist with desire. "Ernie, I wan—"

Before she could finish the sentence, he covered her mouth with his and kissed her passionately, their tongues locking like magnets. Ernie wanted to throw her on the couch and ravish her, but he needed to clarify things before he took the situation any further. He stopped suddenly, took a step back and said, "I want you, Jeanine."

"I want you too," she moaned, and began kissing him again.

It took all the strength he had, but Ernie backed away. "Wait a minute—I need to tell you something," he said sternly.

"Tell me later," she said, looking down at the imprint of his erect sex through his pants. "Right now I want you to make love to me."

"I'm an ex-con," he blurted out. "And I don't just want to have sex with you. I want you to be my woman, Jeanine, but I need to know if you have a problem with my past." He flushed with embarrassment and hung his head.

She didn't seem fazed by his confession. She moved closer and lifted his head with her index finger. "No, I don't have a problem with your past, as long as it's over and done with."

"Trust me—those days are far behind me," he said, looking deep into her eyes.

She rubbed her hands up and down his well-toned arms, something she had wanted to do since the day he walked into the bar. "Well, in that case, I'm yours." Tugging the drawstring on his pants, she said, "Now make love to me."

Ernie picked her up in one quick motion. With her legs wrapped around his waist, he began walking toward the bedroom—but stopped once he saw black smoke coming out of the stove. "Hope you're not starving, because dinner is burned." He carried her into the kitchen and turned off the stove without taking the food out of the oven. His earlier premonition of burning dinner had come true, but he didn't care. Now that he had his woman, he had plenty of time to impress her with gourmet to-go.

"Just starving for you," she whispered into his ear.

"I hope you have a big appetite," Ernie said, "because I'm going to feed you until you're filled."

27

Hilda phoned Lisa first thing to confirm Lyle and her dinner plans. They would be dining at Alain Ducasse, the chic French four-star establishment in the renowned Essex House. Lisa had read countless articles about the famed three-hundred-dollar-per-person restaurant, and she couldn't begin to imagine how one helping of food could possibly be worth what she could feed Justin and herself on for two weeks. Hilda also informed her that Lyle and his driver would be there to pick her up at ten after seven. Obviously, Mr. Johnson was out to make an impression.

Promptly at five o'clock on the appointed day, Lisa did something that was nothing short of miraculous. She actually left the office on time for the day, though on the way out, she was spouting a precise list of instructions to Stephen and Nan. Alain Ducasse was worthy of what Morgan and Dakota would call the full-court press, which included a soothing, scented bubble bath, a body-polishing exfoliant, a fresh blow-dry, a pore-tightening facial, as well as other assorted beauty rituals that would all add up to irresistible. She was thankful that she had the foresight to have Kim, her sitter, take Justin to her house directly from school. Otherwise, sitter or not, there'd be no way she'd have the uninterrupted quiet time that this beauty mission required.

She hurried home, growing more excited with every step. She'd been in a daze since her office tryst with Lyle. Though it had felt incredibly right at the time, afterward she'd been certain that it was a big mistake. What man would respect a woman who had sex with him on the first visit—not even the first date! Particularly a woman such as herself: an unwed mother. Frankly, she'd expected him to avoid her as much as possible, but instead here she was on the way to a famous restaurant with Lyle Johnson, the next chairman of the SEC. Obviously, she'd done something right.

By the time Lyle rang her doorbell, Lisa looked as if she'd stepped out of the pages of *Town & Country* magazine. Her hair was twisted neatly into a sophisticated chignon. She wore an elegant camel-hair 1920s-style suit with a fitted pencil skirt and a short-waisted jacket with a bell cut, along with a pair of I'm-the-baddest-bitch-in-here Chanel slingbacks. Though she'd fretted at the time, tonight she was glad that she'd splurged part of her last bonus on the finishing touches, which were beautiful Tiffany pearls at her neck, wrist and on her ears.

"Wow!" Lyle stood outside her door with his mouth ajar. He knew Lisa was special with that quiet dignity of hers, but tonight she had an alluring sultriness that vividly brought back that explosive evening. It was a magnetic combination.

She smiled lightly at his response. It was just the one she'd hoped for. "Good evening to you too, Mr. Johnson."

"You look amazing," he said, feeling a little befuddled as he stood aside while she locked her apartment door.

"Thank you." When she turned toward him, he looped his arm through hers and helped her down the steps leading to the walkway and the street beyond.

As they approached the black Mercedes sedan, the driver, dressed in a dark suit and bibbed cap, quickly hopped out to open the door for Lisa. Lyle guided her into the sumptuous confines of the car. While she waited for Lyle and the driver to enter on the opposite side, she took a deep breath. She felt like Cinderella going to the ball.

"So how was your day?" he asked once he was settled in next to her. The way he asked the question, he seemed to really want to know the answer.

She shifted in his direction. "It was pretty hectic," she said, "but in a good way. A million last-minute details, temperamental vendors, and overworked employees, but I wouldn't trade it for the world." Now that she was a part owner, she meant it more than ever before.

"You sound a lot like me," he said warmly. "Sometimes I seriously wonder why I stay in a business that is as crazy and nerve-racking as mine is, but you know what?" he asked rhetorically. "I've come to the conclusion that the adrenaline rush is addictive, and that I'm permanently hooked." He held both hands in the air in surrender.

She laughed, understanding him completely. "I see your point, but I also see huge differences in our jobs."

He looked at her quizzically. "Like what?"

"Well, if you make a mistake, it could mean millions of dollars for a client, but if I make a mistake, which of course

I never do, because I am perfect," she deadpanned, "but if I ever did, it would just be a bad party."

He gave her his famous Lyle Johnson half smile. "You know, it's all still relative. To some of my clients, a million dollars is just a drop in the bucket, but a party is so personal, and"—he held up a finger—"it's something that you can never make up. At least if I lose a million today, I'll have a chance to make it back tomorrow."

"That's true." She'd never thought of it that way, and she was very impressed that he had. In fact, she was impressed that he was even asking about her business, which was more than she could say about David, whose only concern about that matter was the gravy train that it provided.

They chatted easily during the fifteen-minute ride to Midtown. When the car pulled up to the gilded entrance, one of the hotel's tasseled doormen opened her door before the car's engine could even begin to idle. Though she was not accustomed to this sort of royal treatment, with Lyle it felt completely natural. *But don't get used to it,* she warned herself. *It's just a date and nothing more.*

As they walked arm-in-arm into the Central Park South hotel, passersby looked on appreciatively at the attractive couple. Lyle wore a custom-tailored three-button Romeo Gigli suit and a silver-gray thickly knotted tie. The Italian cut suited his swimmer's physique perfectly, Lisa noticed. When they walked through the heavy wood-paneled double doors of the restaurant, it was as if they'd entered into another world.

"Good evening, Mr. Johnson and Ms. Burrows." The maître d' bowed ever so slightly. "I'm Jacques Baptiste. Welcome to Alain Ducasse."

"Good evening," they both replied.

"I'm happy that you both could join us," the nattily dressed host said in a very sexy French accent. "If you'll follow me, I'll show you to your table."

She and Lyle were led through a room of rosewood-covered walls, granite columns, tastefully accented with beautiful contemporary photographs and spectacular objets d' art. She remembered reading that Alain Ducasse had spent more than two million dollars to renovate the space before opening the restaurant to a very eager New York public. His restaurants in Paris and Monaco were legendary, and this one went against every grain of New York dining. For one thing, it sat only sixty-five diners for one sitting per night, which was why it took three months to get a reservation. The fact that they were here within a few days' notice certainly didn't go unnoticed by Lisa. The small guest list also meant that the waiter didn't hover over you and your coffee, silently willing you to sign your check so that he could turn your table into another round of cash. She'd heard rumors that four members of the wait staff were assigned to every table so that your every desire could be anticipated before you had a chance to realize it.

When they reached their intimate table in a back nook, Monsieur Baptiste pulled out Lisa's chair for her before smoothly sliding it closer. "For your purse, madame," he said, motioning toward an expensively upholstered footstool set discreetly next to her chair.

How brilliant, Lisa thought. Where to place a handbag was always such a dilemma when dining out, particularly if it was of any size.

After Monsieur Baptiste began his glide back across the floor, Lisa said, "If you were looking to impress me, you have."

Lyle smiled broadly, pleased with himself.

"This must go over really well," Lisa mused, partly to herself, not really meaning for the words to come out of her mouth.

Lyle sat up straighter in his chair. "What do you mean, 'go over well'?"

"With dates."

"Well, I wouldn't know," he said, adjusting himself in the chair. "I've never brought a date here."

Before Lisa could respond, a table manager appeared as if by magic at her side. He was as pleasant and efficient as Jacques had been, with a demeanor like a butler. Lisa ordered a gimlet with Rose's Lime, and Lyle ordered a Manhattan with French vermouth.

"So where were we?" Lyle asked once they were alone again.

"I think I was extracting my foot from my mouth," Lisa joked lightly.

Lyle held up his hand. "I understand. Believe me, I'm aware of my reputation with the ladies."

"Still, it's none of my business, and I was out of line to go there."

"Apology accepted," Lyle said. "But since you did, that gives me some leeway to ask about your dates."

Lisa tossed her head back and laughed. "Unfortunately, there isn't a lot to tell, considering that I have a six-year-old son. Between him and Caché, there really isn't a lot of time for dating." Lisa waited for the shocked you-can-bring-the-check-now look. She was fully aware that being a single mother was not the biggest turn-on for eligible bachelors such as Lyle Johnson. Still, she figured she'd tell him straight up and get any pretenses out of the way. If he couldn't take it, she'd simply enjoy the night for what it was.

"What's your son's name?" Lyle asked, leaning forward.

"J-Justin," she answered, surprised at his interest. She didn't detect any shock, repulsion, or apprehension.

"Tell me about him."

While they sipped cocktails, she told him all about Justin, from his birth and his close call with death to how well he was doing now.

When the third member of their table tag team came over, he covered the specials and every aspect of the gourmet cuisine, making each dish sound utterly irresistible. After he floated away, they discussed the menu, trying to decide between a tasty array of appetizers and entrées. When number three returned a few minutes later, Lyle ordered for them both, a simple act that made the evening all the more special. Likewise, he conferred with number four, the sommelier, for the perfect wine to complement their choices.

Though she'd been excited about the date to begin with, her expectations were a bare minimum. Even after their office tryst, she still expected Lyle to be a jive, self-centered playboy who'd try some cheap, tacky tactics to get her back into bed. So she was pleasantly surprised that he was charming, sensitive and thoughtful throughout dinner, and even better afterward, when he walked her to the door. He thanked her for spending the evening with him and kissed her lightly on the cheek. When his lips touched her, again she felt that spark that had led to an inferno the week before. They both did, for their lips sought each other for a passionate kiss that she never wanted to end. She ran her hands along the muscles down his back, wanting desperately to feel his body in the flesh. *But not tonight,* she chided herself. If she and Lyle were ever going to have a serious relationship, she'd have to slow things down. Besides, as far as she knew, his socialite girlfriend was still on the scene.

She gently pulled away. "I really must get inside," she said, hoping that he understood.

"Can I see you over the weekend?"

"Sure," she said. She liked the sound of that.

He waited on the curb until she was safely behind the door. He was a gentleman to the end, she thought. And a sharp contrast to what awaited her on the other side of the apartment door.

When she walked in, still feeling the glow that lingers after a perfect evening, it quickly dimmed when she found David sprawled out on her couch. With a beer tucked between his thighs, he was wearing a stained wife-beater T-shirt, grungy jeans and a nasty sneer.

"What are you doing here?"

"I came to check on my s-s-son," he slurred.

She was puzzled, knowing that Justin was at his sitter's and there was nobody to open the door for him. "How did you get in?" she demanded.

Pleased with himself, he managed a lurid smile and pulled a duplicate key from his pocket. "I made it for emergencies," he said.

"Who do you think you are, showing up here? This is my house, and I thought I made it clear that you are not welcome."

He looked at her through a haze of alcohol, surprised that she wasn't happy to see him. He pulled himself up from the couch and reached for her. "Come on, baby. What about us?"

She could smell the rancid odor of beer and cheese Doritos on his breath. "If you aren't out of here in fifteen seconds, I'm calling the police."

"You what?" He stepped closer to her, rearing his head back, as if seeing her for the first time. "Where have you been anyway?" he bullied, as he gave her the head-to-toe once-over, taking in the sexy saddles, the tight skirt and the carefully applied makeup.

"It's none of your business where I've been." She fixed him with a glacial expression.

If she wouldn't address his questions about her obvious date, he knew one subject that would give him some leverage. "Where's my son?" he asked, wearing thin the tired excuse.

"That's not your business either."

"I am his father."

How did I ever allow myself to think there was anything redeeming about this pitiful excuse for a man? Lisa wondered. "You are a sperm donor. Nothing more," she spat.

"Bitch!" he yelled, barely restraining himself from pouncing. How dared she talk to him like that? He remembered a time when she was begging on his doorstep, and now, just because she had a job, an apartment and some bank, she thought she could dis him. *Hell no*, he thought.

"Get out!" she shouted.

Her defiance caused him to snap. He yanked his right

hand high across his body, ready to pimp-slap that smug expression from her face. Lisa stumbled back, shocked, with her hands held up to defend herself.

"Don't you even think about hitting her."

Both David and Lisa whirled around. Lyle was standing in the entryway holding Lisa's purse.

David's hand fell to his side. "Who the fuck are you?"

Lyle dropped the bag on a nearby chair without letting David out of his sight. He strolled casually between the two of them until he was within inches of David's face. "If I were you," he said calmly, "instead of wasting what brain cells you've got left trying to figure out who I am, I'd be trying to get the hell up from outta here—while you still can."

David stared at him, confused. But something in this brother's street demeanor told him that he should just follow orders for now and maybe ask questions later.

Lisa watched in shock. For yet another time tonight Lyle had surprised her. What happened to the spit-polished, Ivy League banker gentleman that she'd just had dinner with? Standing in her living room right now was an I'll-kick-your-ass home boy.

David smartly decided to cut his losses for the night. He snatched his sweater from the back of the sofa and stalked out of the apartment.

Lyle went to Lisa. Holding her by both shoulders, he searched her eyes. "Are you okay?"

She took a deep breath and shook her head. "Yes, I'm okay." But she was still shaking from the onslaught.

He held her close, softly kissing her forehead. "Are you sure?"

"I'm positive," she insisted. "Thank you."

"I'm just glad you left your purse in the car."

"So am I."

He pulled away. "You must be exhausted. I'll call in the morning to check on you. Be sure to use the bolt locks. Okay?"

Lisa smiled at his concern. "Okay." As he started to leave, she called after him. "Watch out for David, outside."

He flashed a broad smile. "Oh, I'm not worried. At heart, I'm still a boy from the wrong side of Newark."

28

Business at the bar was booming, and Ernie couldn't help but think that he had a hand in its success. But let Tess tell the story, she had single-handedly brought Street Signs from the brink of bankruptcy and transformed it into a thriving moneymaking machine. After catching her in the office the other night with the checkbook spread open on the desk, he knew that his gut feelings about her were on the money.

"Yeah, she's got them all fooled," he spoke to his reflection, "but she ain't fooling me. I've been around the cell block too many times to fall for the okeydoke."

Ernie dressed in a pair of black gabardine slacks and an ice blue V-neck sweater. Lyle was right: first impressions in this industry were vital. He had watched numerous times as a moderately dressed guy lost out to the tailor-dressed one. He had to admit that when he first came to the bar dressed in faded cords and flannel shirts, he was often on the receiving end of a disapproving look or three. But that was in the past. Now that he had a woman to impress, he wanted to look his best.

With the generous salary that Lyle paid him, Ernie could

afford to skirt around the city in the back of a taxi instead of on the bus. He leaned his head back on the headrest in the rear seat of the cab and relaxed. As the taxi pulled up in front of Street Signs, Ernie reached into his pocket and took out the leather fob that held the keys to his kingdom. He paid the driver and got out. It was early Saturday morning, much earlier than he usually came in, but Ernie wanted to get a jump on what he knew would be a busy weekend. Besides, the more he did now, the less he'd have to do at closing, which meant he might even have some time to spend with Jeanine.

Ernie headed back to the office, ready to roll up his sleeves. As he walked in the doorway, he got a flashback of Tess sitting behind the desk looking shady. "She said I forgot to pay a new vendor," he mumbled and walked over to the safe. "Let's see what vendor she could possibly be talking about."

He quickly turned the combination lock to the left, then to the right and back to the left. He pulled the knob, opened the small vault and removed the checkbook. At the desk, he sat down and started from the first page, scrutinizing the check stubs, for any inconsistencies. He was certain that Street Signs used the same vendors on a regular basis. Satisfied that the entries added up, he began closing the book when his eye caught sight of something irregular.

"What the hell . . . ?"

There on the last page, on the last check stub scribbled in barely legible chicken scratch, was a check made out for cash. When he looked at the amount, he nearly flipped out of the chair.

"Twenty-five thousand dollars!" He couldn't believe his eyes. He knew of no large expenditures that the bar had incurred. He immediately picked up the phone to call Tess. When her voice mail came on, he barked into the receiver, "Tess, it's Ernie. Call me at the bar as soon as you get this message."

He hung up and dialed Lyle to ask him if he knew about the suspicious check, but before the call went though, the front buzzer rang.

"Why would she write a check for over twenty grand?" he wondered as he made his way to the front door.

"I have a package for Contessa Dubois," said the FedEx deliveryman. "Can you sign for it?" he asked, clearly in a hurry.

"Sure." Ernie signed for the package and walked back inside the bar.

He sat at one of the bar stools, put the package on the bar and rubbed his temples, still thinking about the check. "Why would she write a check for over twenty grand? She ain't got no reason to steal—she's part owner. It just doesn't make sense." He thumped his fingers on top of the envelope.

What is she hiding? He looked down at the envelope and thought about opening the package. *No, I can't do that.*

He got up to take the envelope to the office, but a nagging voice in the back of his mind kept saying, *Open it, open it.*

Ernie sat back down and turned the package over in his hands. It looked like a standard express package, nothing unusual.

His instincts had kept him from getting busted many a time. He had learned to listen to his gut, and his gut was seldom wrong. Ernie ripped the tab and dumped the contents on the bar. His mouth fell open in shock as he read the note:

Now you're going to make me act ugly. I told you to deliver $50,000 to the P.O. Box posthaste, but you're dragging your feet. If I don't get the money by tomorrow, the next package will be sent to your partner. And let's see how he takes to being in business with a cross-dressing thief.

Ta-ta

Attached to the note was a rap sheet. He read the familiar-looking paper. Tyrone's offenses made his own dull in comparison. "I knew it!" he said, slapping the paper across the bar. All along, he'd felt that something was wrong with her. Boy, was he right, since she wasn't a her at all, but a him! It also explained why she was trying to pilfer funds: to pay a blackmailer.

Ernie clutched the paper in his hand. Finally he had the tangible evidence to nail Tess/Tyrone—whatever its name was. *What a stroke of fortune,* he thought, *finding this load of paydirt.* He walked behind the bar to call Lyle, but got his voice mail, both at home and on his cell. Boy, did he have an earful for his little brother. . . .

Tess hadn't stepped a foot into Street Signs, or on the street for that matter, since she got that disturbing message from Ernie. Had he discovered the fraudulent check? And more important, had he reported it to Lyle? She was nearly paralyzed with fear, not sure whether to fight or flee, so she decided to stay in seclusion until she could get a handle on things and assess her next move.

She edged over to the phone. "I better call the bar," she groaned, and held her breath as the line rang.

"Street Signs. Jeanine speaking."

Tess was relieved that Ernie hadn't picked up the phone; she'd been prepared to hang up if he had. She covered the receiver with her right hand and lowered her voice. "Jeanine"—she coughed—"I've come down with a horrible case of strep throat, and won't be in tonight." She coughed again. "As a matter of fact, I probably won't be in for the rest of the week."

"You must be feeling bad, because you sound just like a man. Hold on, Ernie's been looking for you. I'll put you through," she said, not giving her the opportunity to decline.

Tess quickly hung up. *Shit, I hope he doesn't come up here.* She made a beeline for the front door and double-bolted the locks, just in case Ernie was bold enough to pay an unexpected visit.

She nervously bit her acrylic fingernail, until it popped off. *What am I going to do?* When the answer didn't come to her, she put another nail in her mouth and began to chew. She racked her brain to think of a reasonable explanation for the check she'd written, while busily nibbling each ruby lacquered nail until they all fell off, one by one, and were strewn like litter across the living room floor. After annihilating the last one, Tess looked down at her bare hands. Without the decorative window dressing that the fake nails provided, they really were quite masculine, which made her think of Tyrone. She was so preoccupied trying to solve Tess' mess that she hadn't thought about him. It was easy enough to put him out of her mind, as she paraded around as Tess every day, but with the threat of exposure looming over her, it was time for some serious damage control. That is, if it wasn't too late. Suddenly, she had an epiphany.

She reached for the phone and quickly punched in 411. "The Second Precinct," she said into the receiver.

Once the call was connected, a man with a thick Brooklyn accent picked up the line. "Second Precinct. Sergeant Murphy here."

The last blackmail note had included a copy of Tyrone's rap sheet, and Tess needed to find out if the police were still on his tail before she made any drastic moves. "Hello, Sergeant," she said, laying on the old Tess charm, "I was wondering if you could help me?"

"What can I do for ya, miss?"

She hesitated, thinking twice before continuing. She knew she was taking a dangerous chance, but at this point she didn't have much of a choice. "I may know the whereabouts of someone who was wanted by the police a while back, but I don't know if he's still wanted or not." Tess figured that if any of the precincts knew the status, this one would, since it was the hellhole that Tyrone had initially been dragged through. They'd most likely be coordinating any recent efforts, if there were any.

"Look, lady," spat out the gruff policeman, "concealing that type of information is a criminal offense. If you got a tip that'll bring a fugitive to justice, I suggest you come down and make a report. Or call the tip hotline."

Her heart was racing like a thoroughbred's poised at the gates of the Kentucky Derby. "Officer, I'm not trying to conceal anything. For all I know, he's already behind bars. It's just that I saw someone that fit the description of a Tyrone Nathaniel Thomas," she said, slyly slipping in Tyrone's name. She knew that if she straight up asked if they were pursuing him, she would never get the information she needed. Tess only hoped that the officer took the bait.

"Hmm." He hesitated. "That's ironic. Someone just reported seeing him in the vicinity of Broome and West Broadway."

Tess's breath caught in her throat. Did he say that someone reported seeing Tyrone on Broome and West Broadway? *That's my block!* She nearly dropped the phone. *Oh, shit!*

"Is that where you saw him, ma'am?"

"No—no," she stuttered. "I saw him in Harlem," she lied, hoping to steer the bloodhounds in a different direction.

"Well, don't worry. There's an APB out on him. He won't be cruising the streets of New York for too long. You can count on that. Thanks for yo—"

Tess hung up before the officer could express his appreciation. She threw the phone on the sofa, ran to the window and peeked through the thin slats of the miniblinds. Fortunately, there were no blue-and-white squad cars staked out in front. Armed with this new information, Tess knew it was just a matter of days, or maybe hours, until the lights of New York's finest were flashing outside her window.

"I ain't going back to jail," she declared. She was beyond upset. She had complied with the blackmail notes to the letter. Obviously the extortionist wanted more than money. He wanted Tyrone behind bars and had no doubt tipped off the police as to his whereabouts.

Tess slapped herself on the forehead. She felt like a complete dunce. "Damn it, I should've seen this coming when he sent the rap sheet with the last note."

She slumped down in the window seat and put her head

in her hands. "No, no, no," she moaned repeatedly as hot tears stung her eyes. They rolled in a stream down her cheeks, carrying remnants of mascara, eyeliner and rouge along for the ride.

Resigned, she wiped the back of her hand across her eyes and shook her head at the remaining traces of her disguise. Suddenly, she knew what she had to do; there was no other choice. As much as she loved her luxurious loft with its opulent furnishings, it was time to leave it all behind. Once again she would be on the lam, trying to stay a few steps ahead of the law.

What had begun as a stroke of fortune—inheriting Edmund's estate, moving back to New York and investing in Street Signs—had rapidly unraveled. She had to liquidate, which meant putting the loft on the market. Unfortunately, though, she didn't have the luxury of time on her side. She had to assume that the cops would be beating down her door any minute, dragging her off to a five-by-ten-foot prison cell.

Tess gathered herself up, wiped her tearstained face, went over to the sofa and reached for the cordless. She knew what she had to do, and that was to flee, quick, fast and in a hurry. She dialed 411. "May I have the number for Spence Ellis Realty?" She held the line as the call went through.

"Spence Ellis Realty. How may I direct your call?" asked a chipper voice.

"Contessa Aventura Dubois, calling for Mr. Ellis," she said in a snooty tone.

"Hold on, please."

"Well, if it isn't the Contessa," Spence sang into the receiver. "What can I do for you this afternoon?"

"I need to sell my loft ASAP, but I can't wait around for

it to go to market. I'm sure you have a list of clients with ready cash yearning for a space like this," she said, getting right down to business.

Spence paused for a few seconds. "Actually, Tess, the market has taken a turn for the worse. People are holding on to their purse strings. But with a little time, I'm sure we can find just the right buyer."

"I told you, I don't have time to go through a long drawn-out process," she snapped into the phone.

"Well, I don't know what to tell you, because—"

Click. Tess hung up.

She called the only other person who could possibly help her in this time of despair. She dialed and listened impatiently as the phone rang several times. Just as she was ready to hit the END button, someone picked up the line. "Hello?"

Tess exhaled audibly into the receiver. "Hey, it's me."

"Tyrone? That you?"

"Yeah, man. It's me."

"What's wrong? Sounds like you just lost all your money." Jimmy laughed into the phone.

"Bite your tongue. With all my drama, that's the last thing I need to worry about. Actually, that's partially why I'm calling." Tyrone went on to tell Jimmy the latest development in the blackmail scam.

"Damn, man, whatcha gonna do?"

"I gotta leave—that's what I gotta do. But I need for you to do me a big favor."

"What is it?" Jimmy's tone was anxious.

"I need for you to sell the loft and send me the cash."

"What you mean? How'm I supposed to sell your loft? My name ain't nowhere on the deed."

Tyrone exhaled again, sounding annoyed. "Just listen, and I'll tell you what to do." He began instructing. "First, I'm going to transfer the loft into your name. Then you can call the Realtor—his name is Spence Ellis—and list the loft. I just called him, and he doesn't have a buyer in mind yet, but I'm sure he'll find one soon. I just can't wait around until he does. You can sell all the stuff in here and keep that money. You should get a pretty penny for most of the furniture, not to mention the paintings. I just want the money from the loft."

Jimmy was shocked. "Man, are you serious?"

"As cancer," Tyrone said.

"Where you gone be?" Jimmy seemed slightly confused. "I mean, where am I suppose to send the money?"

"I'll call you once I get settled." Tyrone exhaled, but this time it was a sigh of relief. He had misjudged his old friend, thinking that he had been the blackmailer. He should have known better. Jimmy would always be in his corner. "Thanks, man. You're a good friend."

"Don't mention it, T. You can count on me."

Tyrone hung up the phone and for the first time that day felt as if things were somewhat under control.

29

As Lisa showered the next morning, embarrassment replaced the many other emotions that battled within her. Why did Lyle have to witness the seedy underside of her life, especially on their first real date? It was one thing to accept a child in a new relationship, but an ignorant, drunk and crazy ex was a different matter. She wondered if he'd had second thoughts about seeing her again.

So she was pleasantly surprised when he called the next morning at ten. "Thanks again for having dinner with me last night."

"I should be thanking you. For everything."

"You can, you know."

She smiled into the phone. "How might I do that?"

"Meet me for coffee."

"When?"

"I'm on the Lower West Side, but I'll head uptown. Why don't we meet at Sarabeth's at Eightieth and Amsterdam— say, at noon?"

"Cool."

She had planned to pick Justin up that morning, but called Kim to make sure that it was okay to swing by in the early afternoon instead. When she arrived, Lyle was already seated and sipping a glass of fresh-squeezed orange juice. "Hi, there."

"Long time, no see," he said, standing up from the table to greet her in a tight hug.

She glanced at her watch. "Yeah. Almost twelve whole hours."

"You see, now I'm afraid to let you out of my sight."

She hung her head low and quietly said, "I'm really sorry about last night."

He reached out and covered her hand in his. "It's not your fault."

"I know, but—"

"No buts about it. Listen," he said, growing serious, "I want you to take out an order of protection against him." When she didn't respond right away, he pushed on. "I've seen guys like him before, and you shouldn't take him lightly."

"He's a jerk and an idiot, but after last night, I really don't think that I have to worry about him, because he's also a coward."

"That may well be true, but we don't need to take any chances."

Lisa noted the *we* and was touched. She slowly nodded her head. Not only should she be thinking about herself, but more important about Justin as well. As desperate as David was, what would stop him from kidnapping her child?

"You're right."

"Good. As soon as we finish breakfast, we'll stop by the police precinct on West One Hundred Twenty-sixth Street. We can file a complaint and get the process started."

"I can do this by myself," she insisted.

He gave her a big smile. "I don't have anything better to do on a Saturday."

"Okay. If it'll make you feel better."

"I can guarantee you that it will." Since leaving her apartment the night before, he'd been so consumed with worry about her that he'd hardly slept. He had been tempted on more than one occasion to go back to be sure that she was okay.

An hour later, they walked into the Twenty-sixth Precinct and stood in the entrance, looking for someone to talk to. The hustle and bustle of the police station was unnerving for Lisa. She begin to question whether this step was really necessary.

"Excuse me. We need to speak with someone about a restraining order," Lyle said to a passing female officer.

"Have a seat, and someone'll be right with ya," she said, gesturing to a row of adjoining chairs as she continued walking.

As the minutes passed, Lisa fidgeted more and more. Consumed with nervous energy, she stood and began pacing the small space. Lyle stood too. "You're doing the right thing," he said, hoping to calm her nerves.

She gave him a tight smile and continued to pace. Lyle stuffed his hands into his jeans pockets. When he felt his cell phone, it occurred to him that it had been awfully quiet. As he pulled it out, he remembered that he'd turned it off before picking Lisa up last night and hadn't turned it on since. He pushed the ON button and returned it to his pocket. He was about to walk up to the desk and try to hurry things along when a picture on the wall caught his attention. He walked closer to the black-and-white mug shot and stared at it hard, turning his head left and right, as if trying to visually adjust the image in his mind.

"What is it?" Lisa asked, noticing his strange expression.

"I know this sounds crazy, but this guy looks familiar to me."

Lisa couldn't imagine him knowing anyone on a wanted poster. She stepped closer to the grainy photo, and frown lines spread across her forehead. Finally she processed what she was seeing. "Oh, my God!" she gasped.

"What is it?"

She began to read the smaller print on the poster:

> Subject: Tyrone Nathaniel Thomas, black male, 6'2" and 160 lbs.
> Wanted for grand larceny and forgery. Alias: Blake St. James.

"This is the guy who conned Morgan and skipped bail."

"Are you sure?"

"I'm positive. I remember the story," she said, giving him the abbreviated version of the Caché con.

Lyle continued staring at the mug shot. "But why does he look familiar to me?"

Before they could put the pieces together, Lyle's cell phone rang.

"Hello," he answered, distracted. Seconds later he said, "You've got to be kidding! Don't do anything until I get there. Sit tight." He hung up the phone looking as though he'd been punched in the gut.

Now really worried, Lisa said, "Lyle, what is it?"

"That was Ernie," he answered in shock. "It's about Tess—or should I say, Tyrone."

*   *   *

Ernie was pacing the bar like a caged tiger while Jeanine quietly simmered behind the bar. After his discovery, she had been his second phone call.

"I just wish I could get my hands on that lying, dirty, cross-dressing motha." Ernie was pumping his fist into the palm of his hand, grinding it in, while Jeanine looked on thinking, *I wouldn't want to be her—or him.*

Jeanine shook her head. "I knew there was something off about her." Her trained photographer's eye caught the nuances that most people overlooked, but Tyrone had fooled her too.

"I should just go up there and beat the money out of him," Ernie said, heading for the door.

"I don't know if that's such a good idea."

"Why not? I think it's a great idea."

"I'll give you one good reason: Lyle."

"What do you mean? He's the reason I'd like to squash that twit like a bug."

She walked around the bar and came face-to-face with him. "Listen, if you do anything that might garner press, including marching into a fancy apartment building and pummeling a resident, scam-artist transvestite or not, you can rest assured that this whole mess will end up in the papers, especially considering Lyle's nomination." When she saw that she had his attention, she continued. "And if that happens, he can kiss the nomination good-bye. You know how politicians are. They're afraid of their own shadows."

Ernie stroked his chin. "You're right. So what do we do? We can't let her—I mean, him—get away with this."

"I have an idea," she said, taking a seat on one of the bar stools.

Before she could outline her plan, Lyle and Lisa came bustling through the door.

"Where is she?" Lyle asked, looking around as though expecting to see Tess holding a bag of money.

"You mean him?" Ernie rolled his eyes.

"I'm gonna—"

Before he could complete his sentence, Ernie had steered him toward a chair and said, "Before you go flying off the handle, you should listen to Jeanine. She made some really good points."

While Lisa stood next to Lyle with her hand on his shoulder, Jeanine went through the reasoning she'd just completed for Ernie.

"You're right," Lyle said, shaking his head. "Senator Neuman would hang me out to dry if he got wind of me being involved with an embezzling fugitive transvestite."

"Don't worry. We'll figure something out," Lisa said.

Lyle turned to Ernie. "I guess I should have listened to you, huh?"

"I'm not one to say I told you so," he said, "but I told you so. I knew something wasn't right with her from the start."

"You were so right. I guess things aren't always what they seem." He thought about Yvette and how perfect she'd seemed on the surface as well.

"The important thing now is what to do about it."

"Does she have any idea that you are on to her?" Jeanine asked.

Ernie thought about the call he'd made. "No. I did call, but I can make up an explanation for it."

"Okay, then this is what we do," she said as the four of them huddled around a cocktail table, planning to con a con.

30

The two-thousand-square-foot loft that had once been her refuge, a safe haven where she could kick off her Choos, slide off her fake locks and privately depad her Wonderbra, was no longer a sanctuary. Now it felt more like a holding cell whose walls seemed to grow closer and closer with each hour.

Tess had boxed most of her personal items; she didn't attach address labels, because she was still deciding in which direction to flee. She thought about catching the red-eye to L.A., but there were already enough fake boobs, butts and lips out there—hell, silicone could be L.A.'s cash crop. She also knew that in the land of La-La, she wouldn't be anything special. Not that she wanted to bring unnecessary attention to herself, especially now, but she did enjoy standing out in a room full of lusty men. She thought about making a break for the Windy City, but Chicago was just too cold with winter lingering around nine months out of twelve. The cities along the Eastern corridor—Philly, Baltimore, Washington—were too close for comfort. Now that the hounds

were sniffing around, she had to choose her escape route
wisely. Europe was completely out of the question. With the
exchange rate favoring the euro, she would barely have
enough cash to last longer than a few months. In fact, this
couldn't have happened at a worse time, since the bank was
closed and she didn't have access to what money she had
left. To make matters worse, there was a thousand-dollar
daily limit on ATM withdrawals, barely enough to get her
out of New York, much less any safe distance away. Which
was her biggest problem. Where should she run? Cops
would certainly expect Tyrone to show up in a major metropolis. They probably already had his mug shot plastered
in precincts and post offices throughout the country. Tess
also had to assume that the description underneath the
black-and-white glossy described Tyrone as a cross-dresser
trying to conceal his identity as a woman. Though the police
didn't have any mug shots of Tess, there was that photo that
ran in "Talk of the Town," so she definitely had to proceed
with caution.

With melancholy, she drifted though the loft, taking a visual inventory of her treasured possessions. She ran a lazy
hand across the expensive chintz fabric of her custom-made
sofa. The material had been flown in from Paris and had cost
her a mint, but at the time she didn't care. She looked over at
the Bang & Olufsen stereo that was worth a small fortune
and winced as she shook her head. The thought of leaving
behind the high-tech entertainment system and her library of
compact discs and DVDs was physically nauseating. She had
spent countless hours on the Internet ordering classic black-
and-white films, most of which had been restored and digi-
talized to DVD. Her music collection rivaled that of many

radio stations. When the cash was flowing, there was nothing that Tess denied herself. Even down to her groceries, every single item in the kitchen was gourmet. She averaged at least a thousand dollars a month at Balducci's, the gourmet specialty shop. Only now when the money was no longer flowing did she feel foolish for wasting it on pricey imported water at five dollars a bottle. But that was now water under the proverbial bridge.

There were so many items she wanted to pack up and take with her, but she had to travel light. It pained her that she couldn't take all her clothes. The couture evening gowns would definitely have to stay; they were much too bulky to fit inside her luggage. Even the majority of her wigs would have to remain behind. She stood in the doorway of the boutique-sized closet and tried to decide what would stay and what would be practical to take with her. She was taking only a carry-on and a garment bag. Still, it was hard to walk away from Dolce, Prada, Fendi, Manolo, and Louis V. Designers she had always ogled from a distance, on someone else's back. She took the sleeve of a black silk Fendi blouse and rubbed the delicate fabric gently across her face. Now that she had the designers in her possession, she didn't want to let them go.

In the midst of her pity party with her designer friends, the phone rang. "I ain't answering that. It might be Ernie," she said, eyeing the cordless phone on the nightstand as though it were a coiled cobra ready to strike. After three rings, the phone stopped and went through to voice mail. She continued packing without bothering to check caller ID or her messages; she didn't have any time to waste. Finally satisfied with her choices—two pair of black slacks, two turtlcnccks, a jersey wrap dress, one navy pin-striped business suit, a pair of sling backs, and a pair of loafers—she locked the luggage and carried it to the front door.

Tess wrapped herself in a black trench coat, flipped up the collar, tightened the belt around her slim waist and took one final look around her prized domain. She turned off the lights, "Bye, loft," she said softly. As she opened the door, the phone rang again, and again the call went through to voice mail.

Maybe it's Jimmy, she thought, and walked over to the phone to check messages.

You have two new messages, announced the automated voice after she had punched in her code. *Press one to listen to your messages.*

She pressed the corresponding number and waited for the messages to play.

Tess, this is Ernie. Jeanine told me you've been under the weather, but I was hoping you were feeling up to coming in later. Lyle's in Washington, taking care of some last-minute nomination stuff, and I have to leave early tonight. My mom is sick, and I have to catch an early train to Jersey. I wouldn't ask you to get out of your sickbed, but tonight's going to be busy. We're booked for two birthday parties. If you can come down and help Jeanine close up, that would be great. If not, I understand. Okay. I gotta run.

Tess held the phone to her ear and listened to the second message.

Hey, man. Jimmy. Just wanted to let you know that the transferred deed was delivered by courier, so it's all set. Don't worry. I'll take care of everything.

She erased both messages and put the phone back on its cradle. Tess sat on the edge of the sofa and thought about

Ernie's call. "He didn't mention anything about a check. What the hell is he up to?"

She got up and walked over to the window to make sure the coast was clear, before heading downstairs. She eased open the slats of the blinds and peeked out. The crowd in front of Street Signs was three deep. People were lined up waiting to get into the bar, as if they were giving out money. The women were posing, and the men were flexing, trying to get chosen by the brain-dead doorman. The clog of people seemed to swell by the minute; Tess had never seen it so packed. *I wonder who's having a party?* she thought.

She stood at the side of the window for a minute longer and watched the scene unfold. Black Town Cars and taxis rolled up to the curb one after the other in a procession, depositing even more party people in front of the bar. Just as she was ready to close the blinds, she spotted an imposing figure coming out of the door, trying to fight his way through the hordes. It was Ernie. He waited until a group of women got out of a taxi and hopped inside. Tess watched the cab disappear into the night. She waited at the window for another twenty minutes, thinking that Ernie might double back, but he didn't.

She continued to watch the ensuing commotion taking place in front of Street Signs. *This looks like my kind of party*, she mused. *I bet the cash register is ringing off the hook. The bar must be racking in a mint with all those thirsty people waiting to get in.*

No sooner had she thought about the night's receipts than a tempting idea popped in her head. "Maybe I will close tonight."

Tess stayed glued to the window for the next few hours, watching carefully until everyone had gained entry to the bar. Her mouth salivated at the thought of all that cash ooz-ing out of the register, especially considering her lack of cash when she needed it most. It was tempting, but she couldn't take the chance. But then again, maybe she could. Lyle was out of town, Ernie was long gone and the cops were nowhere in sight. And she could definitely use some traveling cash.

She waited and watched as people slowly began to file out of Street Signs. Soon the bar would be closed. She looked at her watch and knew that Jeanine would also be leaving in about an hour. She knew the closing routine; Jeanine would tally up the night's receipts, separating the cash from the credit card slips, and deposit both in the safe. A bank de-posit wouldn't be made until Monday. But by then she would have made a significant cash withdrawal.

The last sixty minutes seemed to tick by at a snail's pace. She was anxious to get her show on the road. "Come on out, Jeanine. What's taking you so long?" She thought about go-ing down before the bartender left, but coming in now would look too suspicious, and she didn't need the dreaded bitch quizzing her. "Just be patient. You've waited this long. A little while longer won't matter," Tess said.

Then as if on cue, Jeanine came out and locked the front door. Tess watched her walk down the street and around the corner before making her move. Tess checked to make sure that she still had the key to Street Signs. She fingered it and smiled as she left her lookout post by the window and exited the loft for the very last time.

Outside, the night was unusually quiet as she discreetly walked the few short steps from her front door to the bar. Tess had the key poised in her hand as she neared the door. Just as she was ready to put the key in the lock, her hand began to tremble, and she dropped it on the pavement. The sound of metal meeting concrete made a shrill *clong* in the silence of the night.

"Damn it," she mumbled, and bent over to retrieve it. With key in hand, Tess quickly unlocked the door and stepped gingerly inside before closing it behind her.

With her back to the door, she squinted her eyes to adjust to the darkness, scanning the room. The watering hole had become her second home, but now it felt like a desolate foreign land. There were no fawning customers hanging on her every word, no sound of champagne corks popping. The only sound was that of her heart pounding like a piston against her chest. She was so nervous that her legs began to shake, but she willed herself to move. "Come on, you're wasting time. Get the money and get out of here."

Tess crept down the darkened hallway, glancing over both shoulders in nervous paranoia. When she reached the office, the door was closed. She wrapped her fist around the brass knob and slowly turned it until the door creaked open. Tess poked her head inside, and from what she could make out, nothing was amiss. She breathed a sigh of relief and made a beeline straight to the vault, where she deftly turned the combination lock and opened the safe. She reached inside, and much to her delight she felt a huge bundle of cash wrapped in bundles. She couldn't tell exactly how much, but judging from the thickness of the stacks, she figured well over ten thousand dollars. She had an urge to turn on the light and count the money, but knew that she shouldn't waste any more time. Quickly she stuffed the stacks into her coat pocket and shut the safe. "Like taking a pacifier from a baby," she said, turning to leave.

"Pacify this," boomed a deep voice.

Before Tess could respond, a fist tore through the darkness, landing squarely on her jaw. She stumbled backward against the wall, but before she could regain her footing, a second blow came and introduced itself to her cheek. Like a caged animal, Tess started swinging wildly into the air, not landing a single blow. She was flailing her arms through the air like a churning windmill when suddenly the lights flicked on. She blinked at the sudden change in brightness.

"I see you do fight like a little girl, but we know better. Right, Tess—or should I say *Tyrone?*"

She blinked again, adjusting her eyes to make out the figure standing by the door, blocking her escape.

"Is that all you got?" said the voice.

She looked closer. It was a man in a wig and overcoat. "Ernie?" she asked.

"The one and only." He slid the wig off. "I knew you'd be watching from your window, so I left as Ernie and came back as Ernise. I also knew you wouldn't be able to pass up a chance at getting your grubby paws on some cash. Your gig is up."

It all came down to this, Tess thought, summoning a reserve of courage. Putting it all on the line, Tess charged at him with all her might. She knocked a surprised Ernie back against the doorframe and ran past him like a running back in sight of the end zone.

"You cross-dressing son of a bitch," Ernie yelled from behind. He ran after her and barely grabbed her arm. Tess swung around and caught him with a left hook. He fell back but quickly recovered with a punch of his own and knocked her wig off, sending it sailing through the air. They traded blows, like Rock 'Em Sock 'Em Robots. Amid the churning arms, she managed to connect one that sent him sliding to the floor.

With him down, she jetted out the door. He scrambled to his feet, but it was too late. Tess was down the street and rounding the corner, disappearing like a thief in the night.

"Damn it!" Ernie yelled. "I almost had him." But that was okay. After all, he didn't want Tyrone arrested because of the scandal that would surely follow. He merely wanted to scare the hell out of Tyrone and make sure that he never stepped a foot back on the island of Manhattan.

Ernie limped back inside, rubbing his ribs. "I guess he doesn't fight like a girl."

He looked around the bar and saw Tess' black Tumi luggage parked by the front door, alongside her auburn wig, which lay in a tangled heap on the bar's floor. The reign of Tess was over.

31

Lyle's celebration at Street Signs was just the type of ritzy, exalted occasion that Miss Tess would have worked like a pig rooting for Italian truffles. It was brimming over with the powerful, the beautiful, and those lucky creatures who hoarded both gifts in abundance. Tess would have given her firstborn—if she'd been able to have one—for the thrill of working the roomful of important men, the likes of which were rarely assembled in one place. Including major players on Wall Street, the current and two of the city's past mayors, as well as an impressive assortment of other notable and respected alpha males, including Senator Neuman and Congressman Wesley. The women present were also of the highest caliber, very much *unlike* the hungry females who normally scouted the grounds at Street Signs. This pack had the brains and the bank accounts to accompany the beauty.

Lyle smoothly navigated the steady stream of well-wishers, many vying with each other, without shame, to suck up to the next chairman of the SEC. Meanwhile, the well-stocked bar flowed as freely as water over Niagara

Falls. He disentangled himself from a coterie of suits that encircled him tightly as the men all offered him their most heartfelt congratulations on his now imminent appointment.

Ernie appeared at his side, nodding his head. "Congratulations, little brother. I am really proud of you." Seeing the magnitude of the evening caused him to suddenly realize just how important his baby brother was.

A sincere smile spread across Lyle's face. "Thank you."

Leaning in and whispering conspiratorially, Ernie added, "I'm real impressed that you've got a roomful of uppity white men kissing your ass." They both laughed at the rich irony of it all, rising from the underbelly of Newark to the nexus of power in New York City.

"I have you to thank too. If you hadn't have handled that sticky situation with Tess, tonight could easily have been a wake instead of a celebration." He shuddered to think of the humiliating disgrace that would have accompanied a public airing of his partner's sordid lingerie.

Ernie shook his head, his eyes squinted as he recalled the absurdity of punching a dude who was done up like a chick. "I just wish I could have seen the look on his face when he finally counted all that Monopoly money, or better, that I could've taken him for a little ride. Sick, twisted bastard."

"It's probably best that you didn't." The last thing he wanted was Ernie to end up back in jail for beating, or worse, killing, a worthless con.

"I'm just worried that he might show up again." Ernie didn't like loose ends. But he knew one thing. If he ever laid eyes on Tess, Tyrone, or whatever he wanted to call himself, he would finish the ass-whipping that he'd started.

"After the other night, I don't think you have to worry. I'm sure he's scared straight."

"In his case," Ernie chuckled, "I don't think that's possible."

"You know what I mean." Lyle gave Ernie a hug. "Thank you, big brother. Once again, you saved my ass."

The real irony to Lyle was how, at the two most crucial points in his life, the first being after their father split and the other on the eve of his nomination, the brother he'd written off as a disgraceful degenerate had come through for him.

"What else are big brothers for?" He patted Lyle affectionately on the back.

"There you are."

Lyle turned to find Yvette standing with her hands planted on her hips. She ignored Ernie altogether. "Oh, hi," he said.

"Is that all you have to say to me?"

He glanced at his brother. "Would you excuse us?"

Ernie smirked. "Gladly."

"I don't get a hug?"

Lyle looked at her with barely contained disdain. "Why would you want to hug a low-life wannabe from the wrong side of the tracks like me?"

Yvette's expression froze on her face. She knew at once that she'd overplayed her hand, and now he was holding all of the cards.

"I suggest that you head back to the Upper East Side. I wouldn't want you to get your designer pumps dirty."

She tossed her hair arrogantly and walked away.

Lisa and Morgan watched the exchange from the bar across the room. "Who is that?" Morgan asked.

"His girlfriend."

"Looks to me like more of an ex-girlfriend."

"I guess we'll see."

"I wouldn't worry about her if I were you."

"Hey, I am just happy that everything worked out for him."

"So am I, considering that it could have been a complete disaster." Lisa had called Morgan after leaving the precinct on Saturday and told her about the reemergence of the duplicitous Tyrone.

Just then, Lyle walked over, and with his hand resting lightly on Lisa's waist, he asked, "Is everything set for later?"

"All set," she answered, smiling softly.

"Great." And then he was sucked back into the grasp of New York's elite.

"You two do seem awfully cozy," Morgan noted, eyeing Lisa carefully.

Lisa just continued to smile. "He's a really nice guy, and you know what else?"

"What?"

"I've learned that you really can't judge a book by its cover."

"I see." Morgan had no idea exactly what Lisa was talking about, and at the moment it didn't matter. She was just happy that Lisa was interested in a decent man for a change. Regardless of what happened between her partner and Lyle, Morgan knew that once the bar was set high enough, it would be unlikely that Lisa would ever settle for scum like David again.

After the evening had wound down, and all the guests finally appeared to be gone, Ernie and Lyle sat relaxing in the back office puffing on cigars.

Spence appeared in the doorway, wearing a big smile, as usual. "I have something that belongs to you," he said to Lyle. He strolled over to the desk and laid down an envelope.

Lyle looked at the package and then at Spence. "What could you have that belongs to me?" he said skeptically.

"Trust me. It does." He nodded at the envelope. "Open it, and you'll see why."

Ernie did as instructed. "What?" It was a cashier's check for twenty-five thousand dollars.

"You remember the blackmail note you intercepted?"

Ernie jumped in. "How did you know I intercepted a blackmail note?"

"Because I'm the one who sent it here, hoping you would open it."

"What?" Ernie scratched his forehead. "Why would you do something like that?"

"For sport." Spence laughed, but stopped when he saw the blank expression on Ernie's face. "Let me explain. A few months ago, I had this upper-crusty client by the name of Contessa Aventura Dubois."

Ernie bristled at the mention of Tess' name.

"Anyway, I thought she was a tad weird, but I didn't care because she paid cash for her loft. Well, I thought that was the end of her, until I saw this guy at the club one night who seemed vaguely familiar. Plus, he was flirting with my boyfriend, Kendall. Well, he wasn't exactly my boyfriend." Spence rolled his eyes. "Anyway, when they left, curiosity got the best of me and I followed them. When they arrived at the building, I remembered that I had just sold a unit there a few months before. A couple of days later, I called Kendall and quizzed him about his 'date,' and told him to describe

the layout of the loft to me. Once he did, I immediately recognized the space as the two-thousand-foot loft I'd sold to
Tess. Being the nosy girl that I am," Spence giggled, "I put
two and two together. But it wasn't until I was at Blake's
later and saw a photo that I realized that he was Tyrone. You
see, I wasn't around during the time Tyrone was causing
havoc a few years back. Anyway, I decided to have a little
fun and started sending the blackmail notes. I didn't think he
would resort to stealing from the bar, until Morgan told me
about the check that Tyrone stole from Street Signs. Of
course, I never planned on keeping the money anyway. I just
wanted to pay Tyrone back for impersonating my boy
Blake."

"Trust me—Tyrone won't be impersonating anybody
anytime soon, at least not in New York," Ernie said.

"Give me the scoop." Spence scooted his chair closer and
put his elbows on the desk, so he wouldn't miss one word.

Ernie told him the story of how he set Tyrone up and ran
him out of town.

"Thanks for blowing his cover. If you hadn't, this whole
thing could have been a lot worse," Lyle said.

"Don't mention it."

After Spence was gone, Lyle sat back in his desk chair
blowing billowing smoke rings toward the ceiling with his
legs crossed, ankle over knee. "Wow," he said, shaking his
head, "what a day."

Ernie sat in the opposite chair, also enjoying the calm after the storm. "All's well that ends well. But in the future, do
promise me one thing," he said, pointing his cigar at his
brother.

"What's that?"

"The next time you think about adding a partner, check with me first."

Lyle looked at him with a forlorn expression. "Sorry, I can't promise that," he said, standing up. "It's too late."

Ernie leaned forward in his chair. "Don't tell me—"

"Actually, to be accurate, I'm not getting a new partner. I'm actually getting rid of the bar altogether." He extinguished the remainder of his Zino in the crystal ashtray.

"You're what?" Ernie looked shocked, as if he'd been caught with another uppercut.

"I spoke to my attorney, and she agreed that given my new position, keeping Street Signs could continue to put me in a compromising position. So I'm getting rid of it."

Ernie was crestfallen. He looked around the place that had become a second home and a second chance for him, not to mention that it was a special tie that bound him and his brother. "So what are you gonna do with it?"

"As of this morning it has a new owner."

Ernie already had visions of the unemployment line, if he was even eligible for it. "So who is it?" he asked, though he really didn't care to know.

Lyle reached into his jacket pocket and pulled out papers that had been neatly folded into thirds and slid them across the desk. "You are."

Though he'd heard the words as they left Lyle's mouth, and he started reading the now opened papers, which effectively relinquished ownership of Street Signs to him, Ernie still seemed unable to process what had just happened. "You can't mean that I—"

Lyle interrupted him. "You are the proud new owner of a bar. Congratulations!"

In walked Jeanine, the wait staff and Lisa, who was holding a small cake in the shape of a street sign, with Ernie's name spelled out in lavish chocolate icing. "Congratulations!" they all chimed.

One of the waitresses passed out glasses of champagne, and Lyle raised his to make a toast. "This is to you, Ernie. I love you, man."

Ernie quickly wiped away a tear, not wanting his masculinity further breached, and said, "I love you too, little brother."

32

The sun kissed the horizon good morning as it broke through the clouds, indicating that it was going to be another bright sunny day in the corn belt. The rooster's wake-up song could be heard in the distance. The stale air in the tiny room was disturbed by a whisper of a breeze that gently floated through the weathered curtains. Stretching his lanky body along the twin bed, Tyrone jumped slightly as a coiled spring sprang clear through the ticking of the worn mattress, nearly nailing him in the behind.

"Damn it." He scooted out of the way, rubbed the morning crust from the corners of his eyes, and scratched the stubble that now grew on his face.

He could hear the shop owners along Main Street getting on with their morning ritual. They were already up at dawn sweeping the sidewalks in front of their tiny shops, wiping down plate-glass windows and airing out their little storefronts. Tyrone wanted to linger in bed another hour, but he had his own morning routine to perform. He swung his scrawny legs over the side of the bed, and as soon as his feet hit the cold floor, a shiver ran straight up his spine. He felt like he was in a nightmare, a B-movie version of *The Wizard of Oz*. Only instead of waking up in Kansas, he had woken up in Iowa.

After barely escaping the fracas with Ernie with nothing but the clothes on his back, Tyrone ran all the way uptown to Port Authority. Once inside the bus terminal, he spotted a group of migrant workers boarding a bus. Quickly he filed in line with them and boarded. At the time, he didn't know where the bus was headed and didn't really care, as long as it was leaving New York City. He surely wasn't going to wait around and choose a more suitable destination. His only concern was getting out of Dodge, and a bus full of farmworkers was his ticket to freedom. It wasn't until he locked himself in the smelly toilet to count his stolen cash that he realized that he'd taken a beatdown and abandoned his luggage, all for wads of funny money. He laughed and cried deliriously at the same time.

As he made his way to the dour bathroom down the hall that he shared with two other tenants, Tyrone mumbled to himself, "There's no place like home. . . . There's no place like home. . . ." Fortunately, the bathroom was vacant, so he turned on the shower and stepped inside. Lukewarm water trickled out of the spigot in the plastic shower stall, barely rinsing the suds off as he twisted one way and the other, trying in vain to drench his entire body. Reminiscing about his dual-head marble shower back in New York only made the situation worse, and again he muttered, "There's no place like home. . . . There's no place like home. . . ." This phrase had become his mantra since landing in the corn belt of the Midwest. He had set up temporary housing in a small transient hotel; it was all that he could afford as he waited impatiently for Jimmy to wire him the money from the sale of his loft. Meanwhile his available funds were drying up faster than a corn husk.

After the less than satisfying shower, Tyrone dressed in a pair of Levi's and a plaid flannel shirt, both of which he had bought from the general store down the street, as well as a wardrobe of pseudo cowboy gear. All his exquisite Tess paraphernalia was left behind in his luggage. Besides, this definitely wasn't the place for Tess. She would have stood out like tits on a bull.

Tyrone hoisted up his jeans, buckled the belt tightly around his waist and trotted downstairs to call Jimmy. There were no phones in the single-occupancy rooms, so every morning after his shower, he headed to the lobby and set up a makeshift office in one of two wooden phone booths. They were a throwback from yesteryear, equipped with rotary dials, an overhead light, a pullout wooden seat and accordion doors for privacy.

"Mornin', Mr. Jones."

"Mornin', Henry," Tyrone greeted the ancient desk clerk. He had fabricated the name Marty Jones as his new alias. It sounded generic enough, and suited his new persona just fine until he got his loot and could metamorphose into another fabulous being.

He ducked into the phone booth like Clark Kent and shut the door. "It's time to get out of this one-horse town," he mumbled, and circled the dial, calling Jimmy's number.

I'm sorry. The number you have reached has been dis-

connected. There is no further information available. If you feel you have dialed this number in error, please hang up and dial again, announced the automated operator.

"What?" Tyrone frowned at the silver number dial on the pay phone. "I must have dialed the wrong number." He deposited more change, and redialed.

I'm sorry, the number . . . It was the same message.

What the hell is going on? I just called him yesterday and got his answering machine, Tyrone thought. He sat there for a moment, trying to remember Jimmy's cell phone number. He rarely called it, because most of the time the service was turned off. *Is it 542 or 543?* he pondered, trying hard to remember the prefix.

"Ah, I got it," he nearly shouted, and circled the dial again after depositing another fistful of coins.

"Hello," Jimmy answered after three rings.

"Hey, man, what's up? Why is your phone disconnected? Where are you? You sell the loft yet? You got my money?" Tyrone frantically fired questions at Jimmy, not giving him a chance to answer the first question first.

"Whoa, man, slow down. Where you at?"

"You would know if you returned my calls," Tyrone hissed into the receiver. "I've been calling you for days. Where you been?"

"Uh, I've been around. Where you at?"

Tyrone looked through the window of the phone booth and lowered his voice. "I'm stuck in this one-stoplight, one-horse town in the middle of nowhere, doing nothing until I get my money. So please tell me you sold the loft and have my money."

"Uh—"

Tyrone could hear music playing in the background and someone singing off key. "Who's that?"

"That's Anton." At the mention of his name, Anton seemed to sing louder, his voice nearly coming through the receiver.

"Well, tell him to shut up. I can't hear myself think." Tyrone could hear Anton belting out the lyrics to Cher's hit song "Believe," on one of Tyrone's favorite CDs. Tyrone waited for the music to die down, but it just got louder, with Anton now wailing at the top of his lungs. Tyrone was getting more agitated with each passing second. "Damn it, Jimmy," he finally shouted. "Tell him to shut the hell up!"

"Look, trade, I ain't telling him shit," Jimmy suddenly snapped. "He at home, and he can do whatever the hell he want."

"When did you and that excuse for a boyfriend buy a CD player? Last time I checked you couldn't even afford five-dollar bootleg CDs, let alone something to play 'em on," Tyrone fumed in retaliation.

Jimmy sucked his teeth. "We didn't buy it. It came with our new place."

"What new place?"

"Our new loft on Broome and West Broadway."

Tyrone nearly dropped the receiver from his ear. "Loft? On Broome?" was all Tyrone could manage.

"Yep," Jimmy replied in a cavalier tone. "You heard me right."

"What do you mean? A loft on Broome and West Broad-

way? That's my damn loft!" he shouted, recovering from the
shock.

In a calm voice Jimmy said, "You mean, your old loft.
Remember, you transferred the deed to me, so it's mine, free
and clear. Thank you very much."

"I transferred the deed to you for you to sell it and send
me my money. You know I ain't hardly got no cash left," Tyrone moaned.

"That sounds like a personal problem, my man. You
treated Anton and me like we had the plague when you got
yo' money. You acted like you was too good fo' us, once you
moved into yo' million-dollar loft wit' yo' fancy shit. Now
let's see how you like being on the other end of the whop-
ping stick."

Tyrone could hear Jimmy snap his fingers into the phone,
and could imagine him rolling his neck in unison. "Jimmy,
Jimmy, wait a minute. Calm down—"

Jimmy cut him off cold. "I am calm."

"Man, come on. You can't just leave me hanging like
this. I need the money from the loft. I only got about a grand
left to my name. How long you think that's gonna last?" Tyrone pleaded. The police had gotten wind of Tess and frozen
her bank account.

"You can save your breath, 'cause I ain't selling the loft.
Me and Anton like living the high life. It feels good for a
change—I can definitely say that success is the best revenge,
asshole. And as far as money, why don't you get a *j-o-b* like
everybody else?"

Tyrone sniffled, with tears welling up in his voice. "You
know I ain't like everybody else."

"You're resourceful. I'm sure you'll think of something. You always do. And by the way, this cell number will be disconnected by tomorrow, so don't bother calling me again. And don't forget the cops will be waiting for you if you show up on *my* doorstep." *Click.*

Tyrone didn't get a chance to say another word. He just sat in the booth with the phone to his ear, listening to the dead air. He couldn't believe the turn of events. He was once again a grifter, living on the fringes of life.

Epilogue

The cherry trees were in full bloom on the Hill. The soft pastel pink blossoms were the perfect backdrop for a perfect day, the day of Lyle's official swearing-in as the chairman of the Securities and Exchange Commission. To accommodate his intimate entourage, he'd rented an entire car on the Acela, the express train from New York's Penn Station direct to Washington's Union Station. In addition to his mom, Ernie, and Jeanine, he had invited a small group of friends that included Morgan, Dakota, Lisa and her son. Initially she had declined to bring Justin, thinking that Lyle was just making a polite gesture in extending the invitation to include him. But he insisted that it was genuine, and furthermore said that Justin should see for himself what a black man could achieve. When he told her to consider this a field trip into Justin's future, she finally caved in and agreed to bring him along.

"Is that your little boy?" Lyle's mother asked, motioning to Justin as he sat gazing out of the window.

"Yes, ma'am." Lisa braced herself. She took one look at Mrs. Johnson in her Sunday-go-to-meeting suit and

matching hat and assumed she was gearing up to drill her
with a litany of the usual questions: *Are you married? Divorced? Or just a single mother?*

"What a handsome child." She looked longingly at
Justin. "He reminds me of Lyle when he was that age, quiet
and curious at the same time."

Lisa was surprised. Usually older women couldn't understand the whole concept of single-parenting and were more
than happy to share their feelings on the matter. But Mrs.
Johnson didn't even broach the subject. "That describes
Justin to a tee." Lisa reached over and dusted the top of
Justin's head with her hand. "He's my heart."

Mrs. Johnson nodded her head in the direction of Ernie
and Lyle, then said with the same endearing tone, "I know
what you mean. I'm fortunate enough to have two hearts."

"You must be so proud."

"I am." She beamed. "Both my boys make me proud."

"I hope I can do as good a job as you've done with your
sons," Lisa said, complimenting the older woman.

"From the looks of it," she said, taking another appraising look at Justin, "you're doing a fine job."

"Thank you, Mrs. Johnson."

A short while later, they were pulling into the nation's
capital. Lyle had ordered a caravan of limousines to take the
group to the hearing.

After the ceremony was over, Lyle's small family stood in
front of the Corinthian columns of the Capitol and took
candid shots, committing the historic day to film. Morgan,
Lisa and Dakota stood at the bottom of the steps and
watched on as Mrs. Johnson stood in the middle of her two

handsome sons, beaming from ear to ear. Ernie waved over Jeanine, who stood a few feet away, for her to join them.

Watching Ernie hug Jeanine close around the waist, Lisa commented, "They make such a handsome couple."

"They do seem like a perfect match." Morgan nodded in agreement.

Once the family photo op was over, out of nowhere, a group of blow-dried hanger-ons quickly took their opportunity to cozy up to the new chairman.

"It's amazing how these man-hungry babes seem to show up everywhere," Lisa commented to Morgan and Dakota.

"There's an entire network of money-sniffing wannabes out there ready to snap up eligible men at any given moment," Morgan said, taking in the scene.

"You better go get your man," Dakota instructed.

"He's not my man," Lisa said, watching Lyle smile broadly with a blonde on one arm and a redhead on the other. "Furthermore, if he wants me, he'll have to come for me *and* my son," she said, putting her hand lightly on Justin's shoulder.

The three women stood and watched as Lyle took pictures with the newfound groupies. After the photo was snapped, Ernie walked over and whispered in his ear, "Man, you better watch out for these groupie chicks, and be selective of who you let in your camp."

Lyle looked at Lisa in the distance. "I've already selected who I want to be in my camp."

Ernie followed Lyle's gaze as it landed on Lisa. He slapped Lyle on the back. "Now you're talking. Man, that's a fine woman there. Now that you're officially the chairman of the SEC, you need a good woman who has your back."

"You're right." He raised his arm in the air and motioned for Lisa to come over.

She looked from side to side, thinking that Lyle was signaling someone else. When he continued, she pointed to herself.

"Yes," he called. As she walked up the steps toward him, he yelled out to her, "And Justin too."

ABOUT THE AUTHORS

Tracie Howard is the former Director of Sales for American Express. A graduate of Georgia State University with a degree in marketing, she also worked for the Atlanta Committee for the Olympic Games, Xerox Corporation, and Johnson & Johnson. In addition to traveling, reading, and writing, Tracie is an avid golfer. She lives in Hoboken, New Jersey. Visit her Web site at www.traciehoward.com.

A jewelry designer who secured a stockbroker's license while working on Wall Street, **Danita Carter** is constantly reinventing herself. A native of Chicago, she has had her work featured in *Essence* magazine as well as in international jewelry competitions. She currently lives in Manhattan. Visit her Web site at www.danitacarter.com.

SUCCESS
IS THE
BEST
REVENGE

Tracie Howard
and
Danita Carter

A CONVERSATION WITH TRACIE HOWARD AND DANITA CARTER

Q. How did you begin writing novels? Do you have literary backgrounds?

A. TRACIE: *Revenge Is Best Served Cold* started out as a fun "what if" conversation over cocktails in a midtown Manhattan bar. Danita and I thought the story was so compelling (especially after a couple of glasses) that we decided we had to write a book about it. Up to that point, neither of us had contemplated writing as a career.

DANITA: Stockbroker and Insurance Agent. I also design fine jewelry for private clients and boutiques.

Q. Is it difficult to collaborate on a novel?

A. TRACIE: For us, it's always been a fun process. We conceptualize the story lines over a bottle of champagne (some habits are hard to break!), and from there we carry on individually with separate chapters and connect periodically, or when one of us feels as though we're being pulled in a different direction. We never feel wed to our own or collaborative ideas. This process, which we've fine-tuned, allows us plenty of room to let the story grow organically.

DANITA: Not at all, first of all you have to be on the same page with your writing partner. Once you realize that it's about the story and the characters, then it's smooth sailing.

Q. Do you physically write together?

A. TRACIE: Fortunately, the Internet allows us to be on different sides of the country, as we often are, and still collaborate seamlessly.

DANITA: Initially we meet for a story conference to hammer out the details of the story and the characters. Then we lay out the first ten chapters and go to our respective homes and write. Though we write a synopsis, the story may change, so we work ten chapters at a time.

Q. What advice can you give to first-time writers?

A. TRACIE: Only strive to write a novel when you feel you have a story that you are *strongly* compelled to tell. If you don't believe a hundred percent in it or aren't totally excited every day about it, you can't expect others to be, whether they are agents, publishers, or readers!

DANITA: Start with a simple idea, preferably a subject you know about. Then fictionalize it to the nth degree, and just start writing. Keep in mind that writing is about rewriting, and unless you write, there's nothing to rewrite.

Q. What message do you want most to get across to readers?

A. TRACIE: One of the reasons that Danita and I were so excited about writing *Revenge* is because of the shortfall of stories depicting African-Americans in upscale, mainstream environments. Our main characters could be white, yellow, purple, or blue. They matter most as people, and their ethnicity is secondary. I'd like to add that dimension to our portrayal in the media at large, be it publishing, film, or TV. Since *Re-*

venge was published, I've noticed a trend in this direction, so hopefully we had something to do with that.

DANITA: That it's FICTION, and often we don't have the same views as our characters. Even though we like Gucci, Pucci and Fiorucci, we are two of most down-to-earth people you'll ever meet!

Q. Are your characters people that you know?

A. TRACIE: I hate to be so trite as to say, "They are an amalgamation of many people, blah, blah, blah. . . ." But the fact is, especially with first-time writers, it's true. What I've seen, however, is the more experienced I become as a writer, the less I draw on familiarity, even though the core traits of some characters sometimes do bring a particular person to mind, whether it's an actor, a model, or someone I know.

DANITA: I like to take bits and pieces of people—some of them I know and some I meet in passing. For example, if someone has an infectious laugh that's unforgettable, I might use it as a character trait, or I might use someone's unique walk. Basically my characters are a composite of different people coupled with my extremely vivid imagination. Occasionally our friends think they see themselves in our characters. I guess that's one of the hazards of being friends with a writer.

Q. What is your process for writing?

A. TRACIE: When I begin thinking of main characters, I like to visualize their lives, so I cut out pictures of how I imagine that they might live: their houses, their cars, their kids, and a picture of a face that might even belong to them. I put these images on a big board and sometimes sit and gaze at them, allowing them to fill my imagination, and hopefully spill out magically onto the page.

DANITA: I take real-life situations (since life is stranger than fiction) and totally fictionalize the circumstances. For example, I'll go to a great party, spot a couple across the room, and make up a story for them in my head. The story could be anything from adultery to espionage. A few years ago, I bought this great little book called *Writer's Block*—it's actually shaped into a small block. On each page there's a suggestion or exercise to get your mind in writing mode, and it's worked for me on several occasions.

QUESTIONS FOR DISCUSSION

1. In your opinion, do you think success is the best revenge? If so, has that been a driving factor in striving to achieve your personal best?

2. What was your favorite story line in this novel? Was it the romance between Lisa and Lyle? Was it one of the many tales woven by Tess? Or was it the complex relationship between Lyle and Ernie?

3. Prejudgments are dangerous. Without knowing the facts, you could prematurely discount a friend or family member, as in Lyle's case with Ernie. Is there a personal situation in your life that needs reassessing?

4. Shallowness is such a poor trait. Just ask Yvette. It cost her a relationship. Loving someone for who they are and not what they have is a much better quality, wouldn't you agree? If given the choice, would you choose love or money?

5. Tyrone is quite the chameleon. Who do you think he's going to change into next?

6. Was it right, under the circumstances, for Jimmy to keep Tyrone's condo? Is it ever okay for a thief to be robbed?

7. Was Tyrone morally to blame for Edmond's death? Was he entitled to his inheritance?

8. Despite his many games—legal and illegal—do you feel sorry for Tyrone and somehow hope that he'll get away with his deceptions?

9. Why do women sometimes hold out hope for men like David? Can a zebra ever change his stripes? If not, do David and Tyrone have that inability in common? Can a person ever change his or her character?

Kimberla Lawson Roby believes that Tracie Howard is "breaking new ground in African-American fiction."
Antonio "L.A." Reid calls Howard's novels "sexy, stylish and sophisticated."

Turn the page for a sneak peak at Tracie Howard's most scintillating novel to date—the provocative story of a dangerous game featuring three players, two women and one man, in which getting even is just the beginning . . . and passion can run as deep and dark as revenge.

Don't miss

NEVER KISS AND TELL

Coming in November 2004
from New American Library

A run through Central Park was like therapy for Brooke, not to mention it was a whole lot cheaper. She ran five miles every Saturday and Sunday to help unload the stress that accumulated after a fifty-hour week of seeing troubled patients. Their problems ran the gamut from simple boredom, to full clinical depression and extreme paranoia. In one-hour chunks of time, they unburdened their most personal demons on her desktop. One of her long-term patients, Sarah, now came to see her twice a week just to have someone to talk to. Brooke suggested that she join a social club instead and save herself the hundred fifty bucks an hour. But if all her patients followed that advice, or discovered the joys of jogging, what would she do with her life?

She downed the last drop of coffee and laced up her Adidas cross trainers. She was nearly out the door when the phone rang. Her heart jumped, just as it had in the office yesterday whenever she saw her phone light up. Though she attempted to ignore it, she knew the cause for her anxiousness was about six foot two and dark as chocolate. She snatched the phone off the hook, though she knew that it could not possibly be him. Only her office number was printed on her business card, which meant she'd have to wait until Monday—at the earliest—for his phone call. Or he might never call. She was certain that a guy as handsome as Taylor collected women's numbers for casual sport.

"Hello."

"Hey, girl." It was Joie. "What's going on?"

"I was just on the way out the door for a quick run." She suddenly remembered their shoe-shopping excursion yesterday. "How many new friends did you pick up?"

"A total of seven, I'm ashamed to say," she said, though she didn't sound the least bit upset.

"At those prices you ought to be," Brooke replied. She was the wrong person to call to admit to shopper's guilt.

"You didn't do too bad yourself, kid." Joie laughed. "Did you make it to your appointment on time?"

"No. In fact, I was twenty minutes late. I got stuck in the elevator. Can you believe that?" Brooke heard a muffled voice in the background.

"You, stuck in an elevator? I'm surprised I didn't hear ambulances from the twenty-fourth floor." Over the years, Joie had witnessed Brooke's claustrophobia up close and personal. On one occasion, they were on a flight from Jamaica when the door to the closet-size restroom jammed, with Brooke inside. When Brooke finally got free, it took the rest of the flight to calm her down.

"You would have if it weren't for this guy who happened to be stuck on the elevator with me." Brooke blushed just thinking about their close encounter.

"Was he a medic?" Brooke joked.

Brooke smiled. "No, but he seems to have a great bedside manner. You should have seen the way he took charge and made sure that I was okay. He was"—she fumbled for the words to describe him—"exquisite. He was so caring and gentle. And did I say drop-dead gorgeous?"

"Brooke?"

She was jolted back to reality. "What?"

"Do I hear what I think I hear?"

"What are you talking about?"

"It sounds like someone's smitten." This was music to Joie's ears. For two years now she'd been trying in vain to get Brooke to give a guy half a chance, but Brooke always found fatal flaws in everyone who'd shown any interest.

"No. He was just a really nice guy," Brooke said unconvincingly.

Joie cut to the chase. "Did I hear gorgeous?"

Brooke blushed again. "An Adonis," she confessed.

"So . . . ?"

"So what?"

"So when are you seeing him again?"

"I don't really know."

"Don't tell me you blew him off." Given Brooke's history, Joie would not have been surprised if her friend had. She had no idea how Brooke managed to live a celibate life, but on the other hand Joie was having enough sex for the two of them and couldn't understand any woman who would resist something that was so natural and felt so damn good.

"No. Believe it or not, I gave him my card."

"Either he *was* an Adonis, or you were delirious. I can't even remember the last time you gave a guy your number.

This calls for a celebration." There was rustling in the background and the sound of a stifled giggle.

"Not yet. Remember, he hasn't called."

"But he will."

Above the rustle of bed linens, Brooke heard a man's voice and Joie began to laugh.

"It sounds like someone's doing a little celebrating of her own." It was undoubtedly Brent in the background intent on getting some carnal attention. Brent had been Joie's live-in lover for the past nine months. Brooke wasn't sure if theirs was a relationship or a matter of sexual convenience— primarily Joie's.

"One of us has to—"

Before Joie finished the sentence the phone was pulled away and Brooke heard the sound of laughter muffled by assorted deep moans. She pulled the phone away from her ear. "I guess I'll talk to you later," she yelled and hung up, shaking her head. Though sometimes she envied Joie's easygoing attitude toward sex, she did worry that perhaps her friend was a little to easygoing about it, but who was she to talk? She hadn't had sex with a warm body in almost two years. Certainly, vibrators—however efficient—didn't count.